SWORN

CORPSE WHISPERER
THE SERIES

H.R. BOLDWOOD

OLIVERHEBERBOOKS

"H.R. Boldwood is the Janet Evanovich of zombie hunters. She's fierce and funny and smart, just like her heroine. She's rejuvenated the zombie genre with her fresh new take, in a kick-ass, take-no-prisoners, balls-to-the-wall series you're going to want to read, time and again."

— CHRISTIANA MILLER, AUTHOR OF
SOMEBODY TELL AUNT TILLIE SHE'S DEAD

CONTENTS

1. Rules, Shmules   1
2. Happy Horseshit   7
3. The Full Moon Brings 'Em Out   18
4. Civics 101   29
5. Meatbag Melee   37
6. Injunction Dysfunction   46
7. Secrets and Dreams   54
8. Just Plain Awkward   62
9. Holy Humping Hedgehogs   66
10. Anger, Anxiety, and Asshats   71
11. Saunter and Swagger   81
12. The Odd Couple   86
13. Liar, Liar Pants on Fire   93
14. Coming Clean   99
15. The Girl from Ipanema   110
16. Riders on the Storm   119
17. The Dark Angel   123
18. Now We're Cooking With Gas   130
19. The Stuff of Nightmares   139
20. Slam, Bam, and Wham   143
21. Nowhere to Run   154
22. Talk About Toxic   160
23. The Flaming Arrows of Evil   168
24. A Bunch of Crybaby Gossips   177
25. That Dimwitted, Shit-for-Brains Horndog   184
26. Someone Call for a Murderous, Life-Sucking Devil?   193
27. The Sound of FUBAR   200
28. That Crazy Hoodoo Mambo   208
29. Glints of Gold and Stinky Yellow Dust   214
30. Never Ever Ask That Question   220
31. Prelude to a Clusterfuck in D Minor   230
32. Code Zushi   235

33. 'For Like the Grass They Will Soon Wither'   243
34. This Almost Never Happens   249
35. I'll Try to Bleed Slower   256
36. Shit-Out of Miracles   264
37. Casualties of War   271
38. How Could You?   280
39. Upside Down is Only a Point of View   286
40. A Mama's Love   294

Acknowledgments   303
About the Author   305
Also By H.R. Boldwood   307

This book is affectionately dedicated to Lisa Morton, friend and mentor, without whose unfailing support and encouragement The Corpse Whisperer series would not exist. Thanks for believing in me and cheering me on.

It's also dedicated to Joseph Daniel Back, my spouse, whose eagle-eye and tireless logic reign in my ridiculously right-sided brain when it wanders off. Thanks for understanding and for reading these chapters so many times you could probably recite them by heart.

Last but not least, it's dedicated to the memory of two of Allie Nighthawk's biggest fans:

Rick Burdick who faithfully served as my law enforcement and weaponry expert, and Barbara Kuroff, a wonderfully gifted writer and delightful friend. I wish both of you were here to read the rest of the series as it unfolds. But I know you're up there smiling.

1

RULES, SHMULES

"Get your hands off my Harley."

I leveled my gun at the intruder's bald head and racked the slide. He froze at the metallic *click-clack*, inched his hands into the air and slowly pivoted toward me.

"You...Allie Nighthawk?" he asked, squinting beneath the moonlight at the paper in his hand.

"I'm not going to say it again. Step away from the Lowrider."

He backed off with a shrug. "Bank One says it belongs to them, now. You should've made the payments, lady."

It was just after midnight on a muggy May Saturday in Cincinnati, and the weekend was already in the crapper.

Welcome to my world.

"They'll get their money," I said, keeping the bastard in my crosshairs. "Go on now, leave—before Hawk here has second thoughts."

He eyed my gun, then turned and climbed back into the cab of his flatbed. "Nice piece. Semi-auto?"

"Custom 9 mm. Nighthawk."

Baldy slammed the door of his truck and cranked the engine. It turned over slower than a ninety-year-old hooker, belched smoke and backfired, the sound echoing against the Cape Cod houses that lined Pitty Pat Lane.

Little Allie, the mouthy voice that squats in the back of my head, couldn't resist. *Maybe the neighbors will think that was a gunshot and fall back to sleep.*

In Little Allie's defense, my neighbors have heard worse sounds coming from my house.

The brain bitch, as I like to call her, knows how to push my buttons. She's also the closest thing I have to a conscience. The two of us are a package deal. We live in the real world where zombies aren't just on television, where their numbers increase every day—a world where necromancers will stop at nothing to gain power. When it comes to corpse management, we're number one. No brag, just fact. We do our best to keep our 'work' at the office, but every once in a while, a bit of the batshit crazy follows us home.

By now, the blue-haired biddies of Pitty Pat Lane were surely craning their necks, peering out their windows, and watching the live edition of *Repo Man Uncut*. Come morning, the HOA's mailbox would be bursting with a fresh batch of complaints against me. It's hard to blame my gum-grinding neighbors really. Like I said, when you live down the street from a corpse whisperer, you see some strange shit.

"I'll be back," Baldy yelled, as he rumbled away in his truck.

"We'll be waiting," I shouted, brandishing Hawk in his wake.

Nonnie Nussbuam, my seventy-year-old, next-door neighbor, reached my side in record time. She was spry, for a fossil.

"Miss Allie, that man stealing your motorcycle?"

"That depends on your definition of steal," I said, trudging back to the house.

"Bah. You no fooling me. He repo man."

Nonnie, the Palermo-born widow of a low-level mobster, spoke a subset of English/Italian/Yiddish all her own. I suspected, given her knowledge of who and what a repo man was, that she learned most of her English from reality shows.

She grabbed my arm and jerked me to a stop. "Is true?"

"Don't worry about it," I mumbled. "Go back inside. It's late."

"Is true. You no look at me. What happened with big new FBI job?"

"They haven't paid me for the last job yet, and besides," I said, wrenching my arm from her bony fingers, "they only want me as a consultant. It's not a weekly paycheck."

Normally, I subcontract with the Cincinnati Police Department. But on my last case, CPD and the FBI formed a joint task force, headed by Assistant Director Horton (aka Director Dickhead), to babysit a mob informant named Leo Abruzzi. He'd been bitten by a rotter a few weeks earlier, and though he'd taken his medication to stave off the symptoms, he ended up dying before it was all said and done. I was still nursing some wounds from that case, the invisible kind that take a long time to heal.

Nonnie trailed me into my house and was instantly greeted by my bulldog, Headbutt, and my African Grey, Kulu.

"What about the zumbas?" Nonnie asked, scratching Headbutt's roly-poly stomach. "Someone must kill the zumbas. Why not you?"

"Zombies, Nonnie. And the police got pretty good at taking them down once I showed them how it's done. Taught myself right out of a job, is what I did."

She took my hand and squeezed it. "I have monies. Plenty monies. My Mortie, God rest his soul, he left me—"

"No. I refuse to take money from you. There's got to be another answer."

Nonnie tightened her grip on my hand and stared deep into my eyes. "You also raise the dead, no?"

"We've been through this before, and the answer is still no,"

I said, prying her fingers loose. "I have rules. A moral code. I won't raise every Tom, Dick and deadhead, just because I'm broke."

Shoulders slumped, Nonnie wandered back to her house. I should have known that would never be the end of the conversation. Unless Nonnie hears what she wants to hear, conversations never die; they just circle back like boomerangs, and slap you upside of your head when you aren't expecting them.

Not two mornings later, she showed up at my door, on the pretense of missing 'the terrible twins,' Headbutt and Kulu. She'd pet-sat them for me when I worked on the task force a month or so ago and the three of them had bonded.

The twins are a lot like me—a little rough around the edges and not so fond of rules. But they tolerate Nonnie and love to chow down on her leftover rugelach. Nonnie does my laundry and cooks for me, too. We have a standing dinner date at her house every Tuesday at six.

I spent my early years living next to Nonnie and her wise-guy husband, Mortie, before I went away to a very *special* school for whisperers. As far back as I could remember, her hair had always been bottle-blue and shellacked with Aqua Net, her knee-high pantyhose puddling around her cankles. Mortie passed away maybe eight years ago. Once I settled back in Cincinnati, the crazy old bat weaseled her way into my life so quickly, it was hard to remember how quiet my world had been before I'd invited her into it. I owed her a lot. That made it hard to tell her *no*.

She sat at my kitchen table, clucking at Kulu, and luring me into her web with rugelach and milk. When I least expected it, she sprang into boomerang mode.

"Miss Allie, I hear you say *no raising of the corpses*, but Lucia

4

Falconi, she want you to raise her boy, Rocco. God rest his soul." Nonnie crossed herself, leaned in close, and whispered. "Lucia Falconi has monies."

I rolled my eyes. "Let it go. Raising the dead isn't a game. I made my rules a long time ago."

"But you need monies."

Talk about an understatement. As it turns out, saving the world isn't cheap. I had places to go and promises to keep, not to mention an old nemesis who needed to be stopped before he single-handedly destroyed the world. I'd sworn myself to that cause. But after Leo's case, the bastard had gone underground. No matter. He could run and he could hide, but one day, I'd find Toussaint Le Clerc—or die trying.

In the meantime, I had my rules, and doing what I do without those rules would make me no better than the bastard I was chasing.

"Forget it. I won't raise corpses for stupid reasons."

"Is not stupid. Is for Lucia." Nonnie implored me with her wrinkled brown eyes. "Please, Miss Allie, I ask so little."

I got up and raided the refrigerator for another glass of milk. "Who is this Lucia, anyway?"

"Good friend. Do anything for me. Like you."

"Nice touch," I said, quashing a smile. "And why does Lucia want to raise Rocco?"

"He die from too many of the drugs. Lucia, she think it her fault."

"Guilt is a crap reason to raise a corpse. What your friend needs is a shrink."

Nonnie wrinkled her brow.

"A psychiatrist, Nonnie. She needs a psychiatrist."

Nonnie waddled up behind me, snatched my milk and the plate of rugelach, and held my breakfast hostage. "You raise the corpses for good reasons. Lucia is good reason. She wants the closure. You give her the closure. You need monies. She has monies. Is simple fix to big problem, no?"

"But my rules—"

"Bah! Rules, schmules. Stubborn shiksa." Nonnie stomped out the back door, taking my breakfast with her. She made it about ten feet, then stopped and turned around. "Miss Allie, don't listen to head. Listen to heart. Help Lucia."

As if Nonnie wasn't holding her own in this conversation, Little Allie decided to add her two cents worth, scolding me about doing *the right thing*. That brain bitch had the audacity to remind me, in a very loud voice, that I had chucked the rules out the window more than once in my life. Okay, like lots more than once, but I didn't need a lecture from that overbearing, domineering head hag.

"Fine," I said, wrenching my breakfast from her hands. "You win. Tell Lucia, I'll raise Rocco. But it's going to cost her two grand."

Nonnie beamed. "Is already set. Midnight. Tonight."

"Hold on, now. I'm not digging this kid up—"

"No digging. Visitation tomorrow morning, at Templeman's."

I stared, slack-jawed. "You want me to break into a funeral home to raise this kid? That's illegal. You know that, right?"

"Nonnie do the breaking," she said, with a toss of her hand. "You do the raising."

Swell. What could possibly go wrong?

2

HAPPY HORSESHIT

N onnie pulled into my driveway at midnight ON the dot, in her dirt-brown, wood-paneled, '72 Pinto Wagon. A short, gray-haired fireplug of a woman I presumed to be Lucia Falconi slingshot out of the passenger seat, like a human projectile, and wallpapered herself against me.

"Miss Allie. Oh, Miss Allie," she gushed. "I Lucia. *Grazie. Molto grazie.*"

"Nice to meet you, too, Mrs. Falconi," I said, peeling her off me. "And don't thank me yet. This operation has all the earmarks of a Class A clusterfu..." Little Allie dialed it back. "It's risky. We get caught, it's every man for himself. *Capiche?*"

With a sober nod, Mrs. Falconi trundled herself back into Nonnie's car.

I climbed into the backseat and cut to the chase. "You got my money?"

"*Si.*" Lucia pulled a sock out of her purse and fished out a roll of bills. "One thousand, five hundred dollars."

"Excuse me?"

These old broads. So tight, they'd squeeze a quarter 'til the eagle screamed. "We agreed on two thousand, Mrs. Falconi."

"Please. Call me Lucia."

"Unless you cough up the other five hundred bucks, I'll be calling you a lot of names, not one of which is Lucia."

She threw me a wounded, puppy-dog look. "I old woman. Living on socials securities. Nonnie say fifteen hundred."

"Then maybe Nonnie should raise Rocco."

Lucia waited in stony silence, as if expecting me to break.

Fat chance, sister.

"Well, it's been a real slice of life," I said, opening the car door. "Gotta run."

"Wait. Wait." Lucia dug into her purse and yanked out another sock. "Is Bingo money."

That shyster plucked out a roll of bills big enough to choke a porn star and peeled off five Benjamins.

"Here," she said, smacking it into my open palm. "Take old woman's bingo monies."

"Damn straight," I said, shoving it into my go-bag, beneath the ice pick and the trusty pack of Lays Barbecue chips. They'd both come in handy on our mission. I mentally crossed myself and promised God that if we managed to pull this off without a hitch, I'd try harder to be nice. He probably busted a gut on that one, considering the odds of either of those things occurring were slim to none.

"Let's ride," I said.

Nonnie put the Pinto in reverse and laid rubber as she backed out of the driveway, giving me a lawn job and missing my mailbox by less than an inch. The car coughed and choked its way up the street, belching smoke and noxious fumes, swerving in and out of the lane markers as if Nonnie had had a three-martini lunch. Chances were, I wouldn't have to worry about getting caught breaking into the funeral home. The drive there would likely kill us all.

"Mrs. Falconi... Lucia," I said, doing my best to focus on something other than our impending doom, "I know you want to speak to your son. But what if you don't hear what you want to hear?"

She played with a loose thread on her coat, winding it back and forth around her finger, and finally murmured, "Maybe he forgive me. Maybe not. I love him. This. This he need to hear."

"You do realize, once I wake him up, I have to...return...him to sleep. Permanently."

No need to put too fine an edge on that. The solemn expression on Lucia's face told me that she'd caught my drift.

Nonnie turned off her headlights as we pulled around the back of the funeral home, and then parked beneath the covered portico, where caskets are loaded into the hearse.

"Harder see us here," she whispered, peering left and then right, as if someone might be within earshot—at midnight, in the pitch dark, as we broke into the back door of a funeral home. How many of us could there be?

Clearly, Nonnie had given this operation some thought. Either that, or she had some transferable skills and experience I didn't really want to know about. My suspicion was confirmed when she pulled a small, zippered kit from her pocket and removed a set of pick tools. I silently groaned, wondering if it had belonged to Mortie, and if I'd grow old waiting for her to crack the lock. She slipped the tension wrench in the bottom of the key hole and then inserted the pick. Within seconds, the tumblers clicked and we were in. Nonnie flashed a triumphant grin. I didn't know whether to feel proud, disturbed, or simply relieved at the lack of a security decal on the window.

We pushed inside Templeman's and closed the door behind us. I led our group of unlikely burglars forward, shining my flashlight from side to side. The viewing rooms branched off to the left and right of the main hallway.

"Wait here," I whispered, creeping into the parlor on my left. One sweep of the light told me we were in the wrong room. Not a casket to be found. I returned to the hallway and motioned for Nonnie and Lucia to stay put as I skulked into the other parlor. Sure enough, the casket faced me, positioned against the wall at twelve o'clock. A knot formed in the pit of my stomach. If I was in the right place and doing the right thing, why wasn't I getting a better vibe? I retraced my steps to the hallway and gave the ladies instructions.

"You two stay here until I tell you it's safe to come in. Rocco only crossed over a couple of days ago. Raising fresh corpses is...unpredictable."

If that wasn't a freaking understatement.

Freshies, corpses less than seven days dead, still have muscle memory. They're quick and agile. They also wake up hangry. And while they'll gnaw on anything from Frisbees to mailboxes, they really go for junk food. Supposedly, the fat content stimulates their relentless taste for flesh—which kicks in once they reach the flesh-eater stage, on the eighth day after having been raised.

I pointed at the ladies, reminding them to maintain their position, then stepped back into the parlor, approached the casket, and lifted the lid. Poor kid. It looked like he'd had a hard, if short, life. No hint remained of the life force that right-fully belonged to an eighteen-year-old. Lines etched his face, a face far too gaunt and haggard to belong to a teen. Damn drugs. And damn the dealers for turning addicts into shambling zombies long before they ever die.

I bowed my head and sucked in a breath, centering my mind and heart. Warmth flooded each of my fingertips, one at a time, and then coursed through my hands into my arms. The warmth quickly escalated to an agonizing burn, like it always does when I raise the dead.

I'd placed my hands above the corpse and had begun to do my thing when a shriek from Lucia stopped me cold. "*Madre di Dio! Stop. Is not my Rocco.*"

Nonnie and Lucia, who had crept up alongside me, cringed

and quickly reeled away from the casket. They crossed themselves feverishly and began chanting something from the old country—something with a lot of consonants and phlegm.

I shot Lucia the stink-eye. "What do you mean, that isn't Rocco?"

"Is not my boy." She craned her neck forward, peering over the edge of the casket. "Is old man. Older than me."

"You're sure?" I asked. "Rocco lived a rough life, what with the drugs—"

Nonnie pulled her glasses down her nose and peered at me over the top of the rims. "Try these," she said, taking them off and shoving them at me.

"Oh, for God's sake. Stop that," I said, batting them away.

The codger in the coffin twitched, causing the ladies to scamper further back and shoot him the Italian horned hand, in unison.

Son-of-a-bitch. I knew I shouldn't have taken this gig.

The corpse, suspended somewhere in the galvanized gray space between reanimation and death, resembled a modern-day Frankenstein. The good news was that Lucia had distracted me before I'd raised him completely. If I'd have brought him all the way back, I'd have had to put him down by extreme means. As it stood, I still had a chance to make this go away quietly.

"Sorry, guy," I said, bending over him. "Wrong number. Go back to sleep."

The corpse twitched again, opened his eyes, and shot me an accusing stare.

Like this was my fault, right?

"What the hell are you looking at? Haven't you ever made a mistake? *Go to sleep, you crusty buzzard.*" I brushed my hand down his forehead and over his eyes, letting it linger there, pulling back the energy I'd infused into him. As I drained my life-force from his body, his muscles relaxed. Seconds later, he returned to the world of the dead. Disaster narrowly averted.

Lucia, apparently unimpressed by my power over life and death, merely wrung her hands and whined, "Where my Rocco?"

Good question. There were only two visitation rooms, and Rocco wasn't in either one of them. I closed the lid of Frankengeezer's casket and pulled the Sicilian hen party back out into the hallway. "We do have the right funeral home, don't we?"

Lucia glared at me. "*Si. Non sono pazzo.*"

I glanced at Nonnie for a translation.

"She say, yes. She no crazy."

"Okay, you two. Stay here. *Don't* move a muscle. I mean it. I'm going to find Rocco."

Lucia stuck a stubby finger in my face. "I no pay more monies. Last corpse *you* mistake."

"Did I ask you for more money?" I asked, whapping her hand aside. "Pull that finger back before I bite if off, sister."

I followed my flashlight beam down the hallway, opening additional doors as I came to them. After ruling out the bathrooms and the business office, only one door remained. And it was locked, damn it. When I turned to call for Nonnie, she and Lucia were already at my side. It was like babysitting two-year-olds.

"Didn't I tell you to stay put?"

"Quiet. I working," Nonnie said, nudging me out of the way.

She picked the lock in seconds and pushed the door open.

"Thanks," I said, more impressed than I let on. "Now, stay right here while I...what the hell. Stand wherever you want. Just don't get in my way."

From the doorway, I spied a body bag laying atop a steel gurney in the middle of the room. I moved alongside it and pulled the zipper down. The body appeared to be that of a young male, but I wasn't taking any chances.

"Lucia, is this Rocco?"

Lucia shuffled up beside me and looked down at the face inside the bag. Her eyes clouded with anguish, then quickly darted away. "*Si*. My firstborn."

She began to cry, so I motioned for Nonnie to come get her. Zombies, I can handle. Tears, not so much.

"It's not too late to stop this." I said. "We can leave right now. I'll even give you your money back."

Lucia shook her head. "No. Do it. Before I change mind."

I closed my eyes and called forth the strange and awesome power that brings the dead to life, feeling it surge through me, first searing my fingertips and then my hands, before traveling up my arms. It had been a very long time since I'd attempted back-to-back raisings. I was exhausted. Pain snaked across the nerve endings in my fingers as energy arced from my body into Rocco's. The hair on my arms stood up, and the pungent, familiar smell of ozone hung in the air.

It was time.

I crossed myself, and then lay my hands on his chest. "Rocco Falconi, in the name of God, I command you to rise."

Rocco moaned and Lucia let out a gasp.

I leaned down and whispered in his ear. "Rocco, you will rise."

Rocco sat up sluggishly on the table, wearing the same blank, bewildered stare the dead always have when they are awakened. Lucia, now seated on the mortician's stool, twisted her hands over and over in her lap, crying openly, her grief laid thick and bare. Feelings. Emotions. All the touchy-feely crap that makes me uncomfortable.

Why had I let Nonnie talk me into this?

"Rocco, your mother wants to speak with you," I said. "You will stay where you are and answer your mother's questions. Do you understand me?"

Rocco glanced around the room, his gaze finally coming to

rest on his mother. He nodded, never taking his eyes from Lucia. "Tired. So tired."

I pulled the bag of barbecue chips from my pocket and waved them under his nose. For the moment, I had his undivided attention. On my cue, Nonnie walked Lucia closer to the table, stopping a few feet away from it when I held up my hand.

"Go ahead." I nodded to Lucia. "Ask what you came to ask."

"Why, Rocco?" she sobbed. "Why you do this, *mio bambino*? Was it Mama? You do this because of me?" She stepped even closer to the table. Nonnie eyed me silently, waiting for my direction. I wasn't sure it was a good idea for Lucia to stand next to Rocco, but I motioned Nonnie to let Lucia be. She planted herself beside me at the edge of the table.

Rocco flinched as Lucia's hand touched his cheek.

"Not...you, Mama," he murmured. "Accident. Sleep now," he said, laying back down.

Lucia slapped his face "You no lie to Mama. Tell truth."

I reached over and grabbed her hand so she wouldn't slap him again. "He's not capable of lying, now, Mrs. Falconi. That would require deliberation and intent. He has no choice but to tell you the truth."

She smiled through her tears, but her voice had a razor's edge. "Who give you the drugs, Bambino? Who do this—"

"Wait a minute," I said. "We're not going there. That wasn't part of the deal."

Rocco sighed. "Gino, Mama. Gino Ferrari. Sleep now," he mumbled, closing his eyes.

Lucia's voice turned cold. "Where I find this Gino Ferrari? This monster?"

I didn't like the turn this had taken.

"You got what you came for, Mrs. Falconi. Rocco told you his death was accidental. We need to let him sleep now."

Rocco's eyes remained closed; his hands folded neatly on

his chest. By all appearances, he had already returned to his eternal rest. But appearances can be deceiving.

Lucia reached over the edge of the table, took his hand, and gasped. "*Santa Madre!*" She turned to me, grabbed my hand, and placed it on Rocco's. "See?" she said, with tears in her eyes. "He is warm. He lives. *Is miracle, Miss Allie.*"

"No, no miracle. He's just warm from the reanimation. C'mon," I said softly. "It's time for you to go, now."

"No yet," Lucia begged. "Please, no yet." She squeezed Rocco's hand and choked out a sob. "*Non lasciarmi, piccolo. Ti amo.*"

No leave me. I love you.

That's the sucky part about raising kids. Every parent wants to bring them back, but no one ever wants to let them go the second time around.

I nudged the oldsters out into the hall. "Why don't you and Nonnie wait here while I help Rocco get back to sleep?"

The last thing I needed was for Lucia to see how I would help her son return to his eternal rest. There'd be no gunshot or K-bar knife to the brain, no gore, no zombie guts. Rocco needed to be presentable for his visitation in the morning.

I closed the door and locked it to keep the fossils out of my hair, then jerked the icepick out of my pocket on my way back to the table. In one swift motion, I lifted his head and plunged the pick into his brainstem, at the base of his skull. The mortician might notice the small puncture when preparing Rocco's body for presentation, but no one else would. Little Allie reassured me that since I did all this at Lucia's behest, even if there were a minor kerfuffle, I wouldn't face any serious repercussions.

I believed that load of happy horseshit, too, right up to the point when I heard the front door open and saw the lights come on. Heavy footsteps bounded down the hallway. Nonnie and Lucia wailed at the top of their lungs, screaming Sicilian consonants. The doorknob to the mortuary jiggled, but held.

"Cincinnati Police Department," came a voice from the hall. "Open the door and come out with your empty hands above your head. *Now.* Or we'll break it down and do things the hard way."

Shit, shit, shitty, shit, shit. I knew this escapade would end with me in the slammer. And where was that little brain bitch when I needed her? Why hadn't she been the voice of reason and kept me from tumbling headfirst into a steaming pile of biter dung? What's the point of even having a head-squatting voice in your brain if it doesn't have your back?

I unlocked the door and pushed it open slowly, but before I could emerge with my hands held high, I was rushed and taken to the floor by four of Cincinnati's finest. They cuffed me with my hands behind my back and yanked me to my feet.

"Hi, guys," I said, keeping it light. "It's okay. I'm Allie Nighthawk. Everything's cool."

'I don't care if you're God, Himself," snarled one of the officers, twisting the cuffs a bit tighter. "Things are definitely not okay."

"Didn't you guys get the directive from HQ? This is a training exercise."

Even as those words came out of my mouth, I glanced at Nonnie and Lucia cowering in the corner, and realized they'd sell me down the river for a crust of bread. That sweet, wrinkled prune façade didn't fool me. It was every skel for herself.

"Training exercise. No kidding," the officer said with a snicker. "Since you tripped the silent alarm on the mortuary room door, I'm guessing you must have flunked."

My mouth fell open. "Shut the hell up! A silent alarm—in a funeral home? Who the hell breaks into a funeral home?"

The cop cast me a tired gaze. "I was hoping you'd tell me."

I glanced at his badge. "Listen, Officer Franks, I'm no thief.

Do me a favor," I begged as he hauled me out the door. "You know Rico De Palma—works out of the 51st?"

"De Palma. De Palma," he said, scratching his head. "Is he that, what-do-you-call-it, spook squad guy?"

"The Paranormal Crimes Unit Liaison. Give him a call."

Franks led me to his cruiser and pushed down on my head so I'd clear its roof. "Why the hell would I call that bozo?" he asked.

I slid across the backseat and played my get-out-of-jail-free card. "He's my partner."

3

THE FULL MOON BRINGS 'EM OUT

Seated in Investigation Room One, I tried my best to put a positive spin on the night's events. I don't know why. They had us dead to rights. At the very least, we'd committed B&E. The officers had split us up when they brought us in, taking us to separate rooms. Franks had deposited me in an overly bright, barren room and then left, leaving me to stew about my wise-gal partners, Nonnie the Nose and Lucky Lucia.

I glanced into the two-way mirror and imagined myself in prison stripes. I could pull it off. But Nonnie and Lucia, more round than tall, would look like human awnings. As I contemplated that disturbing visual, Officer Franks opened the door, moseyed back in, and leaned against the door frame. I jumped his ass like a dead battery.

"Where'd you stash the blue hairs?"

"They're being interviewed."

"I'd suggest you check on them."

Franks chuckled. "We don't use rubber hoses on old ladies, if that's what you're worried about."

"I meant the officers."

Tough as nails, Nonnie, the Mafioso widow of Morrie Nussbaum, had the balls and swagger of John Wayne. She could handle an interrogation standing on her head. And unless the poor sap who drew Lucia spoke Sicilian, he'd be banging his head against the wall about now.

I rolled my shoulders, then took a breath and started spinning my story.

"Mrs. Falconi just wanted to talk to her son, Rocco. That's all. I was helping her get closure."

Franks pursed his lips and nodded. "Naturally, you thought the best way to help her was to break into the funeral home in the middle of the night."

"He's getting buried tomorrow. We were out of time. Besides, we had permission to be there."

"Permission?"

"Of course," I said. "Mr. Templeman is an old family friend."

That was tru...ish about our families being old friends. But the permission thing, that was a big fat lie.

"Do tell," Franks said. "That's amazing, considering Templeman's at the desk right now filling out a complaint." Franks pulled a chair from the table, spun it around backwards and straddled it. "Lying isn't the way to win friends and influence people, Ms. Nighthawk. How 'bout the truth this time?"

The silence that followed was broken only by the tick-tick-tick of the clock that hung beside the door. I swiped my hand across my forehead. It came away wet. I was hot, irritated and utterly exhausted.

"How about some water," I said, closing my eyes and laying my head on the table.

"The truth, first."

"I told you the truth. Mrs. Falconi wanted to talk to her son. Where's De Palma? He should be here by now."

"How the hell should I know?"

Our circle-jerk was interrupted by a familiar voice.

"Somebody special order a cop in here?"

I peeled one eye open to find Rico standing in the doorway, all six-foot, one-hundred-eighty pounds of him. With his curly black hair and huge brown eyes, the guy was hot enough to melt asphalt.

Franks stood up. "You must be De Palma."

"Yeah. Thanks for calling," Rico said, shaking Frank's outstretched hand.

"This whack-job claims she's your partner. Is that right?"

Rico shot me the side-eye. "Depends. What'd she do?"

"Broke into Templeman's Funeral Home with a couple of golden girls. Said she had old man Templeman's permission to be there. She didn't."

Rico shifted his gaze to me, and I shrugged.

Franks was on a roll. "Crazy broads. Breaking into a freaking funeral home, in the dead of night, to *talk* to one of the stiffs. Christ almighty, but the full moon brings 'em out. Am I right?"

Rico grinned and clapped him on the shoulder. "You new here, Franks?"

Franks frowned and cleared his throat. "Been on the job twenty years. Moved from Baltimore to Cincy a couple of months ago. Why?"

"Franks meet Allie Nighthawk, Cincinnati's resident zombie hunter. She's also got this freaky-voodoo thing she does. Raising the dead. First time you see it, you swear you'll never drink again. She contracts with CPD on *special* cases. The paranormal kind. And, yeah. We're partners."

"I don't care if she's Buffy the fucking Vampire Slayer. She wasn't on police business tonight. She picked the lock at Templeman's and broke in. That's B&E."

"Actually," I interrupted, "The lock-picking thing was Nonnie."

Rico glared and shushed me with a finger to his lips. "I get it, Franks. You were right to bring her in. But since I made the trip in and everything, if it's okay with you, I'll take it from here."

Franks's face puffed up, looking like he was about to explode, but Rico cut him off.

"I'll square it with your sergeant and even talk to Templeman. Really, I got this. Thanks for the call, guy." Rico pumped Frank's hand like a jack handle. "If you wouldn't mind, could you send the other ladies in here? Might as well wrap everything up together."

Franks may have bristled at Rico's intervention, but he looked relieved at the possibility of being rid of us. He shot me a long, hard stare and then walked to the door, throwing a nod toward Rico. "Fine. You want professional courtesy, you got it. But in the future, stay in your own precinct."

Rico gave him a thumb's up. "I owe you one, brother."

"No. No you don't. I don't want nothing to do with you or that spook-squad crap."

Franks slammed the door on his way out, leaving me in the hands of a pissed-off, sleep deprived Rico.

I steeled myself for the endless stream of ugly that I assumed would spew from his mouth. But I wasn't prepared for the ominous death stare I received. We stood toe to toe, staring at each other in silence, and I caught myself uttering a sigh of relief at the sound of a timid knock on the door.

"Nonnie!" I said, as Rico opened the door. I'd never been so glad to see Nonnie in my entire life.

Rico pulled two chairs out from the table. "Ladies," he said, motioning for them to sit. Lucia, he had never met. Nonnie, Rico, and I were a team of sorts, having bonded over our last case involving Leo Abruzzi.

Don't get me wrong. It's not like we'd all sat around holding hands and singing *Kumbaya*. Leo could be a first-class dickweed, but he had his moments. Turns out, he and I shared a love of ballroom dancing. In a matter of weeks, things, friend-ships, and feelings had complicated my life in a strange, sad way I wouldn't have traded for anything.

Rico leaned down and kissed the top of Nonnie's head. "How you doing, lady? What's this I hear about you picking locks?"

Nonnie bit her lip and turned away, mortified. Probably not because she picked the lock, but because she'd gotten caught.

Rico turned to Lucia and flashed his perfect smile. "I don't believe we've met. I'm Rico De Palma, Miss Nighthawk's part-ner. Nice to meet you..."

"Lucia. Lucia Falconi," she purred and extended her hand.

He brought it to his lips, and brushed it with a kiss. The freaking brown-eyed douche-waffle. Lucia did everything but swoon.

Rico coaxed her with a smile. "Why don't we start from the beginning, Lucia?"

That would take forever. "Let me give you the short and sweet," I said. "I—"

Once again, Rico silenced me with a finger to his lips. "Lucia's version, please."

"Seriously?" My face began to burn. "Then Nonnie's going to have to translate, because Lucia doesn't speak much English."

"No need." Lucia beamed at Rico, as if he were Apollo come down from Olympus. "My English fine when I need it."

The old broad had been sandbagging me.

Rico sat across from Lucia and listened intently to her detailed and surprisingly accurate version of the night's events. A bit too detailed, if you ask me, when she included the part about us haggling over the cost of my services. Rico rolled his eyes.

"Don't look at *me*," I said. "This was all Nonnie's idea, Little Miss Lock-Picker."

Yeah. I threw her under the bus. Hard. But she'd have done the same to me, if it had been her ass in the hot seat. She and I, we're cut from the same cloth.

Once Lucia finished confessing to everything but original sin, and Nonnie and I had nothing (that wasn't incriminating) to add, Rico got to his feet and moved to the door.

"I'm going to try to square things with the desk sergeant and Mr. Templeman. They're waiting for me at the front desk. Stay put."

Stay put? *Stay put?* Nonnie and Lucia didn't know the meaning of those words. But, hand to God, when Rico closed the door behind him, they never so much as twitched—the old hose-bags. I stored that away for future reference. Three can play at that game.

I snarled at Lucia. "Rico shows up and suddenly you speak English? What's that about?"

"Che cosa? Non parlo Inglese," she said, with a shrug.

The three of us passed the minutes silently staring at each other in our own pathetic retake of *The Good, The Bad, and The Ugly*. Thankfully, Rico returned moments later with good news.

"Okay, ladies. Consider yourselves sprung. Mr. Templeman has agreed not to press charges. I promised him some of your rugelach, Nonnie. I hope that's okay."

"Of course. And extra for you, *buon amica.*"

"What about me?" I said. "I raised Rocco, and I did it for you. Where's my rugelach?"

Nonnie dismissed me with a wave of her hand. *"Oy.* Yes, yes of course for you. The world no spin for you alone. How they say? Get over yourself."

Well, that was uncalled for. And hadn't this night scored a ten on the shit meter?

As we walked out the precinct door, I soon discovered that the night had yet to hit rock-bottom. Jade Chen, the Channel 10 news reporter and her cameraman, Rip Sacca, were waiting like vultures at the bottom of the steps to devour me.

Jade smirked and brought the mic to her mouth. "Good evening, Cincinnati. We're here at CPD's Third Precinct where The Queen City's resident cadaver diver, Allie Nighthawk, has just been released from custody."

I stopped in my tracks and turned to Rico. "Why didn't you tell me that bitch was here? What were you thinking?"

Rico glared at his lover, Jade, but she ignored him and took the steps like a storm trooper.

"Sorry," he murmured in my ear. "We were...together... when the call came in. She must've followed me."

Of course, they'd been together. That hoochie-mama-dill-weed reporter hates me with the heat of a white-hot yeast infection. Who knows why? Maybe it's because I keep telling her boyfriend that she's a bubble-headed twat-waffle.

I can't help it if the truth hurts.

"Miss Nighthawk, were you present at the midnight break-in at Templeman's Funeral Home?"

"No comment."

"Is it true you raised a corpse?"

"No comment."

"I'd like to get your perspective, Ms. Nighthawk. The ACLU condemns the practice of raising corpses as a human rights violation. What do you say to that?"

"No comment."

"Please, describe for our viewers the damages you inflicted on the funeral home tonight. Is it true your liability carrier has dropped you as uninsurable?"

That little bitch.

I took a deep, cleansing breath and centered myself. "I'm sorry, Ms. Chen. I'm sure you view my 'no comment' responses as unhelpful and aloof. They're not meant to be. They're meant to be dismissive and rude. Now, get that freaking mic out of my face before I tear off your head and shove it down your throat. How's that for a quote?"

Nonnie gasped. Lucia pretended that she hadn't understood me. Rico grabbed me by the arm and hustled us all down the steps past Jade.

"Detective De Palma," Jade shouted, as we made our escape. "Do you have any comments you'd like to make?"

He glared over his shoulder at the camera and mumbled, "Maybe later."

Hurrying on, he stopped after several steps and whirled back toward Jade. "Definitely later."

I crawled across the backseat of Rico's Mustang, leaving the two fossils to duke it out for the front. Lucia, twenty years younger than Nonnie, flatly refused to concede. She crossed her arms and stood back, tapping her toe, waiting for Nonnie to vacuum-pack herself into the car.

Nonnie moaned as she wrestled into the backseat. "*Verkakte* contraption. Is sardine can. How I get out? Such a night."

Rico yawned. "Perhaps you'd rather walk to your car, Nonnie."

"Is only at Templeman's," she said, collapsing into the back seat beside me. "Three blocks away."

"No, dear," Rico said, with a glance into the rearview mirror. "It's at the impound lot. That's where we tow cars when their drivers get arrested."

Lucia, wearing a victorious smirk, slammed the passenger seat back and plopped in beside Rico.

Nonnie smacked the back of Rico's seat. "Feh! How much that cost? I have no monies."

"A hundred and sixty bucks."

Nonnie's eyes glistened with tears. "Miss Allie, what I do? I need car."

"Miss Money Bags up front is loaded," I said, nodding toward Lucia. "She's got at least two loaded socks in that purse of hers." My hand shot forward between the seats. "Cough it up, Buttercup."

Lucia's eyes widened. "No. No, I give you all my Bingo monies. Is gone...empty...no more."

"Then you'd better break into The Widows and Orphan's sock, honey. We wouldn't be here if not for you." I said, making a grab for her purse.

Lucia snatched it away and opened her mouth to argue, but Rico touched her hand and gave her a conspiratorial wink. She melted like permafrost in global warming. Damn his brown eyes. The guy was a freaking fossil whisperer.

"Maybe I look again," Lucia purred.

She made a show of fishing through her purse and raising her eyes, batting her gray lashes at Rico.

"Silly me. Of course," she said. "My Keno money sock. See?"

She flashed a wad of bills, then licked her thumb, peeled off the $160, and gave it to Rico. He flashed his pearly smile at her as he pulled into the impound lot. Once he parked, the oldsters pried themselves out of the car and I slid across the seat to exit after Nonnie. Rico reached around and tapped my shoulder.

"Where do you think you're going?"

"Home with Nonnie. Why?"

"Oh, no, you don't. You're staying here. We need to talk."

"It's five o'clock in the morning. We can talk tomorrow."

"*Now.*"

Well, shit. I'd just made mincemeat out of his girlfriend on the air. I guess I had it coming.

Nonnie and Lucia made a hasty exit, never bothering to turn back to see if I needed or wanted any help. Like rats deserting a sinking ship—cunning, fossilized, blue-haired rat finks.

Rico fixed me in a steely-eyed stare. "This thing with you and Jade has to stop. She's my girlfriend. You're my partner. You don't have to like each other, but you have to find a way to co-exist."

"Don't look at me," I said. "She's the one who uses you to hunt me down like a Bluetick hound, jumping my ass every chance she gets, doing her best to make me look bad in front of the entire city."

"You do a good enough job of that on your own. Cap's already warned you about spouting off in front of the cameras. He's going to be pissed when he sees your interview."

Cap, aka Captain Philip Dorsey of the CPD, heads up the Paranormal Crimes Unit. He's bald with an ever-expanding middle-aged spread and a by-the-book mentality. And he's got issues with me—my mouth, my attitude, basically everything about me. But he knows I'm the best whisperer around, so he gives me a lot of leeway. Enough to let me hang myself from time to time.

Rico was right. Cap had warned me about tangling with Jade Chen on the air. Once again, I'd get my ass handed to me. And once again, I wondered where Little Allie had been when I'd needed her. Why she hadn't intervened—stuck one of Lucia's socks in my mouth. Something. Anything. That buttinsky brain bitch and her ADD were killing me.

Rico's phone rang and Cap's number popped up.

"You don't think he already knows, do you?" I whispered.

Rico shrugged. "Jade wouldn't squeal on you. But she won't pull that interview, either." He lifted the phone to his ear. "Hi, Cap. What's up?" After a few nods and a couple of *uh-huhs*, Rico said, "Text it to me," and disconnected the call. "Looks like neither one of us is going to get any sleep. There's a 311 in progress in Over-the-Rhine."

"A biter call? Can't the cops on duty shoot the damn thing in the head and be done with it?" I asked. "Why do we have to take the call?"

"There are twenty of the bastards, and they've got a delivery truck surrounded at Findlay Market."

"Twenty, you say?"

"Roger that."

"Now, that's something you don't see every day." I settled into the Mustang's leather seat, called Nonnie, and left a message on her answering machine asking her to check in on Headbutt and Kulu. Wrangling twenty rotters could take a while.

"Cap's concerned that this is related to the virus manipulation. He and Director Horton are on their way to the scene."

Swell. Director Dickhead. The day was off to a fine start.

After an expectant pause, Rico finally asked the question I'd been waiting for.

"You think that Toussaint guy has something to do with this?"

The question was inevitable, but it still made me flinch. "It's just a cluster of deadheads. Don't jump to conclusions," I said.

The brain bitch, who'd been AWOL for far too long, finally decided to grace me with her presence. As usual, she was as helpful as tits on a bull.

What the hell's wrong with you? Of course, it's Toussaint. It's time to come clean about your past.

Easy for Miss Goody Two-Shoes to say. But I'd buried the truth three years earlier, along with my father. And as far as I was concerned, it could stay right where I'd left it—out of sight, out of mind, and six-feet under.

4

CIVICS 101

Rico flipped on his lights and headed for Findlay Market. It was only a ten-minute drive from the impound lot, and for that, I was thankful. A little bit of the brain bitch goes a long, long way. I silently told her to stow it, but the loud-mouthed head hag refused to shut up.

Then Rico's voice added to the mix. "What makes you so sure Toussaint isn't involved?"

That was all I needed, those two ganging up on me. For a minute, I wondered if Rico could hear her, too. "I don't know, either way," I said. "Just don't assume anything, okay?"

He shrugged and went quiet, but moments later he came back at me again. "So, tell me about him."

"Him who?"

"Santa Claus," Rico said, rolling his eyes. "Toussaint. Who do you think?"

I slumped deeper into the bucket seat and stared out the window. "I told you before. He's a whisperer like me. And he went bad. End of story."

Rico's twenty questions game was getting on my last nerve. Not that he cared. He continued grilling me as he turned onto

Race Street. "Why did he *go bad*? And what does that even mean?"

"Power...greed. Take your pick," I snapped. "Lord, but you're dense for a cop. The power over life and death can make a person very rich."

Rico pulled curbside in front of Findlay Market and turned off his car. "How do you know him? What is he to you?"

"*Jesus*. Give it a rest, will you?" I opened the door and rolled out of the passenger seat, onto Race Street.

In a few short hours, the market would be teeming with merchants and shoppers alike—a veritable zombie smorgasbord. We'd need to handle the horde quickly and quietly, before sunrise, while the streets were still empty. People tend to find the sight of me butchering biters a little...off-putting. But for some reason, they just can't look away. It's like watching a train wreck. Whether I'm raising a corpse or putting one down, if people are around, they'll cover their eyes and then peek through splayed fingers to watch. When it's over, half of them will think I'm a demon, and the other half, a savior.

No, thank you. Working under the cover of darkness suits me just fine.

Rico joined me and together we squinted down a moonlit Elder Street. "You think these are the biters that can see in the daylight? Or the blind ones?"

"There's only one way to find out," I said, taking his six as we moved on through the darkness.

These days, it was a crap shoot which version of deadhead we might run into. Until recently, biters were elusive. The sunlight burned their retinas, so they came out late at night, kept to the shadows, and lived off vagrants or anything else with a heartbeat. The general public, tucked safely away in their beds, behind locked doors, viewed biters as just another undesirable lurking on the wrong side of the tracks. But once Toussaint started manipulating the Z-virus, the game changed.

The new breed of biters could see in daylight, making them more mobile, and the synthetic version of the virus could be transmitted by injection.

Scary-ass shit, even for a zombie hunter.

Rico pulled a quarter from his pocket and put it between his thumb and forefinger. "Heads they were bitten, tails injected."

I scowled and slapped his hand, sending the quarter skittering across the pavement.

"There is a third option, smart guy. They could have been raised."

"Jesus, Nighthawk. Who pissed in your Wheaties?"

"Yeah, well. You know better."

Rico and I had an easy rhythm for having worked together less than a year. Sometimes, it was easy to forget that he wasn't born into this shit, like me.

"Shh. Did you hear that?" he whispered. "Listen...there it is again."

A soft, but unmistakable, cry for help drifted out of the shadows further down Elder Street. We flipped on our flashlights in unison and scanned the road. The plea came again, this time joined by a distant frenzy of snarls, groans, and moans. We followed the sound a couple of blocks south to a dumpster under siege by a large group of deadheads. A box truck from Avril's Meats was parked curbside, maybe twenty feet away, with no driver in sight.

We took cover behind the rear bumper of the truck, as the biters pinged against the dumpster like a bunch of brain-dead pinballs.

"Do you actually have a plan, or are we winging this?" I asked.

Rico pulled his phone out of his pocket and studied the display. "Cap texted me the delivery driver's name and number." He punched the number into his phone.

Within seconds a muted, tinny version of Pharrell Williams *Happy* floated out from the dumpster.

"Hello?"

"Gary Walker?" Rico asked.

"Yes?"

"Officer De Palma, CPD. I'm positioned behind the rear of your truck. Rough morning, huh?"

The lid creaked open less than an inch and a pair of eyes peeked out. "No shit."

The rotters keened, throwing their bodies against the dumpster, trying to claw their way inside it.

A metallic bang rang out as Gary yanked the dumpster lid closed. "So, do something already. It stinks in here."

"We're working on it," Rico said, rubbing his chin. "Stay on the line."

I raised my eyebrows. "What's our plan, fearless leader?"

"I was hoping you'd tell me."

A sudden chorus of boos and jeers caused us to turn toward Race Street, where a sign- carrying crowd thronged along the Market's perimeter fence. I'd seen the signs before. Freaking ACLU. *Dead Lives Matter. Rotter Rights. Eternal Rest is Meant to be Eternal.*

Rico sighed. "I see your fan club showed up."

"Not to mention your girlfriend and her pet rock," I said, pointing to Jade and Rip, who was filming the fray. "The sun's not even up yet, and the ACLU just happens to appear at the scene of a biter incident, with their Dead Rights signs in hand? I don't think so. I think Jade followed us here and called in the freaking protestors to pump up her exposé."

Jade had been after me to work with her on an exposé about the Z-virus manipulation and the sociopolitical aspect of undeath. I'd turned her down cold. A whisperer like me can't win a debate about the ethics of raising. And when it came to investigating the virus manipulation, Jade had no idea who or what she was up against. I didn't want to be responsible for getting my partner's girlfriend killed.

I smiled and waved at the protestors, making them jeer louder. That's all we needed. A mob of bleeding-heart liberals shredded into zombie sushi (aka *zushi*) on Elder Street. Thankfully, the zombies were laser-focused on the dumpster.

"Isn't this a powder keg?" I muttered to Rico. "What am I going to do? Pull Hawk and blow out the brains of twenty biters in front of a news crew? How long do you think it would take for that clip to show up on CNN?"

Cap, and a couple of suits I didn't recognize, arrived on the scene. Director Dickhead followed several steps behind, wearing his usual tight-lipped snarl. A swarm of officers moved in, and posted themselves along the perimeter of the market to hold the protestors at bay.

"Who are the other two guys?" I asked Rico.

"The guy on the left is Kevin Shoemaker, the Safety Director. I don't know the guy on the right."

Perfect. Yet another talking head. The situation was going from bad to worse.

The delegation moved in and stationed itself alongside us, behind the bumper of the box truck.

"What's your status?" Cap asked.

Rico pointed at the dumpster. "Vic's still taking cover."

"Why haven't you gotten him out yet?" Dickhead asked, crouched last in line at the far end of the bumper, not even bothering to crane his neck for a glimpse at the dumpster. The weasel-wussy douchebag.

"Perhaps you'd like to volunteer to go get him," I said, shifting my gaze to the frenzied horde.

"I'm here in a decision-making capacity, Nighthawk. I'm not an operative."

"Then let's hear your plan, Director. With the media here, I'm guessing you'd rather I not open fire and paint the market

Zushi Red. Who's the new guy?" I asked, nodding at the sweaty, pale-faced stranger plastered beside him.

Sweaty guy, whose eyes had been squeezed closed, whipped his face toward me and cut loose. "I'm Milton Cahill, the city's public relations manager. And dispatching those...creatures... in the public eye is completely out of the question." His words would have carried more conviction if his teeth hadn't been chattering.

"Okay, Milty. What's your plan?" I asked.

Milty's eyes darted from me to Dickhead, then to Cap, next to safety guy, and finally to Rico. When he had everyone's attention, Milty leaned forward, and kept his voice low as he filled us in.

"I say we load those things into the box truck, drive them across the bridge into Covington, and let Kentucky deal with them."

I snorted. "Seriously. Who called this guy in? Catch and release is not an option, here. Next?"

After throwing a devious glance over his shoulder, Dickhead leaned in close. "We could corral them into the truck and then shoot them through the sides so the press can't film it."

"No good," I said. "You can't be sure you'll hit them all in the head."

Cap murmured, "What if we drive the damn truck into the river and just leave them there?"

Milty's eyes went wide. "Are you crazy? The EPA would have a field day."

"This isn't rocket science," I said. "Why don't we drive the truck somewhere private and destroy it—like with C4 or Napalm? Or a javelin missile?"

The safety director stared at me slack-jawed. "Gee, we're fresh out of Napalm and missiles."

"No problem. I've got—"

"Moving on," Rico said, his eyes shooting daggers at me.

"How 'bout we lure them into the truck with a trail of meat, Hansel and Gretel style, then drive them to Ziegler's Scrap Yard and crush the whole mess into a two-by-four Tonka Truck."

"Hello? Remember me?" yelled dumpster-diver Gary, through the open phone line. "That's my truck you're talking about, and roughly $4000 worth of meat."

"You want out of that dumpster or not?" Rico asked.

"Wait a minute," Milty said. "You're forgetting something. Whether the media films you taking down these deadheads or not, they still know the deadheads exist. They've got film of them mobbing the dumpster. You can't just blow these creatures to bits, or crush them into one big zombie cube. They were people once. They need to be identified, humanely dispatched, and properly interred."

"Sure, Milty," I said, with a nod toward the dumpster. "Why don't you go ask one of those *creatures* for his driver's license?"

Cap massaged his temples. "Whatever we do, we can't leave them here. The market's going to open soon." With a quick glance at Dickhead, he announced, "I'm calling the ball. De Palma, Nighthawk, wrangle those biters into the back of the meat truck and take them to the precinct. Back the truck up to the delivery entrance. We'll herd them into a holding cell using catchpoles, and leave them there while we figure something out."

Gary's voice squawked through the open phone line. "Who's going to pay for all my meat?"

"How the hell should I know?" Cap snapped. "File an insurance claim."

I didn't have the heart to correct Cap, or to tell him that most of the losses I'd submitted to my insurance carrier would eventually circle back to his desk for payment one day. Property and Casualty adjusters hate zombies.

Erring on the side of caution, Cap expanded the perimeter around Findlay Market, forcing the media off the block and out of video range. After Rico rolled up the delivery truck door, the two of us unwrapped USDA Prime rump roasts, and blazed a trail of bloody cow flesh to lead the rotters toward the truck. The scent of fresh meat slowly coaxed the biters away from the dumpster. As the sun peeked over the horizon, the last of the deadheads followed the stench of blood, clinging to the shadows to avoid the light. I lifted the dumpster lid and helped Gary scramble out. Rico, perched on top of the truck, waited for the rotters to funnel inside, then rolled the door closed behind them.

The three of us climbed into the cab of the Avril's Meats truck and headed for the 51st Precinct, with twenty deadheads vacuum-packed into the rear cargo hold.

When your day begins like that, you'd like to think things can't go anywhere but up.

But this was a day in *my* life, folks. What were the odds?

5

MEATBAG MELEE

G ary Walker wasn't a happy camper, but who could blame him? He'd spent his early morning hours barricaded inside a dumpster, hiding from a horde of the undead. He drove his box truck through town, toward the 51st, picking bits of lettuce and cigarette butts out of his hair and flinging them out the window. I didn't have the heart to tell him he stunk worse than the deadheads we'd corralled into the back, so I hugged the passenger door, cranked down the window, and hung my head outside. It could have been worse. Poor Rico was sitting right next to him.

"Who's going to explain this to my boss?" Gary whined as he pulled into the precinct's parking lot. "All that meat. And the truck. We can't haul food in it anymore. It's ruined."

Gary switched off the engine, and I opened the door. Rico shoved me out so hard, I almost face-planted onto the blacktop.

"Your boss can get a copy of the police report in a day or so."

"This isn't over," Gary said. "The city's going to pay for this."

Rico glanced at me and shrugged. "Maybe we should've let the biters eat him."

Gary's face blazed. "Just unload those bastards and give me back my truck."

"Sorry," Rico said, taking the keys from Gary's hand. "Right now, it's evidence. We'll get it back to you when we're finished processing it."

"Perfect. Just perfect. It better come back clean," Gary yelled. "I'm talking decontaminated, fumigated, detailed. The whole nine yards."

"I thought you said you couldn't use it anymore?"

"Not for hauling food, but it still runs."

Rico waved down a squad car on its way out of the lot and asked the officers to take Gary home. I held back a laugh as Rico opened the rear passenger side door, shoved Gary inside, and walked away before the badges realized they were transporting a human dumpster. Rico whirled around, and grabbed another officer on his way inside the precinct.

"Hey! See that truck? Make sure nobody messes with it. And no matter what you hear going on inside, *don't open it.*"

As we entered the door of the 51st, different smells invaded my nose—the tang of burnt coffee, the spicy marinara of Ricardo's Pizzeria next door, and the ghostly hint of stale cigarette smoke that permeated the old oak desks from decades past. Disparate as they were, those odors always made me feel at home, as if I'd found my tribe.

Rico and I threaded between the desks and hiked down the long hallway toward Cap's office. When we rounded the final corner, the large, empty space outside his door struck a nerve. Cap's secretary, Miriam Miller, had called that area her office for twenty-five years, before she was murdered a month or so ago. In fact, her death was tied to the Z-virus manipulation case we'd been working. Miriam, a graying, persnickety battle-axe, had been totally devoted to Cap, and vice-versa. Walking past that vacant space every day had to haunt Cap.

A multitude of voices drifted out of Cap's door, Dickhead's

being the most familiar. "Before we put the bastards down, we need to learn as much about them as we can. Are they the sighted variety? Or the sun-blind kind? How the hell did they all end up in—"

"A meatbag mob?" I asked, finishing his sentence as we entered Cap's office. "That's a good question."

It was standing room only. Kevin Shoemaker and Milton Cahill had snagged the two crusty red chairs across from Cap's desk. Director Dickhead stood behind the chairs and Rico filed in beside him. I copped a squat on Cap's credenza and did my best to bring everyone up to speed.

"It was hard to tell what kind of biters they were at first, all clustered around the dumpster in the dark. But once the sun came up, it didn't take long for those bad boys to start lunging for the shadows. They're definitely the sun-blind variety. And freshies too, judging by the minimal amount of decomp."

Shoemaker, the safety director, squirmed and ran his hand across the top of his shiny bald head. "As far as I'm concerned, it doesn't make a bit of difference what variety they are. There're twenty of those monsters and they need to go away quickly and quietly."

"Yes. Quietly," Cahill echoed. "Those creatures are a public relations nightmare." He leaned in closer and lowered his voice. "The ACLU and the media will be all over this. Those creatures were people, once—not so long ago, according to you, Ms. Nighthawk. They had lives, and families, and names. We can't just blow them up, or smash them to smithereens. What would the public say if we annihilate them without at least attempting to find their next of kin?"

I tilted my head back and stared at the ceiling. "Maybe we should put their faces on milk cartons."

Rico smothered his laugh with a cough. Cap shook his head at me and sighed.

Dickhead scowled and moved toward the door. "I'll be

leaving now. Since these biters are the original, garden-variety kind, I have no interest in what you do with them or how you do it."

"You should," I said, as he walked past me. "Zombies aren't social butterflies. They don't seek each other out, go clubbing, or hang out with their BFFs. They're eating machines. The fact that twenty of them horded together should interest you. This was no accident."

Dickhead stopped in his tracks. "So, you think this...this cluster...is related to the Z-virus manipulation?"

"It's too soon to tell, but yeah. It could be."

Cap glanced at his watch. "That truckload of biters has been parked outside for the last half-hour while we've been kibitzing about public opinion. Milton is right. We'll check them for IDs when we put them down. Do our best to notify the next of kin. We sure as hell can't leave them in the cargo hold. De Palma, back that truck up to the door. We'll grab some catchpoles and guide them into the holding cells."

It's a good thing I wasn't calling the shots. I'm an *act now, think it through later* kind of gal. Plans suck. They almost never go smoothly. I'd have driven the deadheads to the closest bomb disposal facility and C-4'd them into bite-sized zushi bits. Problem solved. Failing that, I had to agree that we couldn't leave them in the truck. Cincinnati in May can get toasty. In another couple of hours, the early morning sun would morph into an inferno. The stench of twenty baked deadheads would have the entire precinct blowing chunks. Cap's hastily conceived plan was low-tech and high-risk.

Nothing new there.

We filed out of Cap's office, grabbed some catchpoles from the equipment room and headed for the parking lot, making sure to turn on all the lights inside the precinct. We wanted these biters to be as blind as bats once they got inside.

I pushed through the precinct door into the parking lot and

let out an involuntary groan. The officer Rico had enlisted to guard the truck stood in front of it with his arms outstretched, holding back a throng of media. The truck rocked back and forth behind him, bouncing on its tires. Shrieks and growls rang out from inside it. The sight of Rip Sacca, shoving his mic closer to the truck, made my heart drop.

Jade's voice rose above the din. "Ms. Nighthawk, is it normal for zombies to cluster like this?"

"No comment."

"Back off," Rico snapped. "This is an active scene, Ms. Chen. You all need to give us some space."

"Captain Dorsey, does this incident have anything to do with the Z-virus manipulation?"

Cap blew her off without so much as a glance. Give the botoxed bimbo a cookie. She wasn't as stupid as she looked.

Jade's eyes shot daggers at me as she lunged toward Rico. "Detective De Palma, what prompted the attack on the deliveryman at Findlay Market?"

"This is an ongoing investigation. *Please*, back up. Let us work here."

Jade jostled through the crowd of reporters until she was only inches from Cap. "Captain Dorsey, is CPD properly trained to handle hordes of this size?"

I couldn't hear Cap's response because Little Allie instantly filled my brain with flashbacks of previous mass attacks: the night the deadheads overran my house while I was protecting Leo, and the night my old partner, Harry Delk, and I were attacked while investigating the Crosley building. The freaking brain bitch. That's all I needed—a trip down memory lane. *Properly trained?* More like baptism by fire.

Cap called out additional officers and widened the perimeter, pushing the media a block south. No doubt their cameras would continue to roll, pulling in tight with their zoom lenses. The entire city would be waiting for this video.

Rico backed the truck flush against the precinct entrance, while Cap and I rolled up the truck door, slid the ramp into place, and funneled the biters into the brightly lit building. Rico climbed on top of the truck to man the roll-down door, in case something went wrong and we needed to abort the operation.

Sunlight filtered into the cargo hold from the small gap between the building and the truck, blinding the biters. They stumbled over each other and what was left of the meat, pushing, crawling, and dragging themselves toward the front of the truck, away from the light.

So much for planning.

I climbed up the ramp and began pulling slabs of meat back toward the door. Those deadheads may have been blind, but they heard me moving behind them, and they smelled the blood. One of them spun and lunged at me.

I flung the catchpole at the bastard's head and instantly realized I had no idea how the damn contraption worked.

"Just slip the noose over its head and pull," Rico shouted.

Really? Like the freaking rotter was going to let me slip a bolo tie around its neck.

The good news is that after a couple of failed attempts, I managed to lasso a biter and drag it, a pole's length away from its snapping teeth, down the ramp, through the building, and into the holding cell. The bad news is that the rest of the horde followed *en masse*, like I was the freaking Pied Piper of Pussbags.

"Just keep them moving," Rico shouted. "I'll lock the cell door behind them."

Sure, now they were going where we wanted them to go, but things went a little sideways at the mouth of the holding cell. Once I deposited my lassoed deadhead, I made it back out into the hall, but there was nowhere to go. The other nineteen meatbags pushed forward through the narrow hallway, forcing me back against the door to the lockup. I had to scale the cross bars to the top of the cell, then swing myself over to a fluorescent light fixture and wrap my legs around it, while Rico corralled the last of the biters. When all twenty of them were safely inside, Rico hit the electronic lock.

"*See*?" I said, jumping down from the light fixture. "*This. This is why I don't do plans. They never work.*"

Rico's eyes twinkled. "Maybe it wasn't the plan. Maybe it was the execution."

Freaking dill-weed.

With the horde safely and privately tucked away, Rico and I returned to Cap's office to settle on the cleanest, quietest method of disposal. If the P.R. guy, Milty, wanted to rifle through their pockets to figure out the next of kin, more power to him, but he could do it *after* we put them down. There was no way we could hold these rotters for days on end, hoping to locate their families. Besides, it would be better this way. Watching a loved one get put down is a sight that will haunt you forever.

I'd been there and done that, and had Toussaint to thank for it. One day, I'd be making good on my promise to hunt him down. Just as soon as time and circumstance allowed. Little Allie planted this thought uppermost in my mind as Rico and I rejoined the 'Biter Disposal Committee' meeting in Cap's office.

Surprisingly, the first face I saw when I entered the room was Dickhead's. So, he'd decided to stay engaged after all. He must have realized I'd been right. There'd been nothing accidental about this horde. I marched across the room and stood him, face-to-face. "I've got a bone to pick with you, Director."

He raised an eyebrow and stared down his nose at me. "You don't say."

"You still owe me for the Leo Abruzzi case. I need that money, and I want it *now*."

With a single nod of his head, he reached into his suit coat and pulled out a check. "It's all here," he said. "Every last dime."

He held the check in front of him, but didn't hand it to me. When I reached to grab it, he pulled it back.

"First things first, Nighthawk. You keep dodging my calls. Are you in, or are you out?"

Damn him, anyway. He'd made me a job offer after Leo died, working as a temporary consultant—apparently that's code for 'we pay you if and when the sun, the moon, and the stars are aligned.' He'd given me forty-eight hours to make up my mind. But after Leo's case, I needed a few weeks to get my head straight. I'd gone off the grid and left him hanging.

"Fine. I'm in," I said, snagging the check from his hand.

Cap steepled his fingers beneath his chin and waited for an explanation.

"Don't worry," I quipped. "Now I get paid to consult with CPD *and* the FBI. Maybe between the two of you, I'll be able to afford a can of tomato soup instead of stealing ketchup packets from the breakroom."

Cap rubbed his face with his hands. "Now that you have your career path in order, let's get back to the task at hand, shall we? How're we going to dispatch these deadheads?"

Before he could utter another word, Chuck Clawson, the desk sergeant, rapped on the doorframe. Without waiting to be invited in, he strode to Cap's desk and handed him a document.

"Sorry to interrupt, sir, but you need to see this pronto."

Cap slipped on his drugstore cheaters, scanned the text, and then tossed the form across his desk. "Well, that's great. Just great. The ACLU's filed a preliminary injunction to keep us from," he picked up the document and searched for the actual language, "'taking any and all actions that may result in the termination of...undead lives.' Are you fucking kidding me?"

Milty's eyes grew wide. "The litigation could take years. This is horrible."

"That's a lot of stink," I said. "You're gonna need a *shit-ton* of Renuzits."

Dickhead barked a response, but whatever he said was drowned out by the blare of a siren screaming through the building.

"*Sweet baby Jesus,*" Cap said, scrambling out of his chair. "That's the holding cell alarm."

6

INJUNCTION DYSFUNCTION

"What the hell?" Cap said, rushing into the hall. "That's an electronic lock."

The siren continued to blare as Cap grabbed a couple of officers from the bullpen, and posted them at the doors, to make sure none of the biters escaped the building. The rest of the squad brought their guns to high ready and systematically cleared the administrative offices. Rico and I sprinted through the pandemonium, taking down a couple of rotters as we navigated the hallway that led to the holding cell.

Rico reached the cell first and shut off the alarm. A chorus of shouts and curse words rang out from behind the door directly to my left. I took a deep breath, brought Hawk to bear, and burst into the room, coming nose-to-nose with a rotter. It lunged for me, and I spun sideways, pumping a single shot into its temple as it stumbled past. Whirling around to make sure there weren't any more surprises, I found two naked men, eyes wide, mouths gaped in perfect Os, standing beneath what apparently were very cold showers. One of them screamed, "*Shit*," and turned his back to me. The other remained motionless, staring straight ahead, eyes glazed over with that deer-in-headlights look. Rico pushed through the door, gun at the ready, drawing additional shouts from the naked guys.

Little Allie scolded me, telling me to glance away. And I did, after I got an eyeful. But she should have shoved a sock in my mouth. "Good thing I happened along. My gun's bigger than both of yours."

The guy who'd turned his back to me grabbed his towel and wrapped it around his waist. "The d-d-damn thing wandered through the door right before you, looked at us like we were a couple of ham sandwiches, and started closing in. If you hadn't come along when you did—"

A volley of gunfire erupted somewhere down the hallway.

"Sorry. Gotta run," I said, as Rico and I rushed back out the door.

He went right and I went left. Between the two of us, we'd taken out a total of three rotters. There'd been several other blasts of gunfire throughout the ordeal. The only way I could know how many rotters had been downed was by counting their corpses as I cleared each room on my way back to the bullpen. I verified that the bodies were rotters (as opposed to humans) and double-checked that each had been taken down with a headshot. By the time I made it back to Cap's office, I'd counted sixteen. That meant there were four more rotters, either already downed elsewhere, or roaming the part of the building Rico was clearing.

The officers Cap had assigned to maintain the external perimeter had returned to the building when the first shots rang out. They followed me down the hallway, past the holding cell, to provide back-up for Rico. Not fifteen feet from the locker room door, two more rotters lay crumpled on the precinct's linoleum floor. That brought the total count of downed rotters to eighteen, leaving only two unaccounted for.

As we pushed further through the hallway, I heard scuffling up ahead, then a louder, more distinct thud. Rico's voice joined the mix, followed by a single, unmistakable *pop* of a gun. I broke into a dead run and reached the end of the passage to find Rico's Glock laying on the floor. I cleared the corner and found him flat on his back, with one head-shot rotter splayed crosswise at his feet, and another clawing its way up his stomach, snapping its jaws, and clacking its mossy, gnarled teeth.

A primal scream pierced the air, a scream I didn't recognize as my own. I pulled my Ka-Bar, flung myself on top of the rotter, and plunged the knife into its brainstem.

"Did it bite you?" I asked, rolling its carcass aside.

Rico's chest heaved as he gulped for air. I turned his jaw from side to side, looking for bite marks. His neck was clean. I yanked his shirt out of his pants and tore it open. Small, tooth-shaped rips marred the cover of his Kevlar vest.

No, no, no, no, no.

"Did it bite you?" I shouted, tearing at the vest's Velcro straps.

Rico slapped at my hands then rolled onto his side, panting. "I'm okay. I'm okay. Give me...a minute...catch...my breath."

He wasn't the only one breathing like a freight train. I slid down the wall beside him, sucking air like a Hoover. "You're sure? You're sure it didn't get you?"

"No. I'm fine. Damned things...double-teamed me." He took a few more breaths. "Got off one shot, but the bastard was standing so close that it fell on me and knocked my gun loose."

Cap and Dickhead threaded their way through the officers and surveyed the scene.

"That's the last of them," Cap said, staring at the corpses beside Rico. "All twenty of them."

I climbed to my feet and holstered Hawk. "Guess we won't be needing those Renuzits after all."

"Maybe not," Cap said. "But the press will have a field day

with this mess." He grabbed Rico's hand and pulled him to his feet. "You good to go, son?"

"Yeah. Just a little winded."

Cap shook his head and sighed. "That's an electronic lock. How did it fail?"

Rico rubbed his neck and rolled his shoulders. "Maybe there was a power surge."

"Or maybe somebody unlocked the door," I blurted.

"Let's not get ahead of ourselves," Cap said, as we started back up the hall. "We'll know more once we have the lock inspected. In the meantime, all those reporters who were at the perimeter followed the sound of gunfire back to our parking lot. They'll be clamoring for answers, and they won't leave until they get them."

"Good luck with that." Dickhead sneered. "You're on your own."

Cap glowered at him, then stepped in a puddle of zushi and slipped, grabbing the wall to steady himself.

"Jesus," he muttered, shaking brain splatter off his foot.

Twenty rotters makes a lot of zushi.

"Want me to call Splatz?" I asked, navigating around the bio-puddles in some jacked up game of Twister. Splatz is my favorite biohazard remediation service. They're fast and cheap. Plus, I get a *ten percent off* coupon for every referral.

Cap stopped in his tracks. "They got any kind of BOGO rate?"

"Speaking of rates," I said. "Let's do some math. Two rotters in the hallway at two-fifty a pop, one in the shower, and snaggletooth here."

Rico raised his hand. "One of those hallway rotters was technically mine."

"Yours, mine, whatever. Oh, plus the overtime premium pay for the predawn call to Findlay Market to wrangle twenty biters."

I pulled out my abacus, carried the one, and applied the city's ten percent frequent flyer discount.

"That's $1,400.00 even. Who gets the bill?" I asked, darting my eyes from Cap to Dickhead.

Cap harrumphed.

Dickhead waved me off in disgust. "If, and only if, this horde ties back to the task force, I'll consider it."

"Cheapskate."

"Opportunist."

"You make that sound so dirty."

Clearly there was only one answer. I'd bill both of them. End of discussion.

Dickhead ducked into Cap's office while Rico and I cleaned up. A half-hour later, Rico and I followed Cap up the hallway, headed for the press conference from hell.

As we pushed through the door, reporters raced up the steps, thrusting their microphones in Cap's face. Cameramen pushed and shoved, jockeying for position. Protesters carrying signs and chanting, "Dead lives matter," brought up the rear.

Jade Chen emerged from the throng with fire in her eyes. "Captain Dors—"

Cap held up his hand. "At approximately five this morning, CPD responded to an assault at Findlay Market. The victim, Gary Walker, was successfully rescued, and twenty zombies were taken into custody. They were transported here to the 51st Precinct for holding while city administrators evaluated the most humane methods of identifying and neutralizing the undead, notifying their families, and ultimately, re-interring them."

Cap sucked in a breath and then continued.

"At approximately one this afternoon, the electronic lock on the holding cell that housed the zombies failed. These zombies were newly turned and retained a high degree of coordination and muscle control, which allowed them to quickly move through the precinct at large. Extreme measures—"

Jeers and boos rocketed through the crowd.

"We had an injunction," someone shouted.

Cap cleared his throat, then stood a little taller and continued.

"Extreme measures had to be taken to ensure the safety of the city personnel inside the precinct. Even as I speak, officers are attempting to identify the undead. Next of kin will be notified in a professional and compassionate manner."

A chant broke out among the protesters. "Dead lives matter. Dead lives matter."

"We got an injunction! Stop killing the undead!"

"They're *already* dead," I muttered.

Rico elbowed me, and I elbowed him back.

Cap side-eyed us both, then pushed on. "CPD had been notified of the injunction and acted accordingly, in good faith. Extreme measures were only employed once human lives were endangered and no other viable options remained. Security footage from inside the precinct will bear this out."

Jade Chen seized the moment. "The public wants to see that video, Captain Dorsey."

"No," Cap said, shaking his head. "The video is part of an ongoing investigation, Ms. Chen, and therefore, will not be released at this time."

Another round of jeers and chants filled the air.

"Police brutality!"

"Cover up!"

Jade fanned the flames. "What role did Ms. Nighthawk play in today's events?"

That freaking, botoxed biotch.

I stepped forward to respond, but Rico pulled me back. Turns out, I didn't need to worry. Cap had my six.

"Ms. Nighthawk acted with courage, dignity, and the

highest moral fiber. She saved lives today, as did the other officers present. She is an asset to the city. We're lucky to have her."

Hah! Take that, you addle-brained, over-processed bimho.

Cap brought the press conference to a close, promising to provide further updates as warranted. We stepped back inside and watched from Cap's office as the mob dispersed. Then I pulled Rico aside and let him have it.

"What is it with your girlfriend? I'm tired of her taking pot shots at me."

He yanked his arm away. "That's a two-way street, now. Isn't it?"

"Yeah? Well you'd better keep her on a leash, before we're out of a job. She's showing up at all of our crime scenes lately, because of you. This whole mess with the ACLU today was her doing."

"You don't know that."

"Like hell, I don't. I'm not going to have my livelihood jeopardized because you can't keep Mr. Happy in your pants."

"My sex life is none of your business."

"So, get my business out of your sex life. I hope she was worth you almost turning into rotter stew today."

It had already been a long day, that followed an equally long and ridiculous night. We gave each other some space for the rest of the afternoon. As usual, he had a mountain of paperwork waiting for him.

When Jimmy from Splatz showed up, I walked him through the precinct so he could get a handle on the work he needed to do. Then, I remembered Dickhead's check was burning a hole in my pocket. And it was Wednesday. I had places to go and people to see, so I popped my head into Cap's office and told him I was headed out.

Cap glanced up from his laptop. "Plans?"

"Yes."

"Where you headed? Want some company?"

I stopped in my tracks. The last time Cap asked to go somewhere with me was the 5th of never. "Out. And...no."

What the hell was going on with Cap? Didn't he have a job to do? I spun on my heel and hurried out the door before either one of us could ask for an explanation. Even captains and corpse whisperers are entitled to their secrets.

7

SECRETS AND DREAMS

Wednesday nights are special. All week long I run around in black jeans, raggedy T-shirts, and a pair of zombie-stomping boots. But on Wednesday nights, I trade in my zushi-stained work duds for a fringy red salsa dress that Nonnie picked out. (Why Nonnie? Because I know crap about dresses. It's the only dress I own.) Then I slip on the size ten canary yellow dancing shoes Leo Abruzzi gave me, along with a gift certificate for ballroom dancing lessons at Arthur Murray's. That was right before the drug he was taking to keep from turning into a biter failed. Before he died. And before I had to put him down to keep him from coming back.

"Life's too short," he'd told me the night he died. "Don't leave nothing on the table."

For a double-talking, mobbed up douche canoe, the guy made a lot of sense.

So, for one hour a week, I pin up my hair, slap on some makeup, think of Leo, and live my dream.

I was putting on the finishing touches for my big night out when the doorbell rang, prompting Headbutt to raise his head off the floor vent. Kulu imitated the ring of the bell and screeched *Get outta here* from her perch. I opened the door and was surprised to find Rico.

"Ah...hi," he said, looking at me as if he'd never seen me before.

"Hi, yourself."

He stood on the porch, speechless.

"What brings you by?"

"I, ah. I didn't like the way we ended our discussion earlier. About Jade."

His eyes slowly traveled from the top of my head to my breasts, then lingered at my hips before drifting down my legs.

"Why...why are you dressed like that?"

"I'm on my way out."

"It's nice. The dress, the hair. The makeup." He pointed to my feet. "And the shoes. They're...different."

Heat rose in my cheeks. "Yeah. Not very practical for zombie hunting."

He couldn't take his eyes off me. His lips curved into a bemused half-smile that was hot as hell, and yet, a little creepy.

"Date?"

"What?"

"Do you have a date?"

"Oh. Yeah. He should be here any minute, so—"

"I'm sorry," Rico said. "I should have call—"

A red MX5 pulled into the driveway behind Rico's car. I stifled a wince as Sean Ferris opened the door and slid out from behind the wheel.

Rico blinked. "What's *he* doing here?"

Ferris flashed a ridiculously perfect grin and bounded across the lawn to my front steps.

"Hey, De Palma! Good to see you."

It had been a while since they'd seen each other. They shook hands, but I sensed a weird vibe passing between them, a tenseness in the air.

Ferris casually moved beside me, put his hand on my waist, and asked, "So, what brings you by?"

Rico's eyes narrowed. "What brings *you* by?"

Ferris, an FBI agent, had worked with Rico and me on the task force protecting Leo's butt while he waited to testify before the grand jury. Ferris was a damn fine agent and a straight shooter. He was a quick study when it came to hunting Zs, too. The three of us made a kick-ass team—when it came to the job.

But instead of hanging out after work and grabbing a beer, like I do with Rico, Ferris and I go dancing. And we kiss. And we do other things. Things that I don't do with Rico. I didn't think my relationship with Ferris was any of Rico's business, so I'd never mentioned it.

Talk about awkward. It was time for me to come clean.

"Sean, ah, Ferris is taking me to dance class."

Rico nodded and offered a smile, but it was thin and didn't reach his eyes. Early on, there had been sparks flying between Rico and me. But then Jade Chen, that five-feet-two collection of silicone and hairspray, who hates me more than anal leakage, sank her hooks into him. She'll do whatever it takes to get what she wants, and although she's never said it, she resents me working with him. That's okay. It goes both ways. I can't stand the way she uses and abuses my partner.

"Wow. Hey. Good for you guys," Rico said. "You...have a nice time." He trotted down the steps, then turned back and studied us with unreadable eyes. "Nice running into you, Ferris. See you at the task force meeting in the morning. And you," he said pointing to me, "I'll pick you up at 8 a.m. sharp."

"*Mañana*," I said as he started down the driveway.

He stopped short at the sight of Ferris's MX-5 blocking him in. If Rico had been angling for a hasty exit, he wasn't going to get it.

"I'll grab my purse and lock up," I said. "You move your car. And be nice."

Ferris threw me a wink. "I'm always nice, Allie girl."

———

Ferris and I walked into Arthur Murray's two minutes late. This was only our third week. Counting tonight, we'd been late three times. Big mistake. Our instructor, a tiny, wrinkled Bolshevik named Madame Olga, stopped her class, crossed her arms, and tapped her toe on the wooden dance floor, waiting for us to join the class.

"You two, with the banana-boats shoes and the slicky-boy smile, late again. Back row," she said, snapping her gnarly fingers. "And pay tensions, please. No canoodling. Tonight, we Salsa."

We slunk into the back row, took our places, and listened while the tiny gremlin with the white bird's-nest hair shouted instructions like a drill sergeant.

"Ladies. Eight steps. This way," she said, turning her back to the class. "On one, please. Right foots back, one. Left in place, two. Feets together, three. Pause, four. Left foots forward, five. Right in place, six. Feets together, seven. Pause, eight. See? Now, men's steps. Left foots forward, one. Right in place, two. Feets together, three. Pause, four. Right foots forward, five. Left in place, six. Feets together, seven. Pause, eight. Is simple, yes? And begin, on one!"

Ferris's left foot slid forward. I stepped in and mashed it with my right. We started over. Ferris's left foot slid forward. I stepped in and mashed it with my right.

"You're the girl," he whispered. "Follow me. I move forward. You move back."

Certain that the third time was the charm, Ferris stepped forward with his left, and I crushed it with my right. Lather, rinse, repeat. Lather, rinse, repeat.

Sweat broke out on my forehead as a scowling Madame

Olga slipped through the dancers, adjusting, correcting, and tsk-tsking.

"Jesus, this is hard," I said. "She's almost here. Just let me lead."

"Not a chance."

"*Do it.*"

Madame Olga's eyes snapped our way. "Shush. No talking." She turned to the couple beside us and stomped her foot. "No, no with the droopy shoulders. Shoulders back, arms up. Once more."

"Oh, God. Here she comes." I grabbed Ferris's hand, stepped forward and kicked his left foot back. He stuttered for a count, then rolled his eyes, and followed my lead.

"If you ever tell anyone I let you lead, I'm out."

"I can't help it. She scares me."

Madame Olga's eyebrows bunched as her gaze fell on us. She brought her fingers to her chin and watched us for an entire eight-count.

"Is *backwards!*" She finally said, pulling me from Ferris's arms.

She stepped in front of him and grabbed his hands. "Slicky-boy, show how man leads."

On the next one count, Ferris led that crotchety crone across the floor in a flawless Salsa.

"This. *This,*" she cried, "Is how mens Salsa. Pay tensions, class. Notice the feets, the arms, even the hips. Nice rhythm. Very good student." She glanced at me and sighed. "Keep trying, Miss Banana Boats."

Sure thing, you crusty Cossack. Break a hip.

Three weeks into dance class and my dream was fading fast. But I sucked it up and toughed it out, because the thought of Leo sitting on a cloud, laughing his ass off at me, was more than I could bear.

It's amazing how a one-hour dance class flies when you're

having fun. At least, that's what I've heard. I wouldn't know. After class, Ferris was quiet, giving me a little space as I limped back to his car, nursing a blister on my heel. But I don't do quiet very well, so the lull didn't last long.

"What's she doing, watching your hips, anyway?"

Ferris laughed. "Babe. She's a dance teacher. That's her job. She's also old as hell. Don't tell me you're jealous."

"Of course not," I said, climbing into the car.

And I wasn't. Well, maybe a little. The old bat was graceful for a bitchy bag-o-bones. I'd been called a lot of things in my day, but graceful was never one of them

"Want to stop for a drink on the way home?" he asked, as he buckled his seat belt.

"Not really."

"Want some ice cream?"

"No."

"Want to make out?"

Ferris always had the best ideas.

He wasn't ready to cave on the ice cream, so he swung into United Dairy Farmers and bought a pint of Rocky Road. Then he stopped at the liquor store, so I'd have the fixings for a Jack Daniel's slushie. After an awkward and crappy beginning, the night was starting to look up.

By the time we made it home, it was ten o'clock. Ferris turned on the lamp, lay on the couch and switched on the big screen in my living room, while I grabbed some spoons and cups. Jade Chen's voice drifted into the kitchen and brought the night crashing back into the dumpster.

"Amid a media frenzy and ACLU protesters this morning, noted zombie wrangler, Allie Nighthawk, slays twenty so-called 'deadheads.' Film at eleven." I sprinted back into the room at the sound of her voice, stared at the screen, and watched her put the word *deadheads* in air quotes.

That am*bitch*ous, mega-mouthed weasel.

I dove across the couch for the remote, to make her forty-two-inch face disappear. Ferris caught me in mid-dive and pulled me close.

"Turn her off," I whined. "Before I have to throw my shoe at the TV. I can't afford to break another one."

Ferris kissed the tip of my nose, picked up the remote, and turned off the TV.

"Who needs TV?" he asked, nuzzling my neck. "I've got all I want right here."

I giggled. Or maybe it was Little Allie who giggled. It was hard to be sure.

"I thought you wanted ice cream? It'll melt."

"What ice cream?" he said, nibbling on my ear.

This dating thing was fun, but it made me a little nervous. I mean, I'd dated before. I'd had boyfriends, and I wasn't a virgin. But most guys find me a little...intimidating. I'm not everyone's cup of tea. I'm rough around the edges, and as long as I'm being honest, let's face it, God forgot to give me a filter. None of that seemed to matter to Ferris.

When Ferris looked at me, I was exciting. I was pretty and smart, and sexy and graceful. Maybe not graceful, exactly, but coordinated. Okay, so strike graceful. This was our third date, if you could call hanging out with a pocket-sized dance Nazi and twelve other couples a date. But that was earlier. We were here now, just the two of us. I could feel the beat of his heart against my chest. His breath was warm and soft against my neck and smelled like wintergreen. Somehow, it always smelled like wintergreen. When he was angry, his blue eyes turned almost indigo. When he was feeling mischievous, they blazed bright as cobalt. But as I lay there in his arms, his eyes were periwinkle soft, filled with longing, and maybe, just maybe, a hint of something more.

He kissed me, softly at first, then with more urgency, tonguing me long and deep and slow. Suddenly, I realized that it hadn't been nervousness I'd been feeling. It had been antici-pation. And at that moment, there was nowhere else on earth I'd rather be.

He scooped me into his arms and pulled me to his chest. "Let's move this somewhere more comfortable," he whispered, as he carried me into the bedroom.

8

JUST PLAIN AWKWARD

Something was pressing against my nose. I opened my eyes and found Ferris's arm draped across my face. We were lying on the bed. Naked.

What the...? Oh, yeah.

Memories of last night looped through my brain like a video. An X-rated video. I smiled and snuggled back into Ferris, wishing I could stay here all day, under his body, wearing it like an afghan. But the sun was up, my neck was stiff, and I needed a cup of coffee. I picked up Ferris's hand and laid it on my pillow, then untangled our legs and scooted off the bed. On my way to the kitchen, I glanced at my watch. It was 7:50.

"Holy shit!" I screamed. "Ferris, *get the hell up.*"

A soft snore drifted from the bedroom.

"Now!" I shouted, throwing poor Headbutt out the door for his morning deposit.

When Ferris didn't respond, I sprinted back into the bedroom and snatched his shirt, the first piece of clothing I found, and threw it on.

"Seriously. Get your ass up."

He rolled over and covered his head with a pillow, so I

grabbed his arm, yanked him to the edge of the bed and bent down until we were nose to nose.

"Get out of bed *now* before I make you."

He snored in my face and nice Allie disappeared. I reached behind him and rolled him off the bed. He hit the floor with a thud.

"What the hell?" He rolled onto his back and rubbed his face. "Why'd you do that?"

"It's 7:50. Rico will be here in ten minutes."

"And?"

"I don't want him to see you here."

I threw Ferris his pants and he lobbed them onto the bed.

"Why?"

"This," I said, pointing back and forth between us, "is none of his business."

He sighed, slowly climbing to his feet, and then reached for his pants. "Are you ashamed to be seen with me? Or are you a prude?"

"I am *not* a prude."

"So, you *are* ashamed to be seen with me," he said, slipping into his pants.

"No. Of course not. It's just...awkward. He's my partner, for crissake!"

Ferris laughed. "He's an adult, Allie. And so are you. He knows we had a date last night. And I'm pretty sure he knows you have sex."

Until last night, I *hadn't* had sex in a very long time, but Ferris didn't need to know that.

I handed him his shoes and pointed toward the door. "Please. For me, just go."

"Can I at least have my shirt back?"

"No. It's all I've got on."

"We have a meeting with Director Horton in half an hour. I need my shirt."

"This can't be your only clean shirt."

He shrugged. "I was going to do laundry when I got back last night."

"Fine," I said, shoving him out into the hall. "Don't turn around." I ripped off his shirt and handed it out the door. "Now, please go."

When I felt him grab the shirt, I slammed the door in his face.

Ferris's voice drifted in from the hall. "I'd like to do that with you again, Allie girl. Soon. Really soon."

I cracked the door, stuck out my head, and kissed him on the lips. "Me too. Now, get the hell out of here."

The doorbell rang, sending Kulu into a tizzy.

Me? I sprang into trapped badger mode. "Shit, shit, shit! He's here. What am I going to do?"

Ferris squished his eyebrows together. "Maybe...answer the door?"

"I'm naked."

"You get dressed. I'll get the door."

I started to object, but what was the point? The genie was coming out of the bottle and there'd be no putting it back. I slid on yesterday's jeans, grabbed my T-shirt from the bedpost, yanked it over my head, and made it to the living room in time to see Ferris open the door.

"Hey, dude," he said, stepping aside to let Rico pass.

Rico walked inside, eyeing Ferris's bare feet. Little Allie groaned.

I couldn't face Rico, so I spun on my heel and headed back to the bedroom. "Almost ready," I called over my shoulder. "Just let me grab—"

"Nighthawk." Ferris said softly, eyeballing my shirt.

Rico looked on in stony silence.

"Your...shirt." Ferris said. "It's...inside out. And backwards, maybe."

64

"Huh. So it is," I said, without even bothering to look. "Be right back."

I sprinted to the bedroom, slammed the door, and nearly hyperventilated while Little Allie verbally abused me.

Yes, of course, this is not my finest hour. Absolutely, I am a moron. Thank you so much for pointing that out, you haranguing head-hag. And since I don't have time for a meltdown, how about you take a big old gulp of shut the hell up?

I took off my shirt, turned it right side out and slipped it over my head, making sure that the words *Zombie Queen* were on the back, where they belonged. After a few calming breaths, I left the bedroom with my head held high, filled Headbutt's bowls, and let him back in the house. Then I threw some chicken-flavored dog biscuits into Kulu's cage, because she doesn't like the liver-flavored ones.

"Let's go," I said, slipping into my shoulder holster.

Rico, who hadn't uttered a single word since he'd arrived, watched Ferris and me filter toward the door. After staring at the floor and pursing his lips, Rico finally decided to speak.

"I think you guys forgot something."

Ferris and I glanced at each other and then followed Rico's gaze to the floor.

Neither of us were wearing shoes.

"Why don't I just go on ahead?" Rico said, locking eyes with Ferris. "You don't have a problem taking Nighthawk. Right?"

"No problem at all, dude."

Rico left, bounding down the steps to his car. Ferris pushed the door closed and then turned to me, wearing a wicked grin.

I punched him in the chest. "See? I told you that would be awkward."

9

HOLY HUMPING HEDGEHOGS

After saying goodbye to the terrible twins and locking up the house, Ferris and I hustled to his car. If we were lucky, we would make it to the task force meeting on time. If we weren't lucky, humiliation would be the crowning glory of what might possibly be the most mortifying day of my life.

The task force, headed by Director Dickhead, operated under the auspices of the Patriot Act. Its purpose was to locate and apprehend the person or persons responsible for the manipulation of the Z-virus, which brought about a new genus of deadheads that weren't sun-blind. The synthetic strain could be spread by injection, where the original strain could not.

We had our work cut out for us.

I leaned back in the passenger seat and closed my eyes. Rico's sullen stare returned to haunt me. Surely, the brain bitch was screwing with me, making a mountain out of a mole hill. How bad could our encounter this morning have really been? Ferris wasn't as close to Rico as I was. He'd be able to put things into perspective.

"So, now that we've had a few minutes to process things, am

I over-reacting? Was that scene with Rico really as awkward as I thought it was?"

"Oh, absolutely."

"Just checking."

I'm not sure why I bothered to ask. When I step in shit, it's always with both feet.

Ferris pulled into a parking space at the Kenwood FBI office. I checked my watch and inwardly groaned: 8:31 a.m. A minute late and we hadn't even made it inside the building.

We sprinted through the entrance, took the elevator to the third floor, and speed-walked to Dickhead's office. Damned if he hadn't already closed the door. Ferris sucked in a breath and rapped twice. The muffled sound of footsteps filtered into the hall. When the door finally opened, Rico stood on the other side. I scooted past him, unable to meet his gaze.

The cone of silence descended, as Ferris and I eased past the podium, and walked the long green mile toward the two remaining seats on the far side of the table. Dickhead glanced at his watch, and waited until we were seated to pounce.

"Thank you, for gracing us with your presence, Agent Ferris."

Ferris sat up straight and tugged at his collar. "Sorry, sir. Won't happen again."

Dickhead rolled his eyes toward me. "Ms. Nighthawk, perhaps you can use this meeting to play catch-up, since you've been AWOL for the last month. Welcome back."

The sarcastic ass-munch.

Little Allie had apparently lassoed my tongue, because the only response I could manage was a red-faced nod.

Having successfully drawn his pound of flesh, Dickhead circled the meeting back to order.

"In the last several weeks, we have added some depth to the task force." He glanced across the table at three unfamiliar faces. "Cyber Specialist, Agent Kelvin Thomas. Profiler Psychologist, Agent Barbara McMillen. And Bio-terrorism Specialist, Eli Stanton. Agents, meet Special Agent Sean Ferris from the Cincinnati Field office, Officer Rico De Palma, Paranormal Crimes Liaison for the Cincinnati Police Department, and his partner, Ms. Allie Nighthawk, the ah...Corpse Whisperer."

Those last two words stuck in Dickhead's throat like a splintered chicken bone.

Kelvin Thomas looked like your average cybergeek: young, twenty-something, bone-rail thin, with curly red hair. The only things missing were adhesive tape on the bridge of his glasses and a pocket protector. Barbara McMillen, mid-forties, had hawkish features and a stoic intensity. Definitely not the warm and fuzzy type. Eli Stanton was knocking on the backside of fifty, hair solid grey and crew cut. His bright yellow bow tie was an unexpected treat. The group nodded introductions across the table and then quieted, so Dickhead could continue.

"Before Leo Abruzzi passed away, he provided Nighthawk with a thumb drive containing an encrypted second set of books for the Giordano crime family. Nighthawk broke the encryption and identified our prime suspect, Toussaint Le Clerc, whereabouts unknown."

From the corner of my eye, I saw Rico's gaze dart to me.

"The WHO and the CDC have been able to isolate the synthetic viral strain. Currently, they are working on developing an antidote. From a tactical perspective, we've issued a BOLO to the field offices for Le Clerc. We've also issued advisories, urging operatives to keep their eyes open for a newer genus of zombies that are able to see in daylight, and possible injection marks in virus-infected victims."

Dickhead's eyes gleamed as he turned to me.

"We've also issued an agency-wide training video that contains detailed information on zombie physiology, the associated science of Carovescology, and the most efficient means of acquiring and eliminating disease-infected targets."

"Oh, really," I blurted. "And what brain-dead, half-assed *expert* led that class?"

"Why, you did, Ms. Nighthawk. Captain Dorsey was kind enough to share the video of your training session—from earlier this year. March, if I'm not mistaken. The one where the biter got loose. Surely, you remember?"

Holy Humping Hedgehogs.

How could I forget? Talk about a clusterfuck. There was zushi everywhere. Splatz had to come in. Nobody died, and before it was over, I took the corpsicle down, but it wasn't my best work. And they were using it as a training video? My stomach roiled; I wanted to hurl.

Dickhead smirked at me from behind the podium, and added, "Of course, we took the liberty of a few edits. No use belaboring the unfortunate...developments."

One of these days, I would feed him his nads through his eyelids, but not today. At this rate, I'd be downing Xanax by noon.

Dickhead turned his attention back to the group. "Before I let you go, the recent horde attack here in Cincinnati bears discussing. Although the biters involved were of the day-blind variety, we cannot rule out the possibility that they are in some way related to the Z-virus case. According to Ms. Nighthawk, biters are solitary creatures and don't, as a rule, horde. This suggests a potential behavioral change which could be related to viral mutation or manipulation. It also begs the question, did these deadheads randomly wander into a cluster and attack a target of opportunity? Or did some person, or persons, wrangle a gaggle of rotters, with the intention of creating a horde?"

He took a sip of water and glanced around the room.

"We don't know the answer to these questions yet, but they bear close scrutiny. I'll be issuing an advisory, asking our folks to be mindful of any horde activity that might surface."

A crisp rap on the door brought the meeting to a pause. An

agent I'd never seen before entered the room and whispered something in Dickhead's ear. They murmured back and forth a few times, and when the whispering ended, Dickhead's face blanched and he narrowed his eyes.

"Thank you, Evans," he said, as the agent turned to leave.

Dickhead stared out from behind the podium. "It appears we have a more pressing agenda. There's been another horde attack. In New Orleans, at Tulane University."

Tulane? Oh, Sweet Jesus, no, no, no.

I grabbed the arm of my chair and bolted upright. "Did they get the victim's name?"

The director exhaled a long, ragged breath. "It was Leo Abruzzi's son, Vinny."

10

ANGER, ANXIETY, AND ASSHATS

"Is Vinny okay?" I asked.

Dickhead shrugged. "That's not entirely—"

"Damn it! Was he bitten or not?"

"We don't know yet. NOLA field agents are responding to the scene."

Rico and Ferris turned their eyes to me. I didn't have to be a mind reader to know they were thinking about the promise I'd made to Leo. Toussaint had threatened to kill Vinny if Leo testified against him before the grand jury. The only way Leo would give up the information we needed was if I swore that the three of us would protect Vinny. As if that weren't complicated enough, it turned out Leo and Vinny weren't all that close. Vinny didn't even come to Cincinnati for Leo's funeral. Vinny wanted nothing to do with his father, or with us. The kid was twenty-one years old. I couldn't sit on him. I resigned myself to keeping an eye on him from afar. What he didn't know wouldn't hurt him.

But Toussaint *would* hurt him, or worse, if it suited his purpose.

Dickhead scanned the faces around the table. "Agents Thomas and Stanton, consider yourselves on standby. Agent McMillen, and the rest of you, are going wheels up at ten-hundred. Dismissed."

Wheels up? Not in this lifetime.

I chased after Dickhead as he picked up his portfolio and strode toward the hallway.

"Director, I'll take the bus. It's cheaper. Save you some money. Or I can ride my motorcycle."

"Nonsense. The trip will take twice as long. I'm surprised at you, Nighthawk. For someone so concerned about Vinny Abruzzi's well-being, I'd think you'd be moving heaven and earth to get to him."

Yeah. You would think that, but for one small detail.

I looked up to find Rico staring at me with eyes that sparkled like Everclear. "Nighthawk, why don't I give you a ride back to your place, so you can pack a few things?"

Rico lived less than ten minutes from me. Ferris lived across town. That only made sense. So why did it feel so awkward?

After telling Ferris that I'd see him at the plane, I walked with Rico to his car.

"It's the heights thing, isn't it?" Rico asked, as he ducked inside the driver's side door of his Mustang. "You're afraid to fly." His voice shimmied, like he was stifling a laugh.

"Bite me, blue boy."

"Back at you, ballbuster."

His comment was a little too on the nose. I'd gone slightly mental on Leo's case when we had to scale a five-story fire escape to rescue him. What can I say? A fear of heights sneaks up on you when you're dangling fifty feet in the air.

But I'd soldiered up. I'd done my job, saving Leo's bacon. I'd saved Dickhead's too, that day when a biter got the drop on him. So what if I'd almost tossed my cookies in the process?

And why bring that up now, when I was about to get on a plane? I climbed into Rico's car, thinking that was a bush-league move, throwing that night in my face. Then again, after oversleeping and getting the morning off to such a craptacular start, maybe I had it coming.

Rico went quiet as he pulled out of the parking lot, doing his best to pretend I wasn't there. Sullen wasn't a look that suited him. Clearly, the elephant in the room wasn't going anywhere, unless I poked it with a stick.

"So, about this morning..."

Rico stared straight ahead, without as much as a flinch.

Had he even heard me? "I just think we should talk about it. You know, clear the air."

He darted his eyes to the dashboard clock. "You're only going to have a few minutes to throw some clothes in a bag. The plane leaves in an hour."

What the hell? "Did you hear me? I said we should talk about this morning."

"What about it?"

"It was...awkward."

"What you do on your own time is your business."

"Damn straight it is."

Rico's response came slowly, as if he were weighing his words. "But if you start shitting where you eat, things could get complicated. Even dangerous—for all of us."

"Speaking from experience? I know what I'm doing."

"Do you?"

I threw open the passenger door, as Rico pulled into my driveway. Before he could bring the car to a stop, I hit the blacktop running and screamed over my shoulder, "I'll pack as fast as I can."

You arrogant pinhead.

I took the steps two at a time and slammed the door closed

behind me. With my job, I'm always carrying concealed, so after cramming three pairs of black jeans, six T-shirts, a handful of underwear, and plenty of extra mags into my duffel, I thought again and added my Dopp kit and a phone charger. Little Allie put a bug in my ear, and I circled back to my dresser, dug to the bottom of the top drawer, pulled out a small, white box that I'd almost forgotten was there, and tossed it in my bag. Next, I dialed Nonnie and begged her to watch the terrible twins again while I was gone.

She took it well, considering I had no idea how long I'd be away. Maybe a little too well. Knowing Nonnie, nothing ever came easy. She had to have an end game. It's a good thing she wasn't in it for the money, but one of these days she might expect me to cough up a kidney or something.

Kulu fluffed herself into a fat feather duster and squatted on her perch, sulking and muttering Sicilian curse words—words she learned during her last stint with Nonnie, the Nose of Palermo. Headbutt lay atop his favorite floor vent and yawned, then rolled a bloodshot eye at me and turned away. I hadn't even left yet, and I was already in the dog house. Or was it the bird cage?

I tore down the steps, tossed my duffel into the back of the Mustang, and plopped into the passenger seat. Rico backed out of the driveway, headed up Pitty Pat Lane toward Red Bank, and picked up our conversation where we'd left off.

"There's a reason the FBI has rules about fraternization."

Little Allie let out a yelp. "Are you kidding me? You're going to tell Dickhead?!"

"It's not my place," Rico said, shaking his head. "I'm just saying that you should think twice about getting romantically involved with your partner."

"Oh, really? But it's fine for you to play hump-the-ho with your hoochi-mama."

"Hump who?" Rico made the connection and frowned. "It's not the same. And don't call her a ho."

"How is it different? She follows us closer than toilet paper stuck to a shoe."

"But my life isn't in her hands. And neither is yours."

I snorted. "Technicalities. Thanks to her, you could have been zombiefied today."

"You don't know that."

Rico might be right about my life not being in her hands, but she sure made my life miserable.

I did a double take as Rico drove past Madison Road. "Isn't your house back there?"

"Yes, but we're headed to Lunken Airport."

"Don't you have to pack a bag?"

He sighed and threw me a glassy stare. "I have a packed go-bag in my trunk at all times. The day I found out I was on the task force, I threw in extra ammo and enough clothes for a week. I take my job seriously. You should try it, sometime."

"Hey, I keep a go-bag. It's in my locker at the precinct."

True enough, although it paled by comparison, a couple of outfits and a sports bra. Point taken. This task force was international. We could travel anytime, anywhere. I needed to be ready.

Damn. I hate when he's right.

I climbed the steps of the Gulfstream, eyeballing one of its turbine engines. "You're sure this thing's safe?"

Rico chuckled. "Safer than driving I-75 at rush hour." He stood at the bottom of the steps, swept his eyes the length of the plane, and whistled. "She's a beaut. A G5. Sleek and sexy."

Freaking gorgeous. Wait 'til I puke in the aisle, I thought. *He won't think she's so sexy then.*

I made my way down the aisle and found Ferris buckled in and waiting for the rest of us to arrive. The seats were grouped facing each other, with tables in between. Further down the aisle was a couch. It was good to know that after I hurled, I'd have a place to lie down.

I plopped into the seat across from Ferris. Rico sat next to me on the aisle. Barbara McMillen, the profiler, boarded moments later and took the seat beside Ferris. She smoothed her hair with a bony hand, tucking a few loose strands back into a topknot that squatted on her head like a balled-up ferret. Long, spindly legs and Cobbie Cuddlers poked out from beneath her trench coat. She nodded in our general direction and fastened her seatbelt.

Rico glanced around the interior and then nodded at Ferris. "Nice ride. You G-Men travel in style."

"Courtesy of our friends at Homeland Security. Horton wrangled it. The Z-virus is hitting some nerves."

I buckled the seatbelt so tight I almost cut off circulation to my lower extremities. Barbara fished a pair of cheaters out of her purse, then pulled a copy of Science Today from her briefcase and buried her head behind it. Not exactly a social butterfly.

The captain strolled back to introduce himself and announced that we'd be leaving momentarily. Then he closed and latched the cabin door and returned to the cockpit.

I nudged Rico's elbow. "That pilot looks awfully young. Why isn't he flying commercial jets?"

"He's had a couple of crashes."

"What?!" I said, starting to hyperventilate.

"Sorry." Rico grinned. "Couldn't resist."

I yanked the collar of my T-shirt away from my neck. "Is anyone else hot in here?"

The plane began to roll. I sucked in a breath and watched the other planes on the tarmac slip from view. Then, the engines whined, and the plane picked up speed and roared down the runway. My body compressed against the seatback. Within seconds, the jet slowly lifted off the runway and climbed into the air. As if that weren't horrific enough, I watched my hand take on a life of its own and clutch Rico's arm in a death-grip.

"We're flying," I whispered.

"That's the general idea."

Little Allie sprang to life and bitch-slapped my brain. *For God's sake, woman. Get a grip.*

I jerked my hand off Rico's arm and turned away, feeling my face blaze.

Ferris's eyes sparkled from across the table. "Don't tell me you've never flown before."

Rico nodded. "Yeah. She's got a thing about heights, and apparently...flying. Oh, almost forgot. Public speaking, too."

"Good to know," Ferris said, leaning across the table. "So, tell me. How is it that Allie Nighthawk, zombie hunter extraordinaire, who can single-handedly fight off a horde, panics at a little altitude?"

"Yuck it up, G-man. Sooner or later this plane will land, and I'll kick your smug ass."

Barbara peered out from behind her magazine and fixed Ferris in a thoughtful stare. "Actually, recent studies show that warriors often have fears and failings to overcome. It's their ability to rise above those weaknesses, in the commission of their duties, that establishes them as heroes."

"Yeah. What she said." I flipped Ferris off and turned to look out the window. Big mistake. The sight of fluffy white clouds made my stomach roll.

I shut the blind and Ferris laughed out loud. "I'm loving the hell out of this. What were the odds?"

Barbara closed her magazine and squared it neatly on her lap. "Statistically speaking, five percent of the population has acrophobia, the fear of heights, while 6.5% of the population suffers from aviophobia, the fear of flying. These phobias frequently co-exist within a host, causing panic, shaking, vertigo, profuse sweating, heart palpitations, and oral outbursts."

Rico snorted. "Oral outbursts—Nighthawk? How can you tell? That's like twenty-four seven."

"Really? You're gonna poke the bear?" I asked, shooting him daggers.

Barbara's pinched lips melted into a lopsided smile. "There, there, Ms. Nighthawk. These phobias can be overcome with cognitive behavioral therapy that exposes the victim to his or her fears in varying degrees."

The plane banked to the left. My eyes flew wide. "We're turning. Why are we turning?"

Ferris pointed out the window. "That's where New Orleans is."

"In the meantime," Barbara added, "May I suggest a controlled breathing technique to help alleviate your anxiety?"

"No, Babs, you may not."

She scowled at me over the rim of her cheaters. "My name, Ms. Nighthawk, is Dr. *Barbara* McMillen. I hold both an MD and a PsyD as well as an MS in Behavioral Analysis. I have an eidetic memory and speak seven languages. You may call me Dr. McMillen, Agent McMillen, or in more colloquial settings, Barbara, if you must. But at no time may you call me Babs. Have I made myself clear?"

Well slap my ass and call me Fanny. The bony bitch had balls.

"Crystal," I said, having no intention of calling her anything but Babs.

She leaned back and closed her eyes. "Perhaps try visualizing yourself in a calm environment."

"As opposed to 30,000 feet in the air?"

Rico pointed to the electronic flight monitor. "Actually, it's closer to 41,000 feet."

"Work with me, people." Psycho Babs took off her cheaters and clasped her hands beneath her chin. "Ms. Nighthawk, picture yourself basking in the warmth of the summer sun, amid a field of glorious sunflowers. Or listening to the sweet, soothing strains of Debussy's "Prelude to the Afternoon of a Faun.""

"What the...who the hell *are* you lady?"

Babs sniffed and stiffened her back. "No need for language, Ms. Nighthawk. I was merely trying to ease your discomfort."

Ease my discomfort, my ass. Between De Palma and Ferris busting my chops and Babs' sunflower fetish, I was praying for a parachute. The only thing that would have eased my discomfort was a fifth of Jack. Since we didn't have one (massive oversight on my part), I pushed my seat back and closed my eyes, making a mental note to properly stock my future go-bags.

The next thing I know, the pilot's voice flooded the cabin. "Sorry, ladies and gentlemen. We're working our way around a thunderstorm. You might experience a bit of turbulence. Please remain seated with your seatbelts fastened. We'll be arriving in New Orleans in approximately thirty minutes."

Ferris winked at me. "See, Allie? Nothing to worry about. We'll be landing soon."

Rico smiled. "You know what they say about landings. They're nothing more than controlled crashes."

I flipped him off, settled back into my seat, closed my eyes, and tried a gruesome but effective visualization technique of my own: our jet suddenly encountering a sudden microburst and plummeting nose-down toward Earth at 508 miles-per-hour. Simply knowing that this planeload of asshats would be checking out with me made my chakras explode like an expired can of biscuits.

My fear disappeared. The negative energy that had been

churning inside me was gone. I was Allie Nighthawk, dammit. The best of the badass zombie hunters. Toussaint had to be behind the attack on Vinny, and it was time to get on with the chase.

Maybe there was something to this psychobabble crap after all.

11

SAUNTER AND SWAGGER

A black government-issued Suburban was waiting for us when we debarked at the NOLA Lakefront Airport. Our driver, Agent Philip Mouton, still had peach fuzz on his cheeks, and spoke with a down-home drawl.

My stomach growled as I tossed my bag into the cargo hold. It was noon in Louisiana, which made it one o'clock Cincinnati time. We'd been up for hours and hadn't eaten a thing. I slid into the back seat with Rico and Ferris, leaving the front passenger seat to Babs. If I didn't eat soon, they'd be scraping me up off the floor mats.

I leaned forward between the seats and took matters into my own hands. "Hey, we've been traveling all morning. Fiorella's is right around the corner. How about a pit stop?"

Phil glanced at me in the rear-view mirror. "Wouldn't mind popping in there myself."

"And it's crawfish season. Doesn't that sound tasty?"

"It surely does, but the field agent in charge already ordered in lunch. He had a feeling you'd show up hangry."

My stomach groaned. It had been a long time since I had a plate of red beans and rice. I could smell them from the car.

Rico cast me a suspicious eye. "Crawfish season? Fiorello's Restaurant? How do you know so much about New Orleans?"

The brain bitch threw a hissy and flicked me hard between the eyes. Damned if my empty stomach hadn't tricked me into opening Pandora's Box. I had a hell of a history with New Orleans, a history I wasn't prepared to share with anyone, let alone Rico. I'd give him the basics, but if push came to shove, I'd whitewash the truth with a big fat brush.

"I went to school here."

"Really?" Rico swiveled toward me. "I didn't know that. Tulane?"

"Yep."

"What year did you graduate?"

"I didn't."

"Oh."

It was an awkward 'oh.' I was hoping he felt awkward enough to drop the conversation, and he did. But that didn't stop Ferris from picking a little deeper.

"Why not?"

"I tried it for a couple of quarters. Sitting in a classroom wasn't my thing."

Ferris snickered. "Talk about a square peg in a round hole."

"Sorry to interrupt," Phil said, turning onto Leon C. Simon Boulevard. "We're almost there."

He pointed out the FBI office and I stifled a sigh of relief. Somehow, I'd managed to finesse my way through that conversation without telling a single lie. It was the facts I hadn't shared that would have curled their toenails.

Phil signed us in at security and then led us to a conference room on the first floor.

"Make yourself at home," he said, unlocking the door and

showing us inside. "Be right back. I'm going to see where your lunch is."

A massive oval conference table with microphones at every seat dominated the room. A podium, projection screen, and audio-visual equipment filled what little space remained. Rico, Ferris, and I walked to the nearest seats, at the front of the room, and sat beside each other. Babs silently strode to the far end of the oval and sat in her own zip code, then placed her briefcase atop the table, carefully squaring it with the table's edge. She folded her hands in front of her and stared impassively at...who the hell knew what? The woman was ten pounds of crazy in a five-pound sack. But the brain bitch just couldn't let her be.

"How's the weather down there, Babs?"

"My, my," she said, slipping her cheaters up her nose. "You are an annoying little gnat, aren't you?"

Rico kicked my foot beneath the table. I kicked him back.

Our game of footsy ended when the door opened. Phil had returned with a food cart. I craned my neck to see what was on it, but the plates were covered with metal domes.

"*Bon appetit!*" he said, as he handed us our plates.

I yanked off the dome and stared at a puny looking slice of ham on white, hold the...everything. "What the fuck, Phil?"

Phil's face flushed. "There's chips and pickles, too. Oh, and sweet tea."

I picked off the top slice of bread and ogled the grey meat-like substance. "We're in the freaking food capital of the world and you bring us...*Oscar Mayer*? Whose lamebrained idea was this?"

"It was mine, Ms. Nighthawk."

The lazy, *Luzianna* drawl came from a suit who had saun-tered into the room with impeccable timing. He carried himself like he owned the joint. Five-ten, trim, mid-forties, maybe, judging by his salt and pepper crewcut. His all-gray moustache suggested he might be closing in on fifty.

"Senior Agent Jake Boudreaux," he said, extending his hand.

I gripped it and steeled myself, preparing for the bone-crushing handshake that follows with guys who feel the need to put me in my place. When it didn't come, Agent Boudreaux earned back a couple of brownie points.

"Sorry about the Spartan lunch. Hectic morning. We'll make it up to you at dinner."

"Damn straight, you will. Bring your credit card. I'm talking everything from *étoufée* to *crème brûlée*."

Boudreaux's eyes gleamed. "So, you're the whisperer I've been hearing about. Looking forward to rubbing elbows with you."

After introducing himself to Ferris and Rico, Boudreaux glanced at Babs, at the far end of the table, and favored her with a nod. "Agent Boudreaux. And you would be...?"

"Doctor Agent Barbara McMillen, MD, PsyD, MS."

"Impressive," he said, though his eyes didn't seem to share that assessment. "And your role on this team, Dr. McMillen?

She slid her glasses down her nose and gazed at him over the top of the rims. "I'm the profiler, Agent Boudreaux. The person who's going to find the un-sub who's orchestrating these zombie attacks."

Rico and Ferris eyed each other silently. The brain bitch screeched so loud my eardrums nearly burst. I opened my mouth to eviscerate Babs, but Boudreaux beat me to the punch.

"You sound awfully sure they *were* orchestrated. If so, I hope you live up to your swagger. In the meantime, you might want to lower your nose a tad. We get some mighty big rainstorms 'round here. Wouldn't want you to drown."

Boudreaux didn't wait for Babs to realize she'd been taken down a peg. "Let's get down to business, shall we? At approximately 0200 this morning, our vic, twenty-one-year-old Tulane student, Vincent, aka "Vinny," Abruzzi, was attacked at the corner of Audubon and Zimpel, while walking to Monroe Hall from his bartending gig at The Boot, a local campus watering hole.

"Witnesses report four zombies, shambling in from different directions, converged on Abruzzi, despite the presence of multiple persons in the vicinity. Many of these folks were screaming to beat the band, which theoretically, should have drawn the biters away from Abruzzi. But those present stated the biters appeared to target him.

"Campus police responded to the numerous 911 calls that ensued. They dispatched three of the Zs with single head shots. Apparently, Abruzzi took one down by himself."

"The kid took one down?" Rico asked, leaning back in his chair. "Impressive. Even the campus police here know to go for the head."

Boudreaux laughed. "Agent De Palma, New Orleans is the land of the undead. We wrote the book on this shit."

I was liking this guy more every minute.

"The campus police reported the attack to NOLA PD, who turned it over to us, based on allegations from Abruzzi that you folks might have a handle on all this. Is that true?"

Little Allie told me to play it close to the vest. "That's a little hard to say at this point. I'd love to talk to Vinny. Where is he?"

"He had an exam this morning. Said he'll be in around three to chat with us. It's a quarter 'til two now. Ferris, why don't you sign out a car from the garage, take your team to the Marriot on Canal and get checked in? Be back here by three."

In slightly more than an hour, I would meet Leo's son, Vinny. I wondered if they would be anything alike. Then it occurred to me that there couldn't possibly be more than one Leo. Right?

12

THE ODD COUPLE

"Nice ride," I said, as Ferris popped the hatchback on our FBI pool car. Judging by the sea of identical SUVs that lined the garage, dark and nondescript were the only game in town. "Nothing says G-man better than a black Suburban with tinted windows."

After loading our gear into the back, we climbed inside, and Ferris chauffeured us to the hotel. We were a bit early for standard check-in, but Cherry, the desk clerk, scanned the reservations and advised us that wouldn't be a problem. The FBI was a preferred customer.

Fluffy robes, cable, and a mini-bar coming up. Life was good.

Cherry handed us the keys. "Two rooms. Two King-size beds each."

An awkward silence filled the air. Ferris looked at Rico. Rico glanced at me. None of us could bring ourselves to peer at Babs.

"There must be some mistake, Cherry," I said. "Check again."

Cherry pulled up the reservation on the computer and wrinkled her nose. "Sorry. You've only got the two rooms."

"Preposterous," Babs said, drumming her long, shellacked talons on the countertop. "We'll require two additional rooms, please."

Cherry blanched. "I'm afraid we're booked solid."

Babs cast me a withering glance, then turned back to Cherry. "Surely, you have at least *one* room."

"I wish I did. It's Thursday, convention check-in day. The Ancient League of Druids and The Disciples of Dag'theth are in town. If we didn't hold back rooms for the FBI, you'd be sleeping in your car."

Little Allie was having a seizure. A night bunking with Babs could push the brain bitch over the edge.

The two rooms were across from each other on the second floor. Babs led the way, trudging down the hall on her long, gangly legs. I followed several paces behind, racking my brain for some brilliant, but as yet elusive, last minute reprieve. Rico and Ferris hung back, whispering, barely within earshot.

Ferris's voice caught my attention. "A hundred bucks, De Palma. You bunk with McMillen. I get Nighthawk."

"Not a chance."

"Seriously. If those two stay in the same room, there's going to be a death match."

"You think? Five to one on Nighthawk."

Ferris grinned. "That's cold, dude. But, yeah. Okay. You're on."

Damn Rico. I'd rather be bunking with Ferris. But push come to shove, I wouldn't mind taking some of that action myself.

Babs stuck her keycard into the lock on room 232, but the green light didn't pop on. She swiped the card a couple more times, giving me a chance to make up the distance between us. When she finally got the card to work and opened the door, I hurried in past her, and tossed my bag on the bed closest to the bathroom and the hallway. Babs might be a braniac, but I wouldn't want her to be my first line of defense if someone uninvited slipped into our room in the middle of the night.

Babs scowled at me as she placed her Burberry suitcase on the far bed, squaring it perfectly with the edge of the comforter, just like she'd squared her briefcase with the tabletop on the plane. She systematically unpacked her clothes, one piece at a time, placed them all on hangers, and then sprayed them with wrinkle release. Curious, I watched as she laid out her toiletries on the sink and lined them up from left to right, shortest to tallest.

Shamed into action, I opened my duffel, pulled out my Dopp kit, and dumped my clothes onto the bed. Then I balled them up and wadded them into a dresser drawer. There. All unpacked.

I walked to the bathroom door and peered around the corner. Babs' lotions and makeup covered the entire top of the sink, lined up with military precision like tiny, collagen-based warriors. She produced a travel-size can of Lysol from her cosmetic bag and sprayed the room from floor to ceiling.

I marveled at the strange and awful enigma that was Barbara McMillen, stepped away from the door, and placed my Dopp kit on the nightstand beside my bed. Babs emerged from the bathroom, grabbed her briefcase and purse, and then left the room without a word. But not before adjusting the thermostat. I followed behind her, mouth agape as I peeked at the temperature display.

Seventy-eight degrees.

I dialed it down to sixty-eight, thought about it, then cranked it back to sixty-two, and closed the door behind me on my way out.

The two of us were destined to go twelve rounds, and Psycho-Babs, aka *The Profiler*, would go down. Hard.

Rico and Ferris stepped out of room 234, looking somewhat relieved to find us both still in one piece. But the day was young. I followed Babs out to the parking lot, and climbed into the SUV, wondering which one of us would snap first. Twenty minutes later, we all filed down the third-floor corridor of the FBI building to Agent Boudreaux's office. When I stepped through his door, I thought I'd fallen into a time machine.

A ghost from my past, five-feet-six with greasy black hair and tiny, close-set eyes stared at me. He wore tight jeans, a gold chain around his neck, and too much Paco Rabanne cologne. When he introduced himself, his thick Jersey accent confirmed that Leo's apple hadn't fallen far from the tree.

"Vinny Abruzzi," he said, swiping his thick, dark curls out of his eyes. "You Nighthawk?"

"I am."

Memories of Leo flooded back. I stuck them in a box and filed them away for another time. But damned if those weren't Leo's eyes staring back at me. Stupid memories. Stupid emotions, and all that other namby-pamby, wimpy crap welling up inside me. I felt my eyes filling and nipped it in the bud.

Corpse Whisperers don't do tears.

When Boudreaux introduced Vinny to the rest of the team, Vinny's sharp brown eyes stayed glued to mine. After an awkward pause, he finally said, "You don't look so tough."

"Yeah? Well, when it comes to biters, I'm the best there is."

"So I'm told," he said, darting his eyes to Boudreaux. "I just figured you'd be eight-feet-tall and bullet proof. Not some Barbie doll in black."

What an irritating pissant. He was even more like his father than I thought.

"And yet, here I am," I said, plopping into a chair at Boudreaux's conference table. "You didn't think you needed my help the last time we talked. What's changed?"

Babs' eyes narrowed. "You've spoken before?"

I brought her up to speed on how Leo had turned state's evidence and had given us information that implicated Toussaint in the Z-virus case. I also mentioned that Leo was afraid Toussaint might retaliate by hurting Vinny. When Leo died, I'd called Vinny to let him know about the funeral, and to offer my protection, but Vinny told me to piss up a rope. He wanted nothing to do with me, or his father.

Vinny squirmed. "Yeah. About that conversation—"

"Save it," I said. "Tell me about last night."

"It's like I told the campus police and everyone else who's asked. I was on my way home, about two a.m., from bartending at The Boot, when I got jumped by four rotters. The creepy thing is, the bastards seemed to be targeting me."

Rico leaned across the table. "How so?"

"They came from different directions, shambled past other people, and came right at me. Just like what happened the day my dad got attacked."

How had he known that?

I looked deep into his eyes, hoping I could read them the way I'd been able to read Leo's. "We never discussed your dad's attack, Vinny. How could you know anything about that?"

"About a month ago, I got a copy of dad's will from his attorney. There was a letter in the envelope addressed to me, telling me how he got bit and turned state's evidence. He told me you said the rotters seemed to be changing, and that maybe some of them could *see*."

Vinny paused and rubbed his face with his hands. "He told me how he took that drug trying to stay alive for a while, hoping we could talk before he...you know. He said you guys always treated him decent, and that it was okay if I couldn't forgive him for being the world's shittiest dad, as long as I knew I could trust you. I've been reading everything I can get my hands on about deadheads ever since. That's how I knew to go for the brain when I took down one of the bastards that attacked me."

The kid had guts. Just like his dad.

"No shit?" I said. "What'd you use?"

"My blade."

"What do you carry?"

"An AK-74 Boker Kalashnikov. Three and a quarter inch blade."

Ferris grinned and leaned across the table. "That's a helluva knife, kid. I'm not even sure it's legal here in New Orleans."

Vinny yawned. "The law says it's okay, as long as it isn't concealed." He slouched down in his chair, locked his hands behind his head, and stretched his legs out in front of him. "But to be honest, I got it in Jersey, when I was sixteen. It wasn't legal there then, and it still ain't now. Whatever."

Okay, so the kid had guts *and* a 'tude.

I couldn't help but smile. Leo was back, maybe not in the flesh, but certainly in spirit. Based on the police report and Vinny's interview, I had to admit the attack looked anything but random. If that was the case, Toussaint was likely behind it, and Vinny was in danger. He couldn't go back to living in his dorm, taking classes, and working as if nothing had happened. He'd be sticking with me, whether he liked it or not.

Vinny's stomach growled. "I been in exams all day. You people going to feed me or what? Let's go to The Boot. I'll set us up—"

"Sorry, guy," I said. "Your schedule is about to change, big time. No more Monroe Hall, no more class, no more working at The Boot, and no more French Quarter, or hanging out in crowds, until we get to the bottom of your attack."

Vinny shrugged. "The only exam I have left is a take-home, and I can do that anywhere. But I need my job. And where the hell am I going to live?"

Ferris pushed back from the table and got to his feet. "I'll have a chat with your boss, and square things away on the job front."

"And for the time being," I added, "You can stay with us at the Marriot."

Vinny's stomach rumbled even louder. "First things first. Where are we going to eat that doesn't draw a crowd? I'm dying over here."

Hmmm. A secluded little place, off the beaten path, that served kickass Creole cuisine? I caught myself smiling. It had been a few years, but I could still taste her gumbo. And when it came to protecting Vinny from Toussaint, no one could help me more.

"I know just the place, Vinny boy. We're going to Mama Femi's."

13

LIAR, LIAR PANTS ON FIRE

Rico and I reclaimed our places in the back seat of the Suburban. Vinny scrambled into the third row, leaving Babs the shotgun seat next to Ferris. I told Ferris to take 46E to St. Bernard Parish, where we'd find the best restaurant in all of Louisiana, nestled in obscurity, on the edge of nowhere, in a tiny patch of land called Meraux. We had a half-hour drive in front of us, and Vinny, like his father before him, didn't care much for the sound of silence. He settled back, looked into the review mirror, and asked, "What's the name of this restaurant we're going to?"

"Mama Femi's," I said. "Best Creole this side of the Mississippi."

"How would you know?"

Snot nose punk.

"I went to school here for a while."

"Is that a fact?"

The car got quiet for all of thirty seconds, before Vinny's brain took a ninety-degree turn.

"Where am I going to sleep tonight? I got like a... whatchamacallit...a regimen, you know? I like it cool, sixty-two, sixty-four. A little white noise, TV, radio, lights off, drapes closed—"

"On a rollaway," Rico deadpanned. "In the room with Ferris and me."

"Not happening, po-po. Vinny doesn't do rollaways."

"You do now. Think of it as expanding your horizons."

Vinny sighed and leaned forward between the seats. "We got to stop at the drugstore. I need my hair gel and deodorant. Toothpaste, toothbrush, mouthwash, and floss sticks—the thick, minty ones. And cologne."

I eyed him over my shoulder. "*Cologne*?"

"For the hunnies," he said with a wink. "Makes 'em hot for the Vin Man. Know what I mean?"

Sweet Baby Jesus! The kid wasn't just his father's son, he was his freaking replicant. Leo 2.0. This was just like old times. I didn't know whether to rip out his gonads or kiss him on the mouth.

"This is adding up," he said. "I'm going to need face wash and moisturizer. And astringent. I hope you guys got some money."

The brain bitch wheedled me to throw Vinny and Babs together in their own hotel room, and let them duke it out over ablutions, counter space, and the thermostat. But frankly, the broad was twelve kinds of twitchy, and the kid was growing on me. Like a fungus, but still...

Vinny pulled a 360 and took the conversation in a new direction.

"This whole thing's wacky, in a cosmic kind of way, isn't it? I mean, what are the odds that both dad and I were attacked by biters?"

Babs popped up her head like a meercat. She swiveled in her seat and stared at Vinny with feverish eyes. "Let's calculate, shall we? By their very nature, zombies are not pack hunters, and therefore, eschew social bonds. They lack the ability to

sexually reproduce, and have no interest in collaborative exis-
tence. They are food-driven, solitary creatures. And highly
territorial. These facts suggest that the probability of a random
attack by a single zombie, on your father, is within normal
limits. The better question, young man, is the probability of
four zombies converging on the Tulane Campus, and working
in tandem to take down prey. Records show no reported zombie
attacks in the history of the university, suggesting the area is not
intrinsically hospitable to the undead. That, coupled with the
previously noted corroborative evidence, demonstrating the
solitary nature of zombies, simply put, suggests a group attack
is highly unlikely, if not empirically impossible."

Vinny's eyes had glazed over after 'let's calculate.'

"Is she for real?" he whispered.

"Certifiable," I muttered. "And I have to bunk with *her*. Bet
that rollaway with Rico and Ferris is looking pretty good about
now."

Five minutes later, we were driving through the streets of
Meraux. How long had it been? Seven, eight years? Could that
be right? It seemed like yesterday. But it also seemed like a lifetime ago, too—before I discovered how truly dark the dark side
gets.

A few new condos dotted the landscape, and a Dollar Store
had sprung up in place of the old Bijou Theater, but the rustic
white frame houses I remembered had stood the test of time. A
little weathered, maybe, and in need of new paint, but solid,
and proudly maintained. Nestled among them was the house of
Olufemi Okoye, more affectionately known as Mama Femi.

The stately two-story, with its wraparound porch and inlaid
brick sidewalk, had sprawled at the foot of Rue de Triumph for
over 200 years. Mama lived on the second floor. Her restaurant,

Mama Femi's, filled the ground floor. The house's gingerbread eaves and hand-hewn rocking chairs welcomed all, while the haint blue ceiling of its portico kept evil spirits away. Mama had taught me that. I smiled at the memory and shoved Little Allie aside when she pondered whether that home-spun gris-gris would be strong enough to keep Toussaint at bay.

Ferris pulled up to the house and parked the Suburban along the curb. We poured out its doors and followed the path of paving stones to the front steps. The screen door on the porch opened from inside and a young couple strolled out. The man held the hands of two toddlers. The woman carried a doggie bag in one hand, and a jar of fresh herbs in the other. Mama had an uncommon touch when it came to growing herbs and mixing tonics. Most folks who stopped by for dinner, or to shop for their herbals, knew Mama as the old Creole woman who fixed the best gumbo in St. Bernard Parish. But others, the conjurers and root workers, the ones who dabbled in magick, knew Mama as a wise and powerful Hoodoo queen.

The Mama I knew was both.

I pulled open the screen door and spotted Mama with her back to me, hunched over a sideboard, stirring a crock of what smelled like *étoufée*. She placed the ladle on the buffet and paused, then tilted her head upward, drew a long, deep breath, and smiled. She was more stooped than I remembered, and her hair had gone to gray. But what had I expected? She was nearly eighty years old.

Little Allie pushed her thoughts across the room. *"I'm home, Mama."*

Mama placed her hand on the sideboard and turned slowly. Her weathered gray-green eyes were moist. So were mine.

"*Ti Kras Zwazo*," she whispered, opening her arms. "*Vini nan Manman*."

Little Bird. Come to Mama.

I crossed the floor in the blink of an eye and wrapped my

arms around the only mama I had known since I was eleven-years-old—when my real mother died. Mama Femi was round as a whiskey barrel, and not much taller. She could sing a baby to sleep or summon hellfire. I heard her do both during the time I spent with her. Holding her close, I whispered in her ear, *"Manman, mwen te manke ou anpil."*

She kissed my cheeks and smiled. "And I have missed you, too." She peered behind me at the rest of my posse. "Come. Sit," she said pointing to a table. "Mama Femi gonna cook someting wonderful for you."

I followed on her heels, offering to help, as she scurried back to the kitchen, but she shooed me away, insisting we would have time to chat once the dinner crowd thinned out. She sent me back to the table with a platter of shrimp and cornbread bruschetta. Little Allie was hoping that the presence of food would instantly derail any probing questions about my reunion with Mama. But I knew better.

Rico eyed me, as he snagged a piece of cornbread. "You want to fill us in?"

"About what?"

"Your touching reunion with Mama...Mama Fefi."

"Mama Femi. And no, I don't. Pass the bruschetta," I said, reaching across the table.

Ferris slid the platter out of reach. "Not so fast. You said you went to school here for a couple of quarters, but *that*," he said, motioning from me, to the kitchen, and back again, "that kind of...connection...doesn't happen overnight."

"Liar, liar," Vinny said, filching some shrimp from the platter. "No bread for you, 'til you 'fess up."

Babs folded her hands neatly on the table and swung her eyes to me. "In point of fact, studies show that humans are quite adept at lying. It seems our capacity to deceive is matched only by our need to trust. Ironic, isn't it," she said, dabbing stray crumbs off the table with her finger tip. "Exaggerations, embellishments, omissions are all part and parcel of that which makes us human."

I cast her my Allie-eye. "Blow it out your ass, Babs."

The cone of silence descended. Damned if it wasn't uncomfortable, with everyone staring at me, waiting for an explanation. Little Allie, who'd started this ball rolling with her telepathic message to Mama, was suddenly and conspicuously quiet. The lily-livered sapsucker.

"I didn't lie," I said, squirming in my chair. "I just forgot to mention that *before* I took classes at Tulane, I...studied...with Mama for a while."

Rico's eyes narrowed. "Studied what?"

"And how long is *a while*?" Ferris asked.

"A few years," I said, glancing back at the kitchen, wishing Mama would save my ass by bringing more food.

Babs settled back in her chair and tented her fingers beneath her chin. "Ms. Nighthawk's reluctance to share the applicable pieces of her past is indicative of deep-seated trust issues. Which, as I previously stated, explains her propensity for lying to others as well as to herself."

That stork-legged psycho-biotch had a death wish. But she also had a point.

Sure, I had trust issues. Issues that had nothing to do with my partners, or Vinny, and everything to do with a past I'd worked hard to forget. And as long as I was telling the truth, I'd known, from the moment we were ordered to New Orleans, that my past with Mama would come up. But I'd also known there was no one better to help me catch Toussaint than my *Manman*, better known among believers as the Hoodoo Queen, Madame Olufemi Okoye.

I glanced at the expectant faces around the table, sucked in a breath, and then shared the story of me and Mama Femi.

14

COMING CLEAN

"This might come as a shock, but I wasn't the easiest child to raise." I glanced around the table, daring anyone to take a cheap shot. Their curious, expectant eyes stared back, and for once, their mouths stayed shut. *Screw it*, I thought. *If they were in for a penny, they were in for a pound, whether they wanted to be or not.*

"I was eleven years old when my mom died. She had this... this...gift. *My* gift. She'd been teaching me how to control it—to appreciate its power. And the importance of rules, a system of checks and balances to keep me centered. She never got the chance to finish teaching me. Dad had no idea how to handle me, or my power. By the time I hit fourteen, I was sassy, sarcastic, and impulsive. Completely out of control."

"As opposed to the way you are now?" Rico asked.

"Do you want to hear the story, or not?"

He raised his hands in surrender, so I began again. "Someone needed to rein me in. Dad didn't know how to do that, but he knew people who did. My mother's...colleagues. That's when Mama Femi took me in."

One of Mama's waitresses swept out of the kitchen with platters of seafood, pastas, and po' boy sandwiches. Mama trailed behind her, carrying a tureen of her gumbo, a favorite in the Big Easy. My nose had an orgasm.

Hands grabbed, silverware clinked, and the focus shifted away from me and my story. For a moment, I thought I'd gotten a reprieve.

Fat chance.

Ferris tossed back some popcorn shrimp. "So, you lived here year-round with Mama?"

"Most of the time. Sometimes, I'd visit my dad. Sometimes, he'd visit me."

Rico blew on a spoonful of gumbo to cool it down. "What, exactly, did Mama teach you?"

"Discipline, self-control. Ethics—and a little bit of hoodoo."

The dinner clatter faded.

"Like...*Voodoo?*" he asked.

"Not exactly," I said. "Voodoo is a religion. Hoodoo is a kind of...magick."

Ferris raised a brow. "You don't believe in that mumbo jumbo?"

Wow. My heart sank. I expected more from him. "With everything you've seen, you *don't?*"

"Sorry. Skeptic—occupational hazard."

"You're an FBI agent, for God's sake. Don't dismiss things that you don't understand. You're better than that."

"The virus, the zombies, I accept." Ferris paused, as if reaching for the right words, and finally blurted, "Superstition, curses, and chicken feet, I gotta go with *no.*"

An awkward silence fell over the table. Everyone resumed stuffing their faces. Everyone except me. I was pissed. As far as I was concerned, the conversation wasn't over.

"And what about my power, Ferris? Where do you stand on that?"

His eyes bored into mine. "I believe in *you*. And your power. I've seen it. It's...tangible. Like the virus and the rotters. They exist. They're *real*."

I shook my head and whispered, "There are more things in Heaven and Earth, my friend. If you *do* believe in me, believe this: The magick is real."

Ferris went silent. Rico scraped the last of his gumbo from his bowl. "So, for the...less informed...at the table, what kind of magic are you talking about?"

Wasn't that a loaded question? What kind *weren't* we talking about? Conjure powder and oils, rituals, spells, cross-me-not barriers, five finger grass, goofer dust. The list goes on. Mama knew them all. Even with my training, I'd barely scratched the surface.

"All kinds," I said keeping my voice low. "Most of the magick Mama practices is for protection." There was, of course, a darker form. The kind Toussaint used. But for that night, under Mama's roof, for very deep and personal reasons, Toussaint and the practice of dark magick weren't appropriate topics of conversation.

Vinny raised the last bite of his po' boy to his mouth. "Were there other kids there with you—like a special Hoodoo Hogwarts school for whisperers? Or did you have a, whatchamacallit, a tutor?"

The brain bitch hissed in my head. *Now you've stepped in it.*

I squirmed and stared at my water glass praying for a diversion. "Yeah. Sure. From time to time, there were other students."

Rico's head snapped up. "Was Toussaint Le Clerc one of those students?"

Mama swept out of the kitchen, carrying a tray of beignets, pecan pie, and bread pudding. I sighed in relief—until she bobbled her tray, nearly spilling the sweets on the floor.

"Toussaint? How you know my *bway*?"

"Your...boy?" Rico darted his eyes to me. I shot him daggers, a silent warning to let it go. Mama either missed the exchange or chose to ignore it.

"Toussaint was my best *apranti*—next to my Allie. How is my sweet *bway*?"

"I wouldn't know," I said, avoiding Mama's gaze. "I haven't seen him in years."

"Nor I. Strange, eh?" She eyed me. "You two used to be...so close. Where could my *bway* be?"

I felt the weight of Rico's stare and looked up to discover Ferris studying us both. Mama finished handing out the desserts, and then silently ambled back into the kitchen.

"Good one," I said, punching Rico's arm. "Mama doesn't know about Toussaint."

"Doesn't know what about Toussaint? And *close?* You and he were *close?* Since when?"

Babs sighed. "I am the profiler assigned to this case. If you were involved with him, you might have mentioned it earlier."

"Back off! Mama doesn't know he went dark. And it was nothing. We were just kids."

The brain bitch blew a freaking gasket. *Just give up all your secrets, pinhead.* She was right, damn it. I felt naked as a jaybird.

Ferris snorted. "Mama knows more than you give her credit for. She sure knew you were lying."

"Whose side are you on, anyway?" I turned to Rico and stuck my finger in his face. "Ix-nay on the oussaint-Tay in front of ama-May."

"She needs to know, Nighthawk."

"Let me handle that."

"Just see that you—"

His phone rang, cutting his lecture short. He glanced at the number and got up from the table with a sigh.

Son of a bitch. I'd know that sigh anywhere. Jade had joined the mix.

Babs scowled across the table at Vinny, who'd been shoving food into his face non-stop. "You should eat slower, Mr. Abruzzi. Chew your food. It isn't trying to escape."

"Hey," he said, sliding his plate out of Babs' reach. "I don't get to eat like this a lot, you know? Mama's a damn fine cook."

I ignored them both and elbowed Ferris. "That bubble-brained twat-waffle needs to take her hooks out of Rico. She's on him like a dog on a bone."

Ferris dropped his half-eaten beignet on his plate. "Why do you even care?"

For the second time that night, the brain bitch nearly took out my ear drums. *See, dumbass? It isn't just me. Ferris sees it, too. You're jealous.*

The freaking head-harpy. What the hell did she know?

Babs quirked an eyebrow at me. "Jealousy is quite common among work partners who've bonded deeply. It's nature's way of—"

I clenched my teeth so hard they almost cracked. "Zip it, psycho-bot. Or next time, I'll—"

Rico had returned to the table and was standing behind me. He slumped in his chair and glowered at me, when I tried to explain why I was so peeved.

"I don't even want to know," he said, waving me off. "That was Jade calling. She tracked us down and caught a flight to NOLA. She wants to follow the investigation for her exposé."

I went vertical, nearly flipping the table on its side. "Damn it, Rico! That's the last thing we need—her sticking her pert, plasticized nose into this case. She's going to get herself killed. Or one of us. Send her back home. *Now!*"

"Chill out," he said, climbing to his feet. "She's at the Maison Dupuy Hotel. I'll Uber there and talk some sense into her. You guys stay put, enjoy the night."

I had my jacket halfway on. "You need more fire power. I'll send her perky ass packing."

Ferris snickered.

"No thanks," Rico said, on his way to the door. "If I wanted this thing to blow up, I'd just throw gasoline on it."

Maybe he was right. Okay, he was absolutely right. But I hate that freaking news floozy with every microbe in my body. He was also right that I should enjoy the night with Mama. I sighed, draping my jacket over the back of my chair, and then silently began bussing the table.

Ferris, unusually quiet, waited until I started for the kitchen to speak. "Where are you going?"

I looked down at the stack of dishes in my hands and then at Ferris.

"Let's go for a walk," he said. "We need to...talk." His eyes darted toward Vinny and Babs. "About the...case."

"I should help Mama," I said, turning on my heel and racing toward the kitchen. I was quick, but not quick enough.

Ferris beat me to the doorway, leaned down and murmured, "While you're in there, give it some thought. Why are you so invested in Rico's life? Maybe then, you can explain it to me."

I'd rather not.

"We can talk about this later," I said, slipping past him into the kitchen.

Mama tried to shoo me back. "Go. Sit with your friends, *sha,* I get this."

"If it's okay with you, I could use a break."

Mama watched Ferris with a bemused smile as he strolled back to the table. "Look at you," she said, turning back to me and taking my hands. "So strong. So beautiful. No wonder he wants you. How have you been, Little Bird?"

I didn't even try to explain my relationship with Ferris to her. Hell, someone would have to explain it to me first. So much had happened since she and I had seen each other last. Where to begin?

"I'm good, *Manman*. Happy."

"Centered?' she asked. "At peace?"

Anything but. "Absolutely."

She looked deep into my eyes, the way she had when I was young and she'd suspected I'd been lying. But she didn't call me on it.

"And your Papa. He is well?"

My eyes began to sting. I cleared my throat and fought for the words. "He's been gone three years now."

There was more. So much more that I needed to share with her about his death. But tonight, our first night back together, I couldn't bear to break her heart.

She pulled me to her chest. "Sweet child, God's will sometimes leaves us empty. But in time, He fills the hole." She stepped back and ran her hands through my thick, black hair. "So, what brings you back home to your *Manman*?"

I shrugged, blinking back a tear that threatened to spill. "I miss your *étoufée*."

"Tsk-tsk," she scolded, "do not lie to *Manman*."

Little Allie cowered in my brain. Suddenly, we'd regressed to the clueless teenagers who could never put anything over on Mama. We'd been busted once again. It was time to come clean. So, I gave Mama the *Reader's Digest* version of how I came to work with CPD and the FBI, making sure to stress that I always keep my rules. *Always* is such an exacting term. I tried not to wince as the word shot out of my mouth. But there was no use trying to fool her. She knows that even though I aim for black and white, I usually end up in the gray. I finished my quick and dirty employment history with, "My...friends...and I are here on a case."

"And Toussaint has something to do with this case?"

"He isn't the angel you remember. Neither am I."

Mama eased herself onto a stool beside the well-worn

butcher-block table. "I hear tings. I know he grows stronger. And I know your heart. There be no darkness in you. The truth this time, child. Why are you *here*?"

I needed her help. And the only way I was going to get it was to tell her about Leo and the virus manipulation. I explained how the virus had been bioengineered to spread more easily, to create more zombies. In Mama's vernacular, bioengineering was akin to root work. Spells and magick were staples of the hoodoo culture—Mama's culture. She'd taught us those things to broaden our understanding of the metaphysical world. Toussaint excelled in root work, in the science of it all. The tortured look in Mama's eyes told me she was putting the puzzle together. I thought I caught a glimpse of guilt in those eyes too, and my heart ached.

The power Toussaint and I shared, the power to raise the dead, wasn't root work or hoodoo. But the reason we were left in Mama's charge was because she understood the veil between life and death, understood the intoxicating power of our wonderful, godawful gift, and the isolating responsibility that came with it. She would consider Toussaint's fall her own failing.

Mama patted my hand. "Is that why you left? Why you and he parted ways? Because he crossed into the darkness?"

I couldn't find my voice. But Mama knew it was true. She *always* knew. With Mama, there was only black and white, never gray. She slowly rose from her chair, shuffled to the doorway, and peered into the dining room. "Good. The night is slow. Your friends are comfortable. The tall, skinny woman is reading a journal, the young man is wooing one of my waitresses, and your man is drinking coffee and checking his phone."

"He's not my man."

Mama snorted. "He is yours, *sha*, whether you want him or not. Come with me."

She led me through a faded velvet curtain strung across a doorway at the back of the kitchen, and I couldn't help but grin. It had been forever since I'd played in Mama's greenhouse.

———

The musky smells of dirt, flora, and mingled herbs met my nose as we crossed into that magical space. Memories of being spellbound as I watched Mama conjure flooded my brain, followed closely by memories of my own spells gone sideways, that had been snatched from the jaws of calamity by Mama.

We walked beneath incandescent lights and followed the main aisle to the center of the greenhouse, where we stopped at a rustic wooden workbench littered with gardening tools, candles, oils, and a mortar and pestle.

Mama lowered herself onto her stool, looked me in the eye, and asked, "What are the two forces in this world?"

The dogma was ever-present. "Good and evil."

"And which path do you follow?"

"The good."

"Then we protect you against the bad, eh?" She worked quickly, anointing her gnarled hands with JuJu oil, a combination of Myrrh, Mimosa, Jasmine, Patchouli, and Galangal.

"As above, so below," she whispered, coating a candle, starting at its center and working her way to the top.

She began to pray aloud. I recognized the words; they belonged to Psalm 23.

She smiled and whispered, "Pray with me, child."

My voice joined hers. "The Lord is my Shepherd; I shall not want. He maketh me to lie down in green pastures: He leadeth me beside still waters. He restoreth my soul: He leadeth me in the paths of righteousness for His name's sake."

Mama continued dressing the candle, this time starting at the center and working her way to the bottom, as we recited the rest of Psalm 23. I'd read that passage so many times when I was a child, that even though I hadn't thought of it in years, the words sprang from me like a song.

"We ask you, Lord, to protect this child against all evil." Mama's eyes began to glisten. "And against those who do the dark works of the left hand. May she rise victorious above all that is malignant."

She let the candle burn as she filled a scrap of red flannel with a collection of herbs, roots and oils, some of which I recognized: dried toadstool, camphor, and powdered jellyfish. She started to stitch the edges of the flannel into a pouch, then almost as an afterthought, crushed a rose petal and sprinkled it into the mix.

"What's that for?" I asked.

She grinned. "What you tink it for?"

I blushed. Of course. It was for love. *Give me a break, Mama.*

She slipped a leather cord through the half-sewn pouch, stitched it closed, then held it in her palms, and blew life into it. Slipping the gris-gris bag around my neck, she said, "Wear this next to your heart. Always. Every Friday, you soak it in whiskey. Keep it strong."

Hey, that worked for me. I could soak it while I was sipping one of my Jack Daniel's slushies.

Mama's face looked like it had aged beneath the incandescent lights. "Last I heard, perhaps a year or so ago, Toussaint was rehabbing a manse in St. Bernard Parish." She started back toward the kitchen, then turned to me with a sad smile. "You should visit a shoppe not far from Congo Square. *Zanj Lan Fé Nwa.*"

The Dark Angel. My heart skipped a beat. That was the childhood nickname we'd given Toussaint when he was nothing more than a charming bad boy.

Mama and I silently made our way, arm in arm, back through the curtain and found Ferris standing in the kitchen with his arms folded across his chest. "Thanks for the amazing meal, Mama Femi. I'm sure we'll see each other again. Right now, Allie and I need to be getting back to the hotel. We have some...unfinished business...to discuss."

Well, shit, I thought. *Mama's busted up rose petal better have some good juju in it.*

15

THE GIRL FROM IPANEMA

The ride back to the hotel was...what's the word? *Awkward.* Babs' nose never came out of her journal. A silent Ferris set his jaw and wrapped his fingers around the steering wheel in a death grip. Vinny whined about us committing *stud-us interruptus* in his efforts to pick up Mama's waitress, Luna. And the head hag bitch-slapped me repeatedly for oversharing, or as she put it, *spewing my secrets like projectile vomit.*

"Is it me?" Vinny asked. "Or is it like really tense in here?"

"How astute," Babs muttered.

When we pulled into the Marriott, my hand was already wrapped around the door handle. As soon as Ferris parked, I tried to make a break for it, but the door wouldn't budge. I hadn't anticipated child-proof locks.

Ferris threw me the side-eye. "Nice try, Slick. Agent McMillen, would you be kind enough to escort Vinny to my room and stay with him until I return? I won't be long." Ferris reached to the back seat, handed Babs his room key, and then glanced at Vinny. "You will remain there *all* night, locked inside, sleeping on the roll-a-way. Or you and I are going to have a problem. Copy that?"

"Cockblocker," Vinny mumbled.

"Horndog."

Babs took Vinny by the arm as he slid out of the SUV. "Come along, Mr. Abruzzi."

The door swung closed behind them, leaving only Ferris and me.

A chill snaked up my spine and woke up the head hag. *You're in for it now, Aliyah Marie.*

I hate when she calls me by my given name. And I swear, I heard her giggle. Ironic, isn't it? The brain bitch had a front row seat to my first lover's quarrel with Ferris.

I sucked in a breath and slowly let it out. "Well?"

Ferris squirmed and stared out the window. "What is it with you two, Allie?" He paused, like he was waiting for an answer. When I didn't give him one, he began again. "You bitch about Jade having her hooks in Rico, but you're...worse. You micromanage his love life. And he..." Ferris twisted his hands around the steering wheel. "Sometimes, he looks at you the way I do. This morning? The look on his face when he came to pick you up and found me there? He has feelings for you too. You know that, don't you?"

I couldn't have denied it even if I'd wanted to. But I couldn't bring myself to admit it, either—to Ferris, or myself. And certainly not to Rico. I was hoping the head hag would pull a pearl of wisdom out of her haughty ass and save me, but she must have been too busy enjoying the show to intervene.

"Well?" Ferris asked.

"Well, what?"

"Damn it, Allie. What do you want?"

What did *I* want? What did *he* want? Sure, we were dating. But we weren't exclusive. The four-letter "L" word had never been spoken. Sure, Rico was hot. And yeah, there was some kind of chemistry between us. But he was with Jade—at least, for now, anyway.

God, I needed a drink.

"Is it hot in here?" I asked, pulling at the neck of my T-shirt. "It is. I don't feel so good."

I rolled down the window and hung my head out like a St. Bernard.

Ferris chuckled in spite of himself, swiveled sideways, and caressed me with his beautiful blue eyes. "Damn you, Nighthawk. C'mere," he said, pulling me close. He kissed my forehead, sending shivers through me. "You don't need to give me an answer tonight. I wouldn't want you to hurl or anything. Not in the agency car."

"Thanks. Good thinking."

"I mean it," he said. "Take your time. Don't tell anyone, but I'm kind of sweet on you, Allie girl. The thing is, I don't like to share. And if you're looking somewhere else, I won't stand in your way." He shrugged. "You could do worse than Rico. He's a stand-up guy."

I kissed Ferris's cheek, inhaled the spicy scent of his Dolce and Gabanna cologne, and almost sighed out loud. This romantic shit was still new to me. I wasn't sure what to say, so I blurted, "I'm...fond...of you, too."

"Fond?" Ferris laughed so hard he nearly choked.

Fond. Yeah, that's right. Of all the words in the English language, I went with fond. Freaking loser. All these *feelings* and *emotions*—all this weeny shit confuses the hell out of me. Somebody give me a roadmap.

Ferris turned his eyes toward the lobby. "Speak of the devil."

Rico had returned and was climbing out of an Uber.

"Call it," Ferris said, opening his door as Rico entered the hotel. "Heads, Jade's headed back home; tails, she told him to pound salt."

I climbed out of the passenger side and grumbled, "Tails."

If I knew Nancy Newshound, she wasn't going anywhere. Ferris and I threaded through the crowded parking lot on our way to the lobby. I'd almost cleared the last row of cars when someone grabbed my shoulder from behind. I spun, leading with my elbow, and connected with a crazed six-foot freshie.

The rotter absorbed the blow from my left elbow and then grabbed my right arm as I followed through with a hook. I pulled my punch at the last second when I realized my fist was headed straight for its teeth. The stinking deadhead jerked my arm toward its mouth, snapping its jaws. I shoved the heel of my left hand into the tip of its chin. It stumbled into the side of a Chevy Blazer, lost its footing, and fell.

A quick glance at Ferris found him tangling with a deadhead of his own. I drew Hawk, squeezed the trigger, and completed a brainectomy on my rotter, but I didn't make it three steps before being brought down from behind.

Hawk skittered from my hand and slid beneath an SUV.

I flipped onto my back and stared into the maggot infested face of a corpsicle.

A shot rang out across the parking lot. Had Ferris taken down his biter? The corpsicle bent down to make a meal out of me, so I snap-kicked its rotting gut, nearly severing it in two. It plopped to the ground in a puddle of liquefied zushi.

I scuttled beneath the SUV and retrieved Hawk, swearing I would never tell Rico that I'd lost my weapon to a biter yet *again*. He'd have apoplexy. What can I say? When you throw down with deadheads, shit happens.

As I belly-crawled out from beneath the undercarriage, something clamped onto my ankle. I looked back and saw my boot squished between the jaws of another rotter. I couldn't get off a clean shot with my foot in the way, so I kicked the meatbag in its face with my other boot. It loosened its grip, and I yanked my foot free.

Once I'd slithered out from beneath the car, I circled around and pumped a 9 mm between its eyes. Allie: three. Biters: zero.

Another shot rang out. My eyes darted back to Ferris. He'd taken down two bogeys, but a third one bulldozed him from behind. The rotter straddled Ferris, ready to drop for the kill.

Ferris pulled his trigger, but the gun misfired.

Rico sprinted out the lobby door, gun at high ready, but he was still maybe twenty feet from Ferris.

"Keep clear," Rico yelled. He brought his Glock to bear, steadied, and pulled the trigger.

Booyah, Baby. This battle belonged to the good guys. Six up, six down, and the parking lot was covered in zushi. Rico grabbed Ferris's hand and pulled him to his feet.

"What took you so long?" Ferris asked.

"I was in the elevator, on my way to the second floor, when I heard gunshots. I got off and took the steps back down. If I hadn't, I'd still be on the slowest elevator in the world, listening to the freakin' Girl from Ipanema, waiting for the door to open."

Ferris put his hands on his knees to catch his breath, then pulled out his phone and called in the attack. Good. Let the Feds deal with the parade of police that would come screaming into the parking lot any minute now.

Little Allie nearly shattered my eardrums. "Oh, my God! Vinny!"

Ferris secured the scene while Rico and I sprinted into the lobby and bounded up the steps to the second floor.

Rico positioned himself along the wall and banged his fist on the door. "Agent McMillen. It's De Palma. Everything all right in there?"

The door opened the length of the safety chain, and the barrel of Babs' baby Glock peeked out.

Rico flattened himself against the wall. "Agent McMillen, holster your weapon please, and open the door."

"*Thank God*," Vinny yelled from inside. "Take that thing away from her before she kills somebody."

The safety chain clinked as it slid across the door. Babs let us in, shaking worse than a crack addict. Vinny scrambled out from beneath the bed and plopped into the desk chair. He reached into his shirt pocket, pulled out a crumpled Marlboro Light, and raised it to his lips. His fingers trembled like he had the DTs when he lit up.

Babs frowned. "That's illegal, Mr. Abruzzi. Not to mention unhealthy."

"Forget you, lady. You *and* your wobbly gun. You scared the shit out of me."

Babs blushed and turned her eyes to Rico. "I heard gunfire and pushed Mr. Abruzzi to the floor. Is everyone all right? Where's Agent Ferris?"

"We're fine," Rico said. "Ferris is outside coordinating with the local PD."

"Another pack attack," I muttered. "We can forget about the element of surprise. Toussaint already knows we're here." I fed Hawk and racked the slide. "From now on, I suggest we all stay locked and loaded."

"Shit. Jade," Rico muttered, pulling out his phone.

Oh, yeah. I'd almost forgotten. "How'd your conversation go?"

"How do you think it went?" he asked, calling Jade. "She's got a job to do and so do we."

He opened the door and stepped out into the hallway.

Fine, I thought. *Catch us if you can, you manipulative man-eating succubus. Just don't expect me to hold your prissy little hand.*

Come tomorrow, we had to find Toussaint, but fast. Taking Vinny with us posed a problem. Leaving him here with Babs posed an even bigger problem. She served a purpose from an investigative point of view, but she didn't have the gravel of a field agent. The thought of taking Vinny to the FBI office for safe-keeping didn't sit well with me either. My circle of trust has never been broad. Knowing Toussaint and his ability to grease palms, I figured we were better off looking after Vinny ourselves.

When Rico walked back into the room, his eyes didn't meet mine. He knew Jade would only get in the way. There was nothing I could do about that. We needed to get on with the business at hand. I told him about Toussaint's manse in St. Bernard, and that Mama suggested we check out the *Zanj Lan Fé Nwa Shoppe*, near Congo Square. I didn't mention the significance of its name. There was enough resentment between us already.

"Good. We've got a place to start," Rico said. "Let's meet downstairs in the coffee shop at nine a.m."

I walked to the door to leave, but then turned and stared him down. "If Jade wants to investigate, fine. But she's on her own. We're not taking her, or her pet cameraman, with us."

Rico's eyes grew dark. "She knows that."

"Does she?"

"I told her so," Rico growled, opening the door, and signaling that it was time for Babs and me to leave. "Right after I told her she was making the biggest, and possibly last, mistake of her life."

I wasn't in the mood for surprises as Babs and I crossed the hall to our room, so I drew Hawk and told her to hang back while I opened the door and had a look-see. No deadheads under the bed, or in the closet, the bathroom, or the shower. Nothing seemed out of place. I holstered Hawk, returned to the door, and ushered Babs inside.

She set her briefcase on the desk and scanned the room. Her eyes landed on my bed and froze. "What's that?"

"What's what?"

"That...*thing*...sticking out of your duffel bag."

Unexpected bonus points to Babs for noticing something I'd missed. A small stick-figure poked its head out of my unzipped duffel. I reached inside, feeling my heartbeat quicken as I picked up the figure for a closer look. It was stuffed with Spanish moss, herbs, and feathers. Shoulder-length black yarn tumbled to its shoulders and was wrapped in a scrap of cotton, on the front of which was painted a bird. A nighthawk to be exact. I brought my fingers to my nose and sniffed. Frankincense, almond oil, and anise. Or was it licorice root? I'd been gifted a voodoo doll that had likely been anointed with Bend Over Oil—used by conjurers to make their victims do their bidding. *Nice try, Toussaint.*

I glanced at Babs. "Hotels usually have a plastic bag in the closet for dirty laundry. Bring it here."

She grabbed it off the shelf and scuttled back, then made a pitiful effort at tossing it to me from several feet away. The bag fluttered limply to the ground.

"Bring it *here*," I said. And open it."

"I don't want to get near that thing."

"Really? A brainiac like you believes in hoodoo?"

"Certainly not, Miss Nighthawk. That doodad has sticks and dirt and...*nature*...in it. Absolutely filthy," she said with a shudder.

Despite her objections, she did as I asked, holding the bag as far from her body as she could.

I dropped the doll inside, twisted the bag closed, and told her to lay it in the bathtub, while I ran to the sink and washed my hands.

In truth, I wasn't as worried as I might have been. This was Toussaint's idea of foreplay, and Mama's blessing protected me. The real evil was yet to come. Still, no harm in being careful.

I told Babs I wanted to take a shower. Once I closed the door behind me, I raided Bab's beauty bag and pulled out a hand-held make-up mirror. I placed it in the plastic bag with the doll, then put the bag on the ground and stomped it. The purpose of the mirror was to reflect Toussaint's magick back to him. Breaking the mirror broke the spell. At least, I hoped so. That's how I remembered it, anyway. I gingerly picked up the bag and tossed it in the trash.

"Are you okay in there?" Babs asked. "Did something break?"

"Sorry. I accidently knocked over your cosmetic bag. Your little makeup mirror is toast. Could you hand me a T-shirt out of my nightstand?"

Babs brought me my *Now go do that voodoo that you do so well* shirt. I slipped it on over my head, walked out of the bathroom, and spied Babs cranking up the thermostat. She eyed me and strolled back to her bed, silently daring me to adjust it.

"Don't you want to take a shower?" I asked.

"No, thank you. Not as long as that...fetish...is in there."

"Suit yourself." I pulled back the covers and crawled into bed, hiding the grin on my face. As soon as she fell asleep, I'd turn the thermostat back. Not ten minutes later, I heard her climb out of bed and head to the bathroom. I threw back my covers and tiptoed to the thermostat. It was dark and I couldn't see what I was doing, so I gave it a good hard twist to the left. No sooner had I crawled back into bed than the bathroom light went off and the door opened.

Babs stood in the dark, hesitating, as if plotting her next move in our game of chess. Finally, she flipped on the lights, and stalked across the room to the thermostat.

"Well, well, well. Fifty-six degrees," she said, turning the knob to the right. "Ms. Nighthawk, have you ever considered the possibility that you have anger management issues, or that you suffer from narcissistic personality disorder?"

"Ha! I do *not*," I said, pulling the covers over my head. "Test results were inconclusive."

16

RIDERS ON THE STORM

Sleep didn't come easy that night. I tried to blame it on the sub-tropical temperature of the room, and Babs' periodic snoring, but in all fairness, Little Allie's mouth was running like a duck's ass: *Every moment since Leo Abruzzi was bitten in that Cincinnati parking garage has been leading up to now. The virus manipulations, the string of murders, the pack mentality of the biters, and the attacks on Vinny were all designed to lead you here—to Toussaint.*

The bastard had been haunting my dreams and messing with my mind for months. He'd even appeared on my laptop screen after Leo died, laughing at me, taunting me, beckoning me. I never told anyone. Especially Rico or Ferris. Why would I? At the time, I'd never so much as uttered Toussaint's name, let alone fingered him as a suspect. Besides, it's not like astral projection was included in law enforcement manuals. Rico and Ferris would have thrown a butterfly net over my head.

Little Allie hissed and said I was full of shit—that the only reason I hadn't named Toussaint was because I couldn't bring myself to admit he'd been playing me all along. Screw her.

Even if she was right, she needed to remember whose head she was in. I wasn't above digging her out with a spoon.

Fine. If the brain bitch wanted me to own it, I'd own it. Toussaint had my number and was plucking my strings like a fiddle. There. I'd said it, but it didn't sit well. I'm nobody's fool.

The digital clock read six a.m., and I was wide awake. Babs flipped onto her back, and a new wave of snores drifted across the room. I climbed out of bed and rummaged through the drawer in my nightstand, pulling out the small white box I'd thrown into my bag as an afterthought. I opened the lid and slipped the leather cord around my neck, fingering the gift that Mama had given me the day I'd left New Orleans—a sparkling piece of obsidian, carved into the shape of a nighthawk. The rich black stone was blessed with Mama's protection. That stone and Mama's gris-gris bag were my shield.

I padded to the door, slipped quietly into the hallway, and hurled a thought into the universe. *Okay, I'm here, you son of a bitch. And I'm coming after you.*

I'd almost forgotten the early morning magic of New Orleans. The "City That Care Forgot" greeted the day in low gear. Water trucks and garbage collectors whisked through the streets, removing yesterday's mess, making way for a new one. It was quiet, and peaceful, and while the mercury hadn't soared yet, as sure as the tide, it would. One by one, the buildings sprang to life and people took to the streets, breathing the humidity, walking their pets, sipping Bloody Marys or coffee spiced with Baileys.

I turned onto Decatur Street, glanced at my watch, and kicked into high gear. Six-fifteen. The perfect time to grab the best treat in all the Quarter: beignets at Café du Monde. By eight, the line of hungry customers would stretch around the block.

I placed my order and carried the small plate of beignets to a street-side table. Since my morning run wasn't over, and it was looking like rain, I ate one, and bagged the other two for later. I wanted to check out The Dark Angel shop on my own, before we pounced on it, flashing badges, asking questions, and making our presence known.

I jogged up St. Ann Street, through the center of the Quarter, and inhaled a collection of smells, some that made my stomach growl, and a few that made it lurch. It felt good to run. My worries about the case faded with every step. Toussaint was strong, but I was stronger, and Mama was protecting me. I could handle this. I made a right on Rampart Street, across from Congo Square, and made a beeline toward a shotgun house less than a block away. Not because I knew the address of the shop, but because the sidewalk in front of it flaunted a black, life-sized statue of an angel. Not exactly subtle, but then, subtlety was never Toussaint's strong suit.

The old frame house, a painted lady, complete with haint-blue tint on the porch ceiling, had been beautifully restored. Nestled between a neon-lit tattoo parlor and a rundown pool hall, the old girl stood out like a rose between two thorns. The smiling sidewalk angel, with its black wings unfurled and its arms outstretched, greeted passersby, beckoning them inside. Who could resist the charms of a dark angel? *Certainly not you,* sniped Little Allie.

Thunder rumbled in the distance as I climbed the front steps. A sign on the door said the shop would open at ten. My curiosity was killing me. Mama hadn't mentioned the nature of Toussaint's business. It could have been anything from psychic readings to pimping cheap tourist tchotchkes, and while Toussaint no doubt had the ability to read people, nickel-and-diming them for geegaws would have been more up his alley. I peered through the window, but the reflection of the glass made it hard to see inside, so I moved closer and tented my eyes with my hands. Rows of shelves filled with glass apothecary jars lined the walls—the kind of jars used to hold herbs, oils, powders and tinctures. Display tables featured crystals, candles, talismans, even tarot decks and bottles of spiritual washes. No tchotchkes here. This shop was the real deal—a spiritual botanica for local Hoodoo practitioners, root doctors, and darker souls who 'served with the left hand.' The black magic workers like Toussaint.

A cold wind swirled through the trees, causing the branches to whisper. For a moment, I swore I heard a laugh riding on that wind.

Don't be stupid, I thought, but the brain bitch had already switched into tactical mode. I whirled from the window, expecting to find someone standing behind me. When no one was there, a breath I hadn't known I'd been holding escaped. *See? It's only the breeze.*

Leaning back toward the window, I cupped my hands again for one last look. The shelves, the jars, and the displays of paraphernalia had all disappeared. There was only Toussaint, on the other side of the glass, floating inches above the floorboards, staring back at me.

He held me in his gaze and pushed his thoughts into my brain. *A gris-gris bag and Mama's necklace? You don't really think they're going to save you. Do you? Tan pral di, Ti Kras Zwazo,"* he said with a wink.

Time will tell, Little Bird.

I turned and ran, stumbling down the steps two at a time, trying to escape Toussaint's laughter. One foot pounded in front of the other as I sprinted back to the hotel, letting the cool spring rain wash over me, hoping it would clear my head. I needed to be centered. The storm I'd been expecting had finally arrived, and its name was Toussaint.

17

THE DARK ANGEL

R ico scrunched his brow. "The shelves completely disappeared."

"And Toussaint...levitated?" Ferris asked.

Babs tilted her head and gazed across the top of her cheaters. "Hallucinations. That's new."

Like I said, astral projection doesn't play well to narrow-minded know-it-alls.

It had been a quarter 'til nine when I made it back to the Marriott. Babs was stepping out of the elevator, into the lobby, as I stepped in.

"Be back in ten," I promised, pushing the button for the second floor.

When the door opened, I trotted down the hall, ducked into the room and tossed my leftover beignets onto the desk. I turned on the shower, and called Nonnie, while stripping out of my rain-soaked clothes. After quick assurances that the terrible twins were fine and hadn't had time yet to miss me, I said good-bye, stepped into the shower, and took a deep breath.

By the time I slid into the booth at the coffee shop, it was 9:05. My damp hair fell in clumps over my shoulders, so rather than have it hanging in my plate, I pulled it back in a scrunchie. I'd been so focused on getting to the coffee shop on time, that I hadn't rehearsed my rendition of the whole dream-walking, soul-traveling...incident. Sadly, it showed.

"I'm not crazy," I muttered.

Vinny shrugged. "Couldn't prove it by me."

Jade and Rip wandered in and walked past us without as much as a sideways glance. They sat in a booth on the far side of the restaurant, well out of earshot. Thank God. Jade would have clung to me like another layer of skin if she'd heard us whispering about an evil, levitating necromancer.

By the time we finished breakfast and headed out onto Canal Street, the rain had passed. Rain often passes quickly in New Orleans. Still, part of me wondered if that little squall hadn't been summoned for my benefit.

Ferris pulled the Suburban up to the curb and the five of us piled in for a road trip. For the second time since sunup, I headed to The Dark Angel.

The vivid hues of the shotgun house on Rampart Street gleamed in the midmorning sun, making Toussaint's apparition fade like a distant dream. But I knew better. I knew what I'd seen. The place had a bad vibe. And while I hadn't noticed it earlier, the smile on the lips of the sidewalk angel never touched its dull, hollowed eyes. There was something sinister about *Zanj Lan Fé Nwa*.

The brain bitch escalated to Defcon 3. *Careful now*, she warned. *Stay frosty.*

For a voice in a head, she can get a little dramatic.

Ferris made an executive decision. Babs would babysit Vinny in the car while the rest of us checked out the store. We didn't know exactly what kind of reception we were going to get, but I doubted that a red carpet would be involved. No use risking Vinny's safety, even if he didn't see it that way.

"This is bullshit," Vinny moaned. "I could help—maybe create a distraction so you can scope out the place, like they do in the movies."

But Vinny got one vote and it didn't count. He was still running his mouth as I climbed out of the car and shut the door in his face. Maybe I'd have been less dismissive if I realized I was about to swallow some humble pie of my own.

"I'll take lead," Ferris said, as we climbed the steps.

I stopped and gave him the stink eye. "Why you?"

"'Cause it's an FBI case. Rico and I can handle the interview."

"And what am I? A potted plant?"

"You wander around. Keep your eyes open."

Oh no, he did not. If Ferris thought that was the end of the conversation, he was sadly mistaken. But we'd have to circle back to that later. Bells tinkled as Rico opened the door to the shop. An invisible cloud of earthy, herbal scents and the sharp-sweet tang of incense billowed around us.

"Hello?" Ferris called.

No answer. We walked deeper inside, eyeing the wooden shelves lined end to end with filled apothecary jars.

"Look," I said, pointing to the jars. "They're...back."

Rico grunted.

Ferris shook his head and muttered something unintelligible. Strike two, FedBoy. And the day was still young.

The labels on the jars contained an impressive list of ingredients. Patchouli, orris root, sandalwood, snakeskin, sulfur, dragon's blood, and more. I opened one of the lids.

"Careful, Miss." A tall black man, with dreadlocks and a winning smile, emerged from the back room. "The jar you hold contains Goofer Dust," he said, gently snatching it from me and replacing the lid. "Very strong. And very dangerous in the wrong hands."

He placed it back on the shelf, and cranked his hundred-watt smile up a notch. He was lean but muscular, with angular cheek bones, one of which featured a jagged half-moon scar.

"Perhaps," he said, nodding toward Rico and Ferris, "I can interest you in a...different...kind of gris-gris. Maybe some Come to Me oil. No?"

That was all I needed. My cheeks burned. "No thanks. I'd like to speak to the owner."

Dreadlock's eyes, almond-shaped and emerald green, bore into mine, as he extended his hand. "Sinjin Lafitte, manager of The Dark Angel, at your service."

A skeleton tattoo peeked out from under his T-shirt sleeve. And not just any skeleton. It was Baron Samedi, the Vodun Lord of Death. We'd seen that same ink on the skels involved in Leo's case. Bingo. We were on the right track.

Ferris swooped in, shaking Lafitte's hand. "I'm Special Agent Sean Ferris, FBI. And this is Officer Rico De Palma of the Cincinnati Police Department."

Ferris and Rico pulled Lafitte aside for a chat, then Ferris glanced back over his shoulder and gave me the high sign to start checking out the joint. I wandered among the shelves, eyes peeled, but stayed within earshot. Ferris might have been running the show, but we were playing in my sandbox now. A supernatural sandbox he knew nothing about. He needed me, whether he knew it or not.

Ferris pulled his business card from his pocket and handed it to Lafitte. "Can you tell me where you were last night, sir? Between ten and eleven?"

Lafitte's smile flickered. "And why would you want to know that?"

Rico lifted a candle from a display table and flipped it back and forth between his hands. "Just answer the question."

"Very well. I was...keeping company...with a dear friend."

"Your *friend* have a name?" Ferris asked.

In my meanderings, I'd come to a door marked *Employees Only*. A twist of the knob found it locked. Another time.

Lafitte's tone took an edge. "A gentleman would never kiss and tell."

Ferris stared him down and closed the distance between them. "Who is the owner of The Dark Angel?"

"Who can say?" Lafitte said, glancing away. "These days with holding companies and conglomerates. It's all so convoluted."

Well, this circle-jerk was getting us nowhere.

"Let's cut to the chase," I said, butting in. "Does the name Toussaint Le Clerc mean anything to you?"

Lafitte's eyes flashed. "I'm sorry. Wh...who?"

The bells on the door jingled again as Vinny walked in, followed closely by a bug-eyed, breathless Babs. "C'mon, Mom," Vinny said. "Let's check out the bongs."

Judas Priest, that brat was his father's clone.

Ferris winced, and Rico hissed under his breath.

The brain bitch soared to Defcon 2. *Abort! Abort!*

Little Allie was right. This recon mission was plummeting into a clusterfuck. But I'm a sucker for lost causes, and somebody had to drive this crazy train, so I stuck my finger in Lafitte's face and let my bitch flag fly. "*Enough stalling.* Tell Toussaint that Allie Nighthawk's looking for him. Want me to spell that? It's N-i-g-h—"

"No need," Lafitte murmured. "Your reputation proceeds you." He turned to Ferris and Rico. "Gentlemen, as you can see, I have customers to attend to. Should you have further questions, I suggest you return with a warrant."

He glanced at me thoughtfully, letting his eyes drop to my chest and linger on the gris-gris bag around my neck. With a flick of his finger, he brushed the bag aside and freed the obsidian bird necklace lodged beneath my shirt. "Such a beautiful bauble. I pray it serves you well."

I slapped his hand away and balled my fist to rearrange his teeth, but Babs' voice warbled from the bowels of the store. "Sir? My, ah, son would like to discuss...*bongs*."

Lafitte's lips curved into a dour smile. "Duty calls. I trust you can find your way out. I do hope we meet again, Ms. Nighthawk."

"Count on it."

With a parting nod, Lafitte drifted to the back of the store to assist Babs and Vinny. Ferris strolled to the door, pushed it open, and then let it close, causing the bells to jingle. Hopefully, Lafitte would believe that we'd left. Ferris hovered at the entrance with his eyes glued to Vinny. The kid was a natural at improv, keeping Lafitte occupied, asking alarmingly knowledgeable questions about bongs and herbs, while Babs, completely out of her element, played the perfect clueless mother. Rico and I moseyed to the checkout counter, out of Lafitte's line of sight, and went to work. Rico quietly riffled through stacks of invoices, packing slips, and correspondence, while I searched the desk calendar and read the random notes scribbled across the dates.

Vinny's voice stopped us cold. "Thanks for your help, sir. I'll take this one. Do you have any in the back that are still boxed?"

Lafitte said that he would check, and then disappeared into the backroom, giving us all time to get the hell out of Dodge. Once we piled into the car, Ferris turned the key, slipped the Suburban into gear, and pulled away from the curb, leaving The Dark Angel in the review mirror.

"Am I good or what?" Vinny asked, as he settled into his seat. "I kept that guy out of your hair, just like I told you I could. Too bad we had to bolt. I really liked that bong."

That earned him a collective eye roll, not that he noticed.

"Hey. You get a load of that guy's ink? The boney dude with the hat and cane. Gangsta, baby."

Vinny didn't know the significance of the tattoo, or that it marked the members of Toussaint's skeleton crew—the asswipes who'd gone after his dad. So, I shared the story and ended with, "Keep an eye out for that ink, kid. We'll be seeing a lot of it before this case is finished."

"Let the bastards come," Vinny growled. "I'm ready."

That crazy ass kid. Just like his dad. Too smart and too cocky for his own good. He was a big, ball-busting bulls-eye who didn't know enough to be scared. And I had promised to protect him. Fucking awesome. Just once, couldn't my job be easy?

18

NOW WE'RE COOKING WITH GAS

Monroe Hall, and any other of Vinny's usual haunts, might have been off limits to him, but he was jonesing for his personal collection of pretty boy toiletries and his fifty-gallon drum of Paco Rabanne, so he wheeled Ferris into stopping by the dorm to pick them up. We stayed in the car with Vinny while Ferris retrieved a laundry list of comfort items and necessities, the most important of which were Vinny's text books and laptop. He still had a take-home exam hanging over his head. From the dorm, we headed back to the NOLA FBI office to meet with Boudreaux.

After nudging Vinny into taking his test, Ferris settled him and his laptop in a conference room, then joined the rest of us as we filed into the room next door, where we'd convened with Boudreaux the day before. We reclaimed our original seats and were quickly joined by Philip Mouton, the agent who'd picked us up at the airport.

The fuzzy-faced kid scurried in with eager eyes that burned over-bright. "Nice to see y'all. Looks like I'll be working this case with you."

I stifled a groan, wondering how many cases the rookie had handled.

The door opened again, and without looking up, I assumed it was Boudreaux coming to join us. But the unmistakable scent of Cajun crawfish lured my nose to the air. My stomach growled. The beignet I'd eaten five hours earlier was a distant memory.

"Kind of stiffed you guys yesterday, in the lunch department," Boudreaux said, as he trailed in behind the food cart. "Thought I'd make it up to you today, courtesy of Fiorello's. Even ordered some bananas foster—you know, *lagniappe*."

A little extra.

That's how you treat your team. If Dickhead were half that nice, maybe I'd be able to stand in the same room with him without twitching like a freshie.

Boudreaux reached for a plate and nodded to Philip. "Let's start with an update on the attack at the hotel parking lot last night."

"Sorry, sir." Philip's freckles blanched as he cleared his throat. "Nobody at the hotel, other than you guys, admits to witnessing anything. And if there was anybody else nearby when the incident went down, they didn't stick around to leave their names."

"Strike one, Agent Mouton. What about the attack on Vinny Abruzzi at Tulane?"

"We've interviewed the known witnesses, and knocked on all the neighborhood doors. The statements were pretty consistent. The biters appeared to head straight for Vinny." Philip swiped his hand across his blonde crewcut. "We did talk to one guy who remembered seeing one of those small U-Haul box trucks in the area. Kind of odd, that time of night. Said it hadn't been there at midnight when he went to bed, but it was there when he got up to pee around a quarter 'til two."

Boudreaux leaned forward. "Any chance your witness got the license number?"

"No such luck," Philip muttered, but a grin played at the corner of his mouth. "So, I called U-Haul and checked the rentals in the area for box trucks that day."

"Good man."

"Four names turned up: Samuel Tucker, Odell Watkins, Sheena Dempsey, and Sinjin Lafitte."

"Holy crap," I yelled, nearly dumping my crawfish onto the floor. "Lafitte's the manager at The Dark Angel!"

"Do tell?" Boudreaux smiled, and nodded at the freckle-faced rookie. "Nice work, young man. But let's stick a pin in that for a minute. Someone want to bring me up to speed on this Dark Angel?"

I opened my mouth to jump in, but Ferris beat me to the punch. "Last night at dinner, we picked up on some intel that suggested our skel, Le Clerc, owns a shop named, *Zanj Lan Fé Nwa*, near Congo Square."

"Ah." Boudreaux nodded. "The Dark Angel."

"This Lafitte guy's the manager," Ferris continued. "Lafitte wouldn't give up the owner's name. Interestingly enough though, he's got the same ink as the skels who came after Leo Abruzzi in Cincinnati. When we asked to look in the back room, he said we'd need a warrant."

"That so?" Boudreaux asked. "Anything else?"

Rico nodded. "We got a chance to snoop behind the counter when Lafitte was...momentarily distracted. Today's date was circled with a note that said three o'clock. Nothing else."

"Although," Babs chimed in, "our source also shared that Toussaint purchased a mansion somewhere in St. Bernard Parish."

"Do we know when?" Boudreaux asked.

I shrugged. "A year, maybe a little more."

Boudreaux's eyes lit up. "Now we're cooking with gas. Agent

Mouton, go sit on The Dark Angel, and see what magic happens at three o'clock. While you're at it, check the property records in St. Bernard Parish for one Toussaint Le Clerc. Take Agent Fairchild with you. He's back in cyber-crimes—about two minutes younger than you, tall, nerdy, kind of pale, looks like he needs some sun."

Philip glanced around the table, wide-eyed, rooted to his chair like a mighty oak.

"Philip?" Boudreaux said quietly. "Git. Now, young man. Anything happens at The Dark Angel, you call in."

Philip nodded, then shook the lead out of his pants and bolted from his chair.

"Agent Mouton," Boudreaux barked. "I mean it. If Lafitte so much as wanders out for a piss, you call it in."

"Yes, sir."

"Kids." Boudreaux chuckled as Philip hit the door on the run. "As for the rest of you, why don't you dig a little deeper into Mr. Lafitte? And keep me posted. Ms. Nighthawk, I trust today's lunch met with your approval?"

"Absolutely, sir."

"Excellent. Couldn't have you thinking I was...what did you call me? Lamebrained. Yes. That's what it was. Lamebrained. Don't forget to pick up Mr. Abruzzi on your way out."

What the...? Why the hell was he picking on me? Okay, maybe I had that dig coming. But I couldn't help but smile. I'd never had my ass handed to me with such style. Cool, shrewd, and wicked smart, this guy. No doubt about it, Senior Agent Jake Boudreaux, for all his backwoods southern charm, had stones the size of casabas.

Boudreaux hooked us up with an empty pod, and we began to fill in all the blanks on Sinjin Lafitte—a.k.a. Sinjin Phillipe,

Lafitte Caron, Phillipe Bisset, and a few other aliases. He didn't have anything major showing in his Louisiana OMV records, and he had *zilch, zip, nada* showing under either property or tax records. But we hit the mother-load under criminal activity: fraud, money laundering, forgery, racketeering, drugs, and that was only going back ten years.

Ferris had requested a report showing known associates when Boudreaux popped his head in the room. "Mouton called in. Saddle up, boy and girls. Lafitte is on the move."

Things were about to get dicey. Taking Vinny with us on a ride-along wasn't an option. He'd have to stay back at the office with Boudreaux and company. I felt a little better about letting him out of my sight, having gotten a sense of the local agents and Boudreaux. Besides, I had a bad feeling that whatever was going to happen at three o'clock would be the stuff of shock and awe.

Ferris raised Mouton on his cell as we sprinted to the SUV. "Do *not* initiate contact, Mouton. Repeat. Do *not* initiate contact. Just keep him in your sights and guide me to you."

We piled in, and Ferris peeled out of the lot before Babs could get the back passenger door closed. She fell over sideways, grasping for her seatbelt, as Ferris whipped the car into a bat turn. *Babs*. Why was she even with us? She was as useful as an HOV dummy, but without the personality.

We followed Mouton's directions and hopped on I-10W. Ferris flipped on his siren and lightbar, hit the gas, and wove through the heavy traffic like a pro.

"Be nice to know where we're headed," Rico mused.

Ferris's eyes never left the road. "My money's on the Warehouse District."

Twenty minutes later, Ferris cut his lights and siren as he

exited at Franklin Street and merged into traffic. We were getting close. For what it was worth, I figured his guess was spot on. The crumbling Warehouse District, that once contained industrial and storage facilities, had been renovated and renamed the Arts District decades earlier. But a few abandoned buildings still remained, anonymous, almost invisible, tucked away among the trendy restaurants and galleries. Whatever Lafitte was up to, one of those buildings would offer privacy, isolation, and fast, convenient shipping.

The kind of place I'd pick.

Ferris spotted Mouton's government issued SUV not two blocks up. When Mouton pulled to the curb, Ferris parked a half-block behind him and called his cell. "You still got eyes on him?"

Mouton hesitated. "That's his Beemer five cars up. I lost him when he got out and took off on foot. I was trying to hang back, give him some space, and..."

Ferris sighed and rubbed his face.

I glanced out the window, noting a shit ton of high-end retail shops and cafes, then spotted a crumbled, abandoned-looking eyesore at the top of the block.

"What do you think?" I asked, pointing to the derelict building.

Rico scanned the names on the store fronts. "Why not? He sure isn't getting his nails done. Let's move."

We took our time climbing out of the Suburban, trying to act nonchalant. Ferris popped the trunk and grabbed flash-lights out of the field box for each of us. We were meandering toward Mouton's SUV when a single gunshot popped.

While Ferris, Rico, and I dove for cover, Babs sank grace-fully to the ground like a wounded swan, leaving her oversized egghead jutting out above the hood like a freaking bullseye. I yanked her to the concrete, then sat on her stomach, and told her to stay put. The last thing I wanted to worry about, while we breached that building, was her bony ass.

Babs' face blazed sixteen shades of pissed off. "*Get your hands off me, you narcissistic, ill-mannered infant.*"

She bucked her hips beneath my ass, sending me sprawling over her head, and onto my back.

She'd caught me off guard and laid me out flat—in front of Rico and Ferris. I'd never live that down. *Note to self: Never, ever touch the psycho bitch again. And if her face ever turns that same patchy shade of magenta, run. Run fast, run hard.*

Another shot popped. People ran through the street, pushing and screaming. Ferris called it in, while Rico hustled pedestrians around the next corner, and out of the line of fire. The four of us hunkered down beside a Taurus, waiting for backup to arrive.

Within three minutes, NOLA PD had swarmed the scene and formed a perimeter to keep the civilians at bay. *Crap,* I thought. *Another dog and pony show. Just what we needed.*

Little Allie moaned. *How long until Jade shows up?*

Boudreaux and his men arrived moments later and gave us the go-ahead to breach the warehouse. Babs stayed behind and filled him in, while Ferris, Rico and I zig-zagged our way toward the entrance. We cleared the corner of the building, then pressed alongside the exterior for cover. Ferris tried the knob on the ancient wooden door. It was locked. He counted down with his fingers: *four, three, two, one,* then kicked the door twice, driving it open.

We rushed inside, slicing the pie, to clear the space. Ferris went straight, Rico went left, and I went right. Not a soul in sight. A line of Boudreaux's agents rushed in behind us, to help clear the five-story structure.

"We'll take the first floor," Ferris told the team leader. "You take two through five."

Clearing the floors wasn't an easy chore. The building had

no power, no lights, and in some places, gaping holes in its concrete flooring. Rusted rebar jutted willy-nilly out of the walls and floors, electrical wires, cable, and insulation drooped from the ceilings. Animal scat, trash and dirty needles lay scattered throughout, which made maneuvering downright dicey. Step in a trash covered hole and plummet to your death. Get stuck with a needle and wonder if the tweaker who dropped it was contagious. Somewhere, amid all that mess and danger, lurked a shooter.

We swept the first floor from side to side and stumbled across a room filled with boxes of laboratory equipment. Now, I wouldn't have known beaker tongs from a Bunsen burner, but somebody needed to check this crap out. The brain bitch screamed *virus mutation* and a chill slithered through me.

What if she was right?

Ferris's radio squawked. "Agent Ferris, report to the second floor with your team."

By the time we made it up the stairwell, the mindless moan of rotters had reached my ears. We followed the noise down the hallway to a steel door that was surrounded by a gaggle of G-men. I shined my flashlight through the window in the door. Maybe a dozen meatbags milled and moaned, mingling like guests at some deadhead dinner party.

I turned to find the G-men staring at me. "What are you looking at? You know the drill. Tap to the head; blow out the brain."

According to Boudreaux, New Orleans was the land of the undead. These guys should be used to this shit, right? Why were they hesitating? A soft cry for help echoed through a hole in the floor. I didn't have time to hold their sensitive hands.

"Deal with it," I yelled, pointing to the meatbags.

Ferris, Rico, and I sprinted back toward the steps. By the time we reached the stairwell, I heard the metallic screech of hinges, instantly followed by a volley of shots behind us. One roomful o' rotters wasted. What else lay ahead?

We'd bounded down to the first-floor landing when a second cry rang out. It came from deeper in the building, maybe thirty yards beyond where we'd found the laboratory equipment. We had to clear each room as we advanced, making it seem like an eternity before we burst through the right door. Some guy was tied to a crappy folding chair, a crumpled gag ejected onto his chest. Blood caked the side of his head; his left eye was swollen shut. Somebody'd done a number on him.

I looked a little closer and my heart caught in my throat. It was Jade's cameraman, Rip Sacca.

Rico tore across the room and dropped to his knees beside the chair. Then he yanked the folding knife from the sheath on his belt and hacked at the ropes.

"Where is she?" he barked.

Rip closed his eyes and moaned.

Rico slapped him and snapped, "Look at me, damn it! *Where's Jade?*"

19

THE STUFF OF NIGHTMARES

Rico's face glistened with sweat as he slashed through the last of the ropes. "Where'd he take her, Rip?"

"I don't know."

"Which way did they go?"

"I...I didn't see."

"Think, damn it!"

"I lost track of them." Rip rose to his feet and rubbed his wrists. "I was too busy getting the shit beat out of me."

Rico grabbed him and pinned him up against a support beam. "Listen, jackass. You were the last person to see her. You're going to recount every second, every—"

Ferris quickly flanked Rico. "Why don't you let me have a crack at him?"

Rico nudged him aside, but Ferris regrouped and stepped in front of Rico, blocking him. "You're too close to this. *Back off.*"

Boudreaux and Babs burst through the door. They'd obviously zeroed in on our location from the radio chatter. Boudreaux hung back, eyeing Rico and Ferris, as if he sensed the tension between them.

After an exchange of silent glances, Rico backed off and let Ferris step in.

"From the beginning, Rip. And don't leave anything out, no matter how insignificant you think it is."

Rip slumped back in the chair and paused, as if collecting his thoughts. Once he started talking, the missing pieces came together. "Jade was beating the bushes for leads this morning when she got this tip from some back-street hoodoo queen about a shop called The Dark Angel. The chick swears it's the real deal, so we drop by, and Jade chats up the manager, some dude named Lafitte. Jade spots the ink on his bicep. She starts asking questions like: 'Where'd you get that tatt? What does it mean?' Then she goes all pit bull on him, asking, 'Who's manipulating the Z-virus?' Lafitte freaks out and shuts down, telling her to take a hike."

Rip sighed and rolled his eyes. "You know Jade. She puffs up and starts spouting piss and vinegar, threatening to finger him in her 'exposé' if he doesn't cooperate."

The air quotes Rip had slapped around *exposé* let me know that I wasn't the only one who thought Jade had bitten off more than she could chew. It was getting hard to breathe, what with the ginormous *I-told-you-so* stuck in my throat.

Rip fidgeted and rubbed his face with his hands. "So, after the guy gives us the boot, I'm putting my camera back in the SUV and Jade's dictating her notes, and two sketchy-looking guys come creeping out the back door of The Dark Angel, hauling a big-ass wooden crate. They load it into the back of some beat-to-shit box truck and take off."

"Any idea what they were hauling?" Rico asked.

"Do I have x-ray vision? No. Jade tells me to follow them, so I do. They end up here. They back the truck up to the loading dock, haul the crate inside, and then start to lower the roll door. Jade's screaming at me to stop the damn door from closing, so I grab one of the steel-transport cases for our equipment, dive out of the SUV, and shove the case beneath the door as it's coming down. Worked like a charm, too. Jade and me, we crawl inside and hide. This big guy walks in across the room, six-four, about two-hundred and thirty pounds. Shoulder-length black hair, thirty-something. Dude has to be the boss, the way these guys kowtow to him. And what they do next, after they open that crate—it's the stuff of fucking nightmares."

Given that Rip had just described Toussaint, I had a pretty good idea about what Rip saw in those nightmares.

"These guys open the crate and some Bob Marley-looking dude sprawls out across the floor. He's still alive, but he's moaning and twitchin', and looking loopy, like he's three sheets to the wind. They're twenty yards away, give or take, so it's kind of hard to hear, but big dude squats down in front of Bob Marley, and asks his goons how long ago he'd been injected. Somebody answered, 'long enough.' Big dude starts whaling on Marley and asking questions, most of which I can't hear. The guy's mumbling like a whackadoodle. Can't make out a word of what he's saying, so I grab my camera, and try to get some pics, 'cause this soiree's got Pulitzer written all over it, right? But I fumble the fucking lens cap. It rolls into the middle of the freakin' floor, and next thing I know, I'm getting the shit beat out of me."

Rico shook Rip's chair. "What about Jade?"

"She begs them to stop beating on me. Then who walks in but that Lafitte guy from The Dark Angel. He gets all worked up, grabs Jade and drags her over to big dude, who he calls Toussaint. Tells Toussaint that Jade and me were in the shop, asking questions and threatening to expose his operation."

Rip started to hyperventilate, but he fought through it, raised his head and stared in Rico's eyes. "Toussaint pulls a .45 from his belt, points it at Lafitte's face and says, 'You brought her to my doorstep, cameraman in tow. If there's one thing I can't abide, it's carelessness.' Then he pulls the trigger, putting one right between Lafitte's eyes. Next thing I know, he blows the head off Bob Marley, and tells his goon squad to throw them both in the crate and dump it."

Rico grabbed Rip's face and squeezed. "*For the last time. What happened to Jade?*"

Rip winced and tried to pull away. "Toussaint slugged her in the jaw. She went down, he tied her up, and told his guys to carry her to his car. Then he gave me a message for Nighthawk." Rips eyes darted to me. "If you want to see Jade alive again, meet him at Congo Square at midnight tonight. You and only you. If you don't show, or if Toussaint gets even a whiff of cop, he's going to inject Jade with the virus."

20

SLAM, BAM, AND WHAM

"*S*on of a bitch*." Rico kicked Rip's chair, nearly toppling him backward.

A silent Ferris gazed at me, his eyes lingering uncomfortably long. He seemed to be trying to communicate, but whatever subliminal message he was sending was getting lost in transmission. Either that, or Little Allie's shrieks of *guilty, guilty* had short-circuited my receptors.

Ah, what the hell did she know anyway?

Jade was the thorn of thorns. The albatross of albatrosses. Toilet paper stuck to the bottom of my shoe. She was conniving, manipulative, and without question, a hoochy mama heifer. But she was also Rico's girlfriend. My *partner's* girlfriend, who had asked for my help with a dangerous exposé. And what had I done? Rather than protect her, I'd given her the middle finger salute and told her to piss up a rope. I might not have been able to read Ferris's eyes, but the fact that Rico couldn't bring himself to look at me made his feelings abundantly clear.

Rico blamed me for Jade's disappearance.

It had been her decision to follow us out here *uninvited*, but if I had helped her when she'd asked me, months ago, maybe today she would be safe and sound at back at Channel 5, ripping me a new one, instead of missing and in harm's way.

What if she died? Sweet Jesus, what if she turned?

Boudreaux's voice called me back from circling the drain. "Let's huddle up. The first thing we do is get a warrant out on Le Clerc for kidnapping and two counts of capital murder. Agent Ferris, why don't you put in a call to Director Horton and ask him to send your bioterrorism guy out here to take a peek at the lab equipment we recovered. What's his name?"

"Eli Stanton, sir. I'm on it."

"Excellent. Now, let's consider this proposed midnight meeting of Toussaint's."

"Consider?" Rico glowered at Boudreaux. "Toussaint didn't give us a suggestion, or even an invitation. He made a threat. Nighthawk *has* to go. If she doesn't show, Jade's as good as dead."

"Like hell," Ferris growled. "You want to send Nighthawk in *alone*? It's a set-up. We need to get the damned warrant and arrest his ass. Period. You don't have any—"

"Any what? Jurisdiction? This isn't about jurisdiction—"

"*Enough.*" Boudreaux stepped between Ferris and Rico. "Somebody want to tell me why you two got your tails up?"

Ferris glared at Rico. "No reason."

"Simple misunderstanding," Rico said. "That's all."

Boudreaux eyeballed the three of us. "Don't piss down my back and tell me it's raining. Out with it."

Crickets chirped. Tumbleweeds drifted across the floor.

Babs folded her arms across her chest and sighed. "In a nutshell, sir, Agent De Palma is dating Ms. Chen, and there appears to be some unresolved...*entanglement*...between the three of *them*." She drew a triangle between Ferris, Rico and me with her finger, like we were blobs of listeria on a slide. "Speaking as a mental health professional, I suggest that for the time being, they try to step back and compartmentalize their feelings, in order to function properly within the team paradigm."

Freaking Babs. I wanted to snap her neck like a twig. Fuck *feelings*—and double fuck *team paradigm*.

"Is that a fact?" Boudreaux asked, turning to me. "Ms. Nighthawk, you got any *feelings* you want to share with the group?"

"Oh, God no, sir."

"How 'bout you two?" Boudreaux side-eyed Rico and Ferris. "Any feelings you want to shout from the mountain tops? Now's the time to let 'em rip, boys and girls. Otherwise, get your sensitive asses in check. You feel me?"

Actually, I did feel him. With all that testosterone flying through the air, nobody had asked me what *I* thought about the meeting with Toussaint. Thankfully, Boudreaux recognized the oversight. "Ms. Nighthawk, since it'll be your ass on the line tonight, maybe we should ask *your* thoughts on the action plan."

"You bet your ass I'm going to meet with Toussaint. The way I see it, we don't have any choice." I glanced at Ferris and instantly wished that I hadn't. His eyes were intense and over-bright. Was it fear I saw? Rico let out a long, slow sigh of relief. At least one of us was happy I'd be meeting with Toussaint.

Having settled on our course of action, Boudreaux sent us back to the hotel to get some rest. The night would be long, unless of course, I bit the dust, in which case, sleep would be totally irrelevant. We collected Vinny from the FBI office, and headed back to the hotel for a quick dinner before relaxing. I decided to bow out. I needed to keep it together, and being the ping-pong ball in a match between Rico and Ferris wouldn't help.

I entered my room with an abundance of caution, and after a thorough search, said a prayer of thanks. No more Voodoo dolls or fetishes. Kicking off my boots, I stretched out on my bed and closed my eyes. Visions of Nonnie and Leo, Rico and Ferris, and even my old partner, Harry, and the terrible twins danced through my head. If I'd been hoping for sleep, my brain wasn't cooperating. I blocked out the visions, censored my thoughts, and found myself slipping down a long, dark corridor. There was peace in that darkness. And solitude. The only sound, the steady beat of my heart.

A small figure hovered at the edge of the void. As the figure drew closer, my heart began to thrum. Screams and moans shattered the solitude. My eyes were closed, but I squeezed them tight, as if that could save me from the monster who had stalked my dreams for years.

But I knew better.

Toussaint appeared and filled my mind with pictures of Jade, her porcelain skin rotting, and slipping off the bone. Pictures of Rico, hating me more with every tear he shed. Pictures of me, flat-eyed, shuffling aimlessly, and living off human flesh. The stink of the horde filled my nose; their frenzied moans whirred in my ears.

I tore myself from the dream, if it really was a dream, drenched in sweat. Then, I hopped in the shower and washed the apocalyptic visions from my brain. Putting on fresh clothes, I reminded myself that those depraved dreams served a purpose: they kept me on edge. And if I was lucky, that might keep me alive.

Babs' keycard rattled in the door. She let herself in and walked toward the beam of light that shone from the open bathroom. She glanced in the mirror and watched me slip the obsidian necklace and Mama's gris-gris bag around my neck, then leaned against the doorframe, and stared at my reflection.

"Ms. Nighthawk, I know you don't value my services, but the truth is, I'm very good at what I do. And I want to help. Trust me. Compartmentalizing your past with Toussaint will allow you to control your emotions during your meeting. Better control means better decisions. Another weapon for your arsenal, no?"

She made a good point, but trust isn't really my thing. I peered into the mirror and gave her a taut smile. "Thanks. I'll remember that."

She stared at my reflection. "I'll be staying here with Vinny tonight. Take care out there. Who knows? When you get back, I might even turn the thermostat down to seventy-two."

"Sixty-eight."

"Don't push it." Babs turned on her heel and left the room for her babysitting detail with Vinny. I tucked Mama's protective gris-gris bag inside my shirt alongside my obsidian necklace, slipped on my shoulder holster, and snapped Hawk inside. Then I slid Baby in place at my ankle, and made sure my Ka-Bar knife was tucked safely in its sheath.

Taking one last glance in the mirror, I chanted the mantra that had carried me through my darkest moments. "I'm Allie Nighthawk, the best of the badass zombie hunters." For some reason, the words rang hollow, so I fired a special thought through space and time. A warning shot, of sorts. "God help you, Toussaint Le Clerc. This time, I'll take you down, or die trying."

I parked our government issued SUV on North Rampart Street, not far from Congo Square. Ferris and Rico were stationed in a surveillance van less than a block away. It was 11:30 p.m.—a half-hour early. I had time on my hands, time to think.

That's usually when things go south for me.

It had been years since I'd last seen Toussaint. How strong had his powers grown? Would I be strong enough to take him down? Did the fire in my gut burn hot enough? Could his eyes, those silky, sea-green eyes still sway me?

So much for thinking and introspection. I'm more about *doing* anyway.

I switched gears and started running the most likely scenarios through my brain, but even that wasn't giving me the warm fuzzies. I knew this man, the way his mind worked. His twisted thoughts and supernatural powers introduced unknowns to the equation. I was trying to predict the unpredictable. Time to turn off my thoughts and slide into autopilot.

I placed the surveillance bud in my ear and gave it a gentle push, lodging it deep inside the canal, out of sight. Then I slipped the transmitter around my neck, flicked the power button to 'on,' and tucked it beneath my T-shirt.

"Sacrificial lamb, check one," I mumbled.

Ferris's voice whirred in my ear. "Affirmative, Drama Queen. Big Brother, out."

Supernatural powers notwithstanding, the presence of two-way communication made me feel less vulnerable. But only a little. Self-reliance was my motto, so I mentally checked off my weapons: the ever-vigilant Hawk, perfectly balanced in his shoulder holster; Baby, my backup piece, perched alongside my ankle; and last but not least, my trusty Ka-Bar knife, tucked safely in its sheath. Feeling their weight, and their familiar contours against my body, gave me a sense of security, even if the odds of me actually getting to use them were slim to none. Given our history, Toussaint would *expect* me to be carrying. No way was he going to let me walk into this garden party locked and loaded. My stainless-steel security blankets would surely be confiscated, and there wasn't a damn thing I could do about it.

"Sacrificial lamb, on the move," I muttered, as I climbed out of the SUV and headed for Congo Square inside Louis Armstrong Park. The park's visiting hours ended at seven. I'd never been there in the dead of night. As I strolled through the deserted park, lost in my thoughts, my boots echoing off the white concrete pavers, I thought I heard a different echo. Softer. Distant. Almost melodic. The echo of *people*. No...*revenants*... from long ago, laughing, dancing, drumming, and singing. An icy finger touched Little Allie's spine, causing us both to shiver. The past lived on in this place. Some of it good. Some of it bad. Some of it worse.

The breeze wafted a voice to my ear. "The spirits rejoice tonight, no?"

I spun, heart in my throat, and stared into the emerald eyes of my past. After all these years, after everything we'd put each other through, everything we'd done to each other, Toussaint still took my breath away.

His brazen eyes embraced me from head to toe. "I am so happy that you are here, *Ti Kras Zwazo*."

Little Bird. Toussaint had christened me that on the day I'd arrived at Mama's, all those years ago. I forced myself to avoid his gaze and to remember why I'd come. "It's not like you gave me a choice. Where's Jade?"

"Safe. For now."

I spread my arms wide. "You wanted me. Here I am. Give her back. *Now*."

"Not so fast, *sha*." He nodded at two of his goons, who instantly started toward me.

"Call them off," I snarled. "Or I'll kill them."

"You'll do nothing of the sort. They are only here to ensure an equal playing field for our little soiree. As you can see, I am unarmed. It's only fair that you are, too."

I did a slow burn as Toussaint's minions patted me down and took my weapons away.

"You know," I said, raising my hands in the air. "If you took Jade to spite me, you're way off base. I don't even like her."

Toussaint laughed. "Oh, but your *partner* does. Or is he... *more*...than your partner? Your thoughts are so muddled, Little Bird. Do you even know? Besides, Jade may only be a gnat buzzing about *your* face, but to me, she and her *exposé* are thorns in the lion's paw."

"Jade?" Her name flew from my mouth like an angry bee. "Jade couldn't find her ass with a flashlight and barbecue tongs. She and her half-assed *exposé* are the last things you need to worry about."

Ah, ah, ah, the brain bitch warned. *Remember: compartmentalize.*

Toussaint shrugged. "What would you propose I do with her? Give her back?"

"Why not? You don't want her anyway."

"Ah, but *you* do." Toussaint put his arms behind his back and began to pace. "So, tell me, why would I do as you ask? Why would I give my wife's murderer *anything* she asked for?"

"I didn't kill your wife. She was sick; I put her down. There's a difference."

"I was healing her, and you took her away from me. You'll pay for that until the day you die. And then some."

It'd been three years since Toussaint exacted the most monstrous form of revenge he could for a crime I didn't commit. Three years since my world crashed down around me. The ache in my heart nearly brought me to my knees. I was done compartmentalizing.

"You sick bastard. You rose my father from the dead for no reason other than to make me put him down. What more could you possibly want?"

"A life for a life, Little Bird...your life."

A band of biters shambled out of the shadows. I did a 360, squinting into the darkness beneath the faded light of the crescent moon. Toussaint's goons and my weapons were nowhere in sight. When I whirled back around, Toussaint had gone too.

Four rotters advanced, moaning, groaning, and snapping their teeth, closing the distance between us with every shuffling step. And me, without so much as a butter knife to make my stand.

God help me if the freaking transmitter crapped out. "*Yo. Big Brother. Sacrificial Lamb here. A little help?*"

I backed up a few paces and squared myself to take on the horde. One of them was a corpsicle—the nastiest of the undead, turned biter more than sixty days back. He was easy to spot, twenty feet behind the others, stinking like sunbaked zushi, and moving at the speed of tree sap. Two were twitching like electrified monkeys, bearing down on me like their hair was on fire. They were freshies—turned zombie within the last seven days. A half-step slower than the twitcher twins, but even more deadly, was a garden-variety flesh-eater that had turned somewhere between eight and sixty days back. Its teeth, the stuff of nightmares, chattered faster than a wind-up toy.

The twins reached me first. A frontal assault would be risky with a high probability of incurring a bite wound, so I resorted to the *slam, bam, and wham* method I teach in my zombie 101 class. I let them rush me, then sidestepped, and stationed myself behind them. Reaching out, I wrapped my hands around the forehead of the closest biter and used spinal leverage to slam it backward to the ground. Then I drove the heel of my industrial-strength, zombie-stomping boot through its forehead and into its brain. Booyah, baby. One down. I rolled sideways to get into position for the second twitcher, but a gunshot popped from behind. The twitcher's head exploded like a brain-pulp piñata.

As I scrambled out of the line of fire, the flesh-eater opened its jaws and dove at my thigh. Rico squeezed his trigger and brought the biter down with a 9 mil, single shot lobotomy. Ferris fired a round though the eyeball of the last of the rotters, the corpsicle that had shuffled to within a few feet of me. I ducked, but not soon enough. Its head exploded like an over-ripe watermelon, bathing me in zushi.

Jesus. Would it be too much to ask for a day without flesh bombs?

Ferris ordered his backup team to conduct a search. They found my confiscated weapons laying in some bushes and brought them back to me, but they didn't find Toussaint. He was long gone. Rico stood, arms akimbo, silently staring into the night, his heart dangling from his sleeve. He would have given his life to get Jade back. Much to my surprise, I would have too.

I walked up alongside him and touched his elbow. "I'm sorry we didn't get her back. But we will. And that crack I made about not liking her..."

Rico waited for me to finish, but I couldn't. My hypocrisy only goes so far. We both knew what would have come out next would have been a lie.

"He's not going to kill her, you know. And he's not going to turn her. She's his bargaining chip."

Unable to look at me, Rico nodded and pulled away. Having no reason to stay, he turned his back, walked to the van, then started the engine and drove off, leaving Ferris behind. The search team came up empty, as I knew they would. The show was over for the night. It was time to pack up the tents, so we could come back tomorrow and start the game all over again.

One by one, the government-issued vehicles pulled away until only Ferris and I remained. He pulled me into his arms and kissed me, holding me so long, I thought he might never let go.

"This is hard for me," he whispered. "Seeing you in danger. Knowing how much that crazy bastard hates you. What really happened with his wife—and your father?"

Hell, that whole damn conversation was a matter of record, now. Boudreaux would be all over it. I'd have to explain everything, but not tonight. I begged off, asking Ferris to let me sleep on it, to give me time to wrap my head around it. Maybe sharing the story—saying it out loud—would help me work through the shit storm of guilt and anger those years had left behind.

No sooner had we climbed into the SUV than Little Allie bitch-slapped my brain for daring to think I needed help. She scolded me, saying that *Psycho Babs and her happy crap mumbo-jumbo* were rubbing off on me.

Was she right?

All I knew, as I drove away from Congo Square, was that part of my prophetic dream had come to pass: I'd failed at getting Jade back, and now Rico hated me with the soul-sucking intensity of a black hole.

That hurt worse than I ever could have imagined.

21

NOWHERE TO RUN

It was a little after 3:00 a.m. by the time Ferris and I made it back to the hotel. We kissed goodnight and parted reluctantly, plodding to our separate rooms. Such a waste. Apparently, nothing gets the heart pumping like a zombie death match.

Who knew?

Back in my room, I uttered a silent thanks that Babs had left the bathroom light on, so I could find my bed. She'd also cranked the thermostat down to seventy degrees, a surprising and bizarrely touching compromise. In return, I decided not to tell her that although I tried, I couldn't get the brain bitch on board with the whole 'compartmentalization' thing. We were making progress, and that was the important thing.

Ah, what the hell, I thought, nudging the thermostat down to sixty-eight. *Baby steps, right?*

I turned off the bathroom light and hopped into bed, praying for sleep, but between being wired for sound and Toussaint haunting my dreams, sleep seemed unlikely. The digital clock on the nightstand struck four. Then five. Sometime later, I drifted off, only to be jolted awake at 7:00 a.m. by

Beethoven's Fifth Symphony—Babs' cell phone alarm. I mumbled that I'd meet them in the coffee shop at nine and threw the covers over my head. Babs left, and the door latched behind her.

Just one more hour, God. Please?

That extra bit of sleep and a hot shower made a new person out of me. I hummed, sipping a K-Cup of generic coffee, and watched the news as I got dressed. Serene, with my mind cranking on all cylinders, I felt focused and ready to take on the day. Halfway to the door, my phone rang, and the proverbial turd in the punch bowl bobbed to the surface.

Nonnie advised that we had two problems, both of which had been long in coming. One was totally Nonnie's fault. The other was ~~a simple mistake, a tragic oversight~~, not even *remotely* my fault. At least, that's my interpretation, and I'm sticking with it.

"Headbutt, he pees through fence onto Winstel's wisteria."

"Don't you remember? You *trained* him to do that so he'd stop peeing on your bushes."

"But now, wisteria is brown. Winstels very unhappy."

"Just handle it. Get creative. Plant something on our side of the fence in front of that flowering crap."

"Then *your* bush be brown."

"See? Problem solved. Next?"

Paper crinkled through the phone line. "You got letter from Hamilton County Treasurer's Office. Oh," she moaned. "Is very bad."

"You opened my mail?"

"It say you owe three years back property tax." Nonnie whistled. "Twelve thousand, eight hundred and fifty dollars, Miss Allie."

"What? There must be some mistake."

The brain bitch giggled.

"I don't owe them money."

Then it hit me. My father had been gone for three years. Had I *ever* paid property tax?

"You sure you no owe them?" Nonnie asked.

"Absolutely." Hell, I didn't have a clue. I'm in and out so much. Mail piles up. Shit gets lost. *Please.* I'm too busy saving the world from the freaking horde to keep track of such minutiae.

Determined to top my mound of misfortune with whipped cream and a cherry, Nonnie read on. "If you no pay, they put lien on house. Miss Allie." Her voice quivered. "They can foreclose. I have monies. I loan—"

"*No.* No loans."

"But your father's house—"

"Just put the letter on the table. I'll deal with it when I get back."

"When?"

"As soon as I can. We'll figure something out."

I said goodbye to Nonnie, asked her to kiss the twins, and told her to warn Headbutt that his ass was mine when I got home. I waited until she disconnected and then sank to the bed. Twelve thousand, eight hundred and fifty. It might as well have been twelve million. I was so broke, even moths avoided my wallet.

Well, fuck The Hamilton County Treasurer's office, I thought. *And fuck the horse they rode in on, too.* I had bigger problems to deal with, like saving Jade's life and bringing down Toussaint. I climbed to my feet, pulled up my big girl panties, and shot life the double bird salute. Sometimes, all you can do is embrace the suckage and power through. And that's usually when you don't have any fucks left to give.

"No breakfast?" Ferris asked, as I skirted the buffet table and slid into the booth beside him. Thoughts of financial ruin had soured my stomach and my mood. I wouldn't be discussing that new found problem with Ferris. He'd hear enough of my secrets as the day wore on. He didn't need to know them all.

Rico hadn't even glanced up to acknowledge my arrival. He sat unsmiling, staring at his half-eaten eggs with red puffy eyes, eyes that were tinged with desperation. He looked...lost. A wave of guilt washed over me. The only way to fix this mess was to get Jade back, and I'd do that even if it killed me. Until then, Rico would have to swallow his anger and trust me, or at least trust the process.

Ferris decided to poke the bear. "De Palma, did you make that call to Horton? Is Stanton coming?"

Rico slid out of the booth, signaling breakfast had ended. "He's supposed to be at the meeting this morning."

We filed out of the restaurant and reclaimed our self-assigned seats in the SUV. Babs' nose gravitated back to her scientific journal. Ferris pulled out of the parking lot, keeping his thoughts to himself. Rico stared out the window, daring anyone to engage him. And Vinny filled the excruciating silence with Vinny-isms on women and the art of living large. By the time we arrived at the FBI office for our 9:30 meeting with Boudreaux, I was more convinced than ever that Leo had found his way back from the other side. Frankly, that was a nicer picture of him than the one that had been squatting in my head: Leo sitting cross-legged on some cloud, scratching his head, wondering why he'd entrusted his son's life to such an inept group of asshats.

Vinny didn't have clearance to attend our meeting, so we deposited him in the visitor's lobby on the first floor. He said he wanted to watch TV, but knowing him, the only thing he'd be watching was the sweet young receptionist who had smiled at him as we'd walked through the door.

We arrived almost ten minutes early and found Boudreaux waiting in the conference room. Agents Mouton and Fairchild scurried in behind us and took seats, just as Boudreaux closed the door. The dour look on his face didn't bode well.

"Agent Mouton, what did you find on your property search of St. Bernard Parish?"

Philip sat a little taller and cleared his throat. "Since our intel suggested Le Clerc purchased the property a year or so ago, I requested records for the past three years, just to be safe."

"And?"

"Apparently requisitions is a bit backed up. I'm still waiting."

"Don't let them put you off too long. If you need me to light a fire, let me know. What about the warehouse investigation?"

"Forensics is still working the scene. Since the biters we found were newly turned, they're going to print them, and run them through AFIS. I told them to leave the room with the lab equipment alone, until Agent Stanton has a chance to check it out."

"Excellent." Boudreaux glanced across the table. "Anybody have a theory as to the identity of the Bob Marley-lookalike from the warehouse?" He paused, waiting for a response that didn't come. "Well then, maybe sooner or later he'll turn up in a missing persons report. If we're lucky, Mr. Sacca will be able to give us an ID off the picture. Agent Mouton, why don't you and Fairchild run down the missing persons leads?"

Ricco loosened his collar and leaned forward. "Marley is dead. We have an *active* missing person case to work. A kidnapped victim who is hopefully still alive. Why don't we focus on her?"

Boudreaux sighed and leaned back in his chair. "What

would you like us to do, Officer De Palma? Reassign all our agents to Ms. Chen's case?"

"She might still be alive, is all I'm saying. Let's start with her and worry about the dead guy later."

"I understand you and Ms. Chen are close," Boudreaux said. "Talk about complicated waters. I empathize. I truly do. But please don't mistake my empathy for weakness. I run this show, Detective. Not you. The best way to find Ms. Chen is to chase down every lead, every ghost, and every fucking bread-crumb, no matter how insignificant they may seem at first blush. You let me worry about who follows up on what and when. We clear on that?"

Rico's eyes grew taut, but he settled back in his chair. "Yes, sir."

Boudreaux turned his eyes to me. "Speaking of complicated relationships, Ms. Nighthawk, what's this about you killing Toussaint's wife—and him raising your dad from the dead?"

And just like that, the spotlight was on me. There was nowhere to run. Nowhere to hide. This would be the first time in my life that I would share the story of me and Toussaint Le Clerc. *Where to begin?* I poured a glass of water, settled into my chair, and collected my thoughts.

"Better buckle up and keep an open mind," I said, glancing around the table. "I couldn't make this shit up if I tried."

22

TALK ABOUT TOXIC

"I met Toussaint the day I came to live with Mama. He was eighteen. Mama told me later that she had taken him in when he was twelve. He'd been living on the streets, picking food out of garbage cans and wearing the same set of rags every day. She started leaving plates of food out for him. At first, he'd eat what she'd left and run away. Eventually, Mama began to watch for him and walk out to the porch with a plate of dessert, so they could chat. Toussaint warmed up over time."

The room was hanging on my every word, so I pushed on. "One day, Mama stood in the doorway and watched him pick up a dead sparrow that had fallen from its nest. He cradled it in his hands and breathed on it. The bird flapped and fluttered, then glided away. Mama said she'd always known Toussaint had the gift, but until that moment, she'd never known if *he* knew he had it. She took him in and trained him—taught him how to use the gift properly. All she asked in return was that he help her around the restaurant when she needed it. That's how Toussaint came to live with Mama."

I sipped my water and let those memories flood back.

"Toussaint had been there longer than me, so he knew a lot

more about using the gift, and things like root working, and hoodoo in general. He was kind and patient, like a big brother, more or less. But by the time I'd turned seventeen, we'd...gotten involved."

I couldn't bring myself to look at Ferris or Rico.

"Mama discouraged it," I said. "She thought Toussaint was too old for me, too much a man, and that I was barely more than a child. I argued with her, telling her that anyone with the powers we had, anyone who had to make the choices we'd had to make, were never children to begin with. Looking back, I wondered if Mama sensed that Toussaint was changing and didn't want me to be influenced by him."

I picked at the arm of my chair and stared at the floor. "It was little things at first. Toussaint started studying black magick, and experimenting with spells. He met a root worker named Sabine and began hanging with a different crowd. The more he dabbled with it, and *her*, the less our rules seemed to mean to him. I didn't want to see it. I made excuses for him, even lied for him. But the day I saw him kill a dog, and then try to conjure it back to life using roots and incantations, was the day I knew he'd gone too far—and that he had no intention of coming back."

The room had grown still. I glanced up and found a table filled with people who wouldn't be satisfied until they'd heard every sordid detail, so I continued.

"Even then, I knew we were on a collision course, and that one day, we'd fight a battle only one of us would walk away from. That was the day I left New Orleans. I was twenty and had no intention of ever coming back. I loved Mama too much to kill her boy. It was easier to leave, to just...run away."

Rico cleared his throat. "What does that have to do with you killing his wife? Or him raising your dad?"

"A couple of years later, I got a call from a root worker in New Orleans who'd been friends with both Toussaint and me.

He said Toussaint had married Sabine shortly after I'd left, and that she and Toussaint were performing experiments on rotters. One of them bit Sabine. She contracted the Z-virus. Toussaint tried everything he'd learned over the years to keep her from turning, but he couldn't stop the disease. Instead of putting her down like he should have, he chained her up. He said he loved her too much to put her down."

My heart began to pound, and my breathing got shallow. The memories I was sharing belonged to a history I'd done my best to forget. But how could they understand my unshakeable tie to Toussaint if I didn't spill everything that had happened? No matter how much that hurt.

"He kept her alive by feeding her people. *Live* people. Hell, what choice did I have? I came back to New Orleans, busted into Toussaint's place, and confronted him in his lab. Sabine was there, chained to the wall, skin sliding off her bones, the sickening stench of death rolling off her in waves. I tried to reason with him, to get him to see how...*immoral* that was. Sabine needed to be put to rest. He told me to get the hell out or he'd kill me. Oh, I got out, all right. Right after I put a nine-millimeter between Sabine's eyes."

Ferris raised his brows. "And he just let you leave?"

"He was out of his mind with grief. He knelt beside her and cradled her body, telling me that my life would be a living hell, and that I would never be finished paying for what I had done. I left New Orleans and struck out cross country, trying to get my head straight, and keeping a low profile.

"Eleven months later, my dad died. I went back to Cincinnati for his funeral, but I didn't stick around. I didn't belong in New Orleans, but I didn't belong in Cincinnati, either. So, I took off again, working odd jobs and keeping my 'gift' under wraps. Until I ran out of money. Dad had left his house to me and it was vacant. I *had* to go home. It was my only play."

Hot tears welled in my eyes. "Toussaint knew my dad had

died, but he took his time, and waited until I'd come home to stay to make good on his promise. He raised my father from his grave and turned him into a fucking rotter. Then he called in a fake rotter sighting, so that I would be the one—the one who had to look my dad in the eye and put him down."

The room fell instantly silent. I couldn't tell whether that was due to the story of me putting a round through my father's head, or to the sight of Director Dickhead, as he burst into the room with the bioterrorism specialist, Agent Eli Stanton.

"Assistant Director William Horton," Dickhead said, shaking hands with Boudreaux.

"I didn't realize you were coming, sir."

"It is my taskforce, Agent."

The flat smile on Boudreaux's face suggested that he wasn't impressed. Dickhead introduced Stanton to the group and instantly tried to hijack the meeting.

"Ms. Nighthawk, I understand you had Le Clerc in your fingertips last night and let him get away. How did that happen?"

The fucking douche-meister.

"We were negotiating a hostage rescue and the suspect double-crossed us."

"Do you usually trust the bad guys?"

"I don't even trust you, sir."

Boudreaux coughed. "Agent McMillen, you're our profiler. You've studied the case file and heard Ms. Nighthawk's brief but candid summary of Le Clerc's youth. It's not much to go on, but if you had to venture an opinion, what are we dealing with here?"

Babs clasped her hands in front of her and looked down her nose. "Le Clerc is a malignant narcissist. He's brilliant, manipulative, methodical, and highly motivated by revenge against Ms. Nighthawk. He's also antisocial and sadistic. Control is of the utmost importance to him, even at the subconscious level. He is a master at metaphysics—"

Dickhead snorted. "Metaphysics?"

"The study of abstract concepts—"

"I know what it is, Agent. It's a load of horseshit."

Babs' eyes narrowed. "If Le Clerc's obsession with Ms. Nighthawk can be exploited, we might push him into making an uncharacteristic error."

Rico pushed away from the table. "*Enough. We've talked about everything except our missing hostage, Jade Chen. We're wasting valuable time—*"

"Detective De Palma." Boudreaux rose from his chair slowly. "We had this discussion mere moments ago. Shall I recap it for you?"

Rico turned to Dickhead. "Sir, we aren't getting any closer to finding Ms. Chen sitting in this room. It's your taskforce. With all due respect, sir, run it."

Whoa, bad move, buddy.

Dickhead's eyes blazed. "You'll cooperate with this investigation and do as you are directed, Detective, or you will be removed from the task force. Have I made myself understood?"

Rico's face flamed. He took a long, deep breath and pulled himself together, before nodding to Dickhead. "Yes, sir."

Dickhead fixed his gaze on me, and Little Allie cringed. "Whatever happened to the tissue samples from the Abruzzi case that you sent to Dr. Christian?"

I'd been wondering about the results of those tests myself, but the backlog at the ECPDC rivaled that of the CPDC.

"I haven't heard back. But it's only been a couple of months, give or take." I looked at my watch. Ten a.m. here equaled four p.m. in Sweden. With any luck, we might catch the good doctor.

I pulled out my phone and called him. "Let's see if the doctor is in."

His secretary, Ilse, picked up, and my stomach lurched. Before working for Dr. Christian, Ilse had worked for Sandoval Latka, the world's foremost expert on the Z-virus. He was mysteriously murdered and injected with the Z-virus. Ilse had taken it hard. Sweet, sweet lady. She wanted to chat, but I hurried her along and asked if the doctor was available for a conference call. She put him on the line and I put my phone on speaker.

"Ms. Nighthawk," Christian said. "It's good to hear from you. We're not finished testing yet, but I do have a remarkable bit of information for you."

"Do tell?"

"It seems we've been, as you Americans say, barking up the wrong tree. We've operated under the assumption that your suspect has been manipulating the actual Z-virus. In a sense, that's true, but the original virus remains unaltered. These tissue samples show a new, chemically manufactured virus which mimics the effects of the organic Z-virus."

"In English, Doc."

"There are now two viruses—one organic, one synthetic."

The room went silent.

"That's better news than you think," Christian finally said.

"Really? How so?"

"It means that the original virus hasn't mutated. The sudden, aberrant behaviors of the Z population—their ability to see in the daylight, capacity to follow directions, and willing-ness to group, are all functions of the new, synthetic virus. Victims of the synthetic virus haven't actually died and been risen. They've merely been injected, so theoretically, in time, that synthetic virus could be reverse-engineered to create an antidote—maybe even a vaccine."

"But the victims who were injected died before they turned," Director Dickhead said.

"Yes, that's right. The synthetic virus contains paralytic agents strong enough to stop a person's heart. As the synthetic virus is assimilated, the corpse turns into a zombie."

"This is Agent Ferris, Dr. Christian. What exactly is *in* this synthetic virus?"

"It's fascinating, really. So far, we've identified traces of tetraodontidae, bufo marinus and osteopilus dominidensis."

What the hell?

Boudreaux rubbed his chin. "Can you dumb that down a notch, Doc?"

"Simply put, the virus contains pufferfish, a marine species known to produce tetrodotoxin, a deadly neurotoxin, as well as members of the marine toad and hyla tree frog species, which also produce toxic substances."

Zombie powder. So, Toussaint's knowledge of root working played into the development of the synthetic virus. The pieces of the puzzle were starting to come together.

"Anything else you can tell us?" I asked.

"That's all for now."

I glanced around the table. "Any other questions?"

"Special Agent Boudreaux here, Doctor. The behavioral changes in biters that you mentioned—their seeing during the daytime, grouping, strategizing, et cetera—manifested over time, not all at once. What does that suggest?"

Christian balked. "If I were to hypothesize, your suspect may have engineered multiple versions of the virus, tested each batch for efficacy, and cataloged the outcomes."

"Dr. Christian, this is Detective De Palma. How long until you can come up with an antidote?"

"Finding an antidote using the tissue samples requires a tremendous amount of trial and error. I wouldn't even hazard a guess. If we had a sample of the actual synthetic virus, the reverse engineering process would move much faster."

"How much faster?"

"That's impossible to say, Detective. But your best bet is to get me a sample of the virus."

Rico's shoulders slumped. I didn't need to be a mind reader to know that he was consumed by thoughts of Jade, whose life hung in the balance.

Little Allie asked how we were going to get our hands on a vial of the synthetic virus.

As if I had a clue.

23

THE FLAMING ARROWS OF EVIL

Boudreaux scribbled some notes in his file and darted his eyes toward Mouton. "How's that missing persons report coming?"

"It's running now. We'll have names, dates, last known location, and pics when it's finished."

"Why don't you take Dr. Stanton to the warehouse so he can get a look at the lab equipment? And call in a sketch artist to draw the...Bob Marley guy...for Mr. Sacca to I.D."

Boudreaux closed his file and stood up, signaling the meeting had come to an end. Babs left to collect Vinny and resume her post as his watchdog.

I pulled Ferris and Rico aside, as we stepped back into the hallway. "We need to visit Mama and have a chat about zombie powder."

"*Zombie powder?*" The disdain in Rico's voice was hard to miss.

I'd had about enough of his piss-poor attitude. "The toxins Stanton mentioned are all found in zombie powder. I don't remember the exact proportions in the formula, but Mama will."

Rico's eyes flashed. "You're wasting time we don't have. We need to be out searching for Jade."

"Where?" Ferris snapped, staring out the window at the city of New Orleans. "It's a big-ass city. Do you have any idea where to look? Give the missing persons report a chance to gel."

"Suppose you do find her," I asked. "What are you going to do if she's been injected? Mama could save Jade's life. Is that a waste of time? You tell me. She's *your* girlfriend."

The second those words tumbled over my tongue, I knew I'd gone too far. Once again, the brain bitch had gone AWOL, leaving me at the mercy of my own mouth. That's almost never a good idea.

There was a fire in Rico's eyes I'd never seen before. "Fine," he said. "You and Mama conjure up some eye of newt and wing of bat. I'll find Jade myself."

He spun on his heel and headed back the way we'd come. Ferris shrugged, strolled to the elevator, and silently pressed the call button. I waited in the hallway, watching as Rico knocked on Boudreaux's door. We were a team, damn it. He shouldn't be out on his own—especially in this city, in these streets, where the magick is real, whether you believe in it or not.

By the time the elevator arrived, Rico had disappeared into Boudreaux's office, where he was no doubt pleading his case for going after Jade. Hopefully, between Dickhead and Boudreaux, one of them would realize how foolish that was.

Rico will come around, I thought. *He's just too close to the situation to see that I'm right.* Little Allie jeered at me from the peanut gallery, wanting to know when *I* had become the voice of reason.

That high and mighty brain bitch thinks she has all the answers. But the truth is, when it comes to Jade, Rico tends to think with his little head, giving him the mental acuity of a radish. Someone would need to reel him in, and I was just the person for the job.

———

Ferris and I arrived at Mama Femi's shortly before the lunch rush. Heavenly smells filled the air as we walked inside, making my stomach growl—an insistent reminder that I'd skipped breakfast. We grabbed a table near the entrance to the kitchen. Mama wouldn't have much time to chat, but that was okay. I knew exactly what I needed to ask her.

Luna, Vinny's love interest from dinner the night before, swept to our table and poured us some coffee. She glanced around the restaurant as if she were waiting, or maybe hoping, someone else would be joining us. Her smile never faded, but the gleam in her stunning green eyes dimmed as she pulled out her pen and took our order. Poor thing. To think that Vinny's unique brand of macho-mojo had worked on her was mind-boggling.

Ferris must have been thinking the same thing. "Luna, Vinny said that he'd like to see you again, but we left in such a hurry last night, he didn't have time to get your number. If you'd like, I'd be happy to pass it along to him—but only if you want me to."

She bit her lip and swept a tangle of onyx curls from her eyes. Their emerald shine had returned. "Sure 'nuff," she said. "I'll write it down for you."

She sashayed away from the table with a lightness to her step.

I snorted and rolled my eyes. "Why would you give numb-nuts that poor girl's number?"

Ferris grinned and tossed me a wink. "I'm a sucker for love."

His eyes lingered on mine, drinking them in. An unexpected shiver rippled up my spine. And then, to my absolute shame, a nervous giggle bolted from my throat before I could pull it back. Holy crap on a cracker. I'd been reduced to a silly, teenaged Luna-girl.

I pushed back my chair and stood up, pointing at Ferris. "That...that...*noise* I just made? Never happened. I'm going to go talk to Mama now. You just stay put."

Ferris's grin turned sultry and his eyes washed over me from head to toe. I headed for the kitchen with a quick glance over my shoulder, only to find his gaze still fixed on me. Damn that man and his ice-blue eyes. They could make a woman forget to breathe.

I burst through the swinging door into the kitchen, nearly knocking Mama and the large platter of appetizers she carried to the ancient hardwood floor. I grabbed her arms to steady her. A plump jumbo shrimp skittered off the edge of the tray and plopped to the floor. Mama let loose a mighty sigh, bringing back memories of her ability to dress me down without uttering a single word.

I mumbled an apology and whisked the platter from her hands. She crooked a gnarled finger toward table three, sending me on a delivery run. When I returned, Mama was waiting for me, brow furrowed, arms folded across her massive chest.

"Lawd, if you don't flit and flutter like a mayfly." Her eyes crinkled as she tried unsuccessfully to stifle a smile. "So, what my mayfly need today?"

"How do I reverse zombie powder?"

The gentle smile slipped from her face, and her eyes bored into mine. "Its poison comes from the puffer fish. One fish can kill thirty men."

I nodded. "It's called tetradotoxcin."

"The devil's dust," she said, with a sniff. Crossing herself, she added, "That powder is not a toy."

"What counteracts it, Mama?"

She closed her eyes and breathed in deep. When she exhaled, her breath filtered out slowly. For the first time since I'd returned to New Orleans, I allowed myself to see how fragile she'd become. Her face had grown gaunt. Her laugh lines and crow's feet had deepened into crevices.

"What beats the devil?" she asked. "A magick that is stronger than evil. That, and the will of God."

Was that all?

Mama conjured the strongest magick I'd ever seen. And she was on the good side of God, to be sure. Me? I wasn't a card-carrying, Sunday-service kind of Christian, but God had given me my gift for a reason. And I had my rules, handed down to me from my mom who was already cloud-sitting in Heaven, waiting for me. I liked to think those things put me on the right side of good and evil. But the time might come when I'd have to put that theory to the test.

Mama patted my hand and bussed my cheek with a kiss. "We never alone in these things, child. 'Let your faith be like a shield, and you will be able to stop all the flaming arrows of the evil one.'"

Ephesians, if I remembered correctly.

Call me crazy, but the image of Toussaint shooting flaming arrows at me didn't make me feel any better.

Mama shooed me back to my table with a promise to research the hoodoo antidote for tetrodotoxin, and after enjoying our second delicious meal at Mama Femi's in as many days, Ferris and I returned to the office with carryout for Rico, Babs and Vinny. Rico's included a beignet as a peace offering. I hadn't liked the way we'd parted company that morning.

Babs and Vinny were hunkered down with Mouton, pouring over the missing person reports. I slid their carryout boxes across the desk, then peered around the office. "Where's Rico?"

Babs gazed at me over the top of her readers. "Gone, I believe."

"Gone?"

"I'm sorry. Was that not clear? Gone—as in no longer here."

I hadn't been back five minutes and she was already twerking on my last nerve. "I can see that. Any idea where he might be?"

"He burst from Agent Boudreaux's office and exited the building into the parking lot. Last I saw, he drove away in one of the agency's SUVs."

"By himself?" The hair on the back of my arms stood up. I shoved Rico's food toward Mouton. "Go for it, but save the beignet for De Palma, or I'll kick your ass."

Ferris was already at the door waiting for me. Together, we made our way down the hall to have a chat with Boudreaux.

"What the hell?" I yelled, barging through Boudreaux's door without bothering to knock.

The solid oak door flew back and smashed into the wall, its knob punching a hole through the sheetrock. Crumbled bits of drywall skittered across the carpet, and a small cloud of dust curled into the air.

Dickhead, seated at Boudreaux's desk with his phone pressed against his ear, glanced up, and beheld me in all my pissed-off glory.

"We'll talk later," he mumbled to the mystery caller. Not

skipping a beat, he slipped the phone into his pocket and cast me a disparaging look. "Repair costs for your temper tantrums will be deducted from your paychecks."

"Where's Boudreaux?"

"I borrowed his office. He'll be back momentarily."

"Whose decision was it to let Rico go off on his own?"

"Mine." He sat a little taller and squared his shoulders. "Why?"

"People go missing in this town every day. What were you thinking?"

"He's a cop, Nighthawk. He can handle himself."

"He's an outsider who's sticking his nose into things he doesn't understand."

"Maybe so," Boudreaux said from the doorway. "But he was right. We had an open missing person's case that needed to be worked. I sent Fairchild out with him. Figured Mouton could run down the missing persons leads himself."

"Fairchild? The twelve-year-old with pimples?"

"Don't test me."

"You, of all people, know what he's up against, or at least you should, Mr. *We-Wrote-the-Book-on-the-Undead.*"

"Even my baby agents fresh from the womb kick ass. They wouldn't be on the streets otherwise. He and De Palma will be just fine. But if you're worried, maybe you should join them." Boudreaux's eyes swung toward the door-knob shaped hole in his wall. "I've got a long-ass memory and a decided lack of patience, Ms. Nighthawk. You'd do well to remember that."

Agent Mouton appeared behind Boudreaux and peered into the office. "Sorry to interrupt. I thought you'd be interested in knowing there's been a spike in the number of missing persons. In the last two months we've averaged seventy-five."

"What's normal?" Ferris asked.

Boudreaux scratched his head and whistled. "Twenty, give or take, factoring in the drunken tourists and nutjobs."

"Interesting," Dickhead said. "But how does that relate to our case?"

Mouton shrugged. "I'm not sure that it does, but if your man Toussaint is responsible for the variance, he's building up an army. An army of the undead. I wonder what he's going to do with that," Mouton mused aloud.

Little Allie had her suspicions, but neither one of us was ready to go there yet.

"One more thing," Mouton said. "A missing person's report was filed a few days ago on a Sherrod Wiley, the head of the governor's advance team. He checked into the Hotel St. Marie and that's the last anyone has seen of him."

The brain bitch squealed so loud the fillings in my teeth vibrated. "Governor? As in Governor *Andrew Thornton*?"

"You're kidding," Mouton's voice wavered. "We only have one, right?"

"Gimme that list," I said, crossing the floor, and ripping it from his hands. When I began to read, bells and whistles went off, the creepy kind that made my skin crawl.

Governor Thornton used to be District Attorney Thornton, the same D.A. who refused to indict me for murder when I put down Toussaint's wife. Why would Thornton indict me? She was already dead. No harm, no foul, no more zombie. Everybody wins, right?

Except, that case was one of those freaking Undead Lives Matter situations...the ones the ACLU digs their claws into. The courts didn't want to touch that puppy with a ten-foot pole. So, rather than indict me and initiate a never-ending court battle nobody in power wanted to fight, Thornton's office refused to prosecute. The ACLU threw a hissy that eventually faded away when newer, more sexy oppressions raised their ugly heads. But Toussaint, never one to keep his feelings close to the vest, had sworn he'd kill us both.

Was Toussaint finally making good on his threat?

I continued scanning the missing persons list and caught my breath when I reached the final name: Henri Abellard. Henri, the root worker who told me that Toussaint had been keeping his infected wife alive and in chains, had been reported missing yesterday—the day of the warehouse incident. It had been a while since I'd seen Henri, but I'd never forget his elbow-length dreads.

Now, I've never much believed in coincidence, but fate? I'll put my money on fate any day, and I had a feeling Lady Destiny was throwing us a bone.

"Agent Mouton," I said, "would you print Henri Abellard's DMV photo and show it to Rip Sacca?"

24

A BUNCH OF CRYBABY GOSSIPS

I caught Ferris's eye and nodded toward the door. "We've got a lot of ground to cover. Rico could be anywhere by now."

"Not so fast," Boudreaux said. "The governor's point man is missing. We've got a new priority."

"Like hell I do. My *partner's* missing."

"Not missing. Working a case. Sherrod Wiley's a high-profile target. As of now, all assets are reassigned."

"You can't assign me anywhere. I don't report to you."

"But you do report to me," Dickhead said. "And since it appears there could be a connection between Toussaint Le Clerc and the disappearances of Henri Abellard and Mr. Wiley, I agree with Agent Boudreaux. Your time is best spent working this angle."

"What about Ric—"

"Asked and answered. He's not on his own, he's with Agent Fairchild, and we have no reason to believe they're in danger."

Philip Mouton grimaced, backed out of the doorway, and made his escape. The sound of his shoes slapping against the Berber carpet echoed down the hallway. My mouth snapped open to launch a new assault, but the brain bitch went cray-cray in the hope of shutting me down. Screw that haughty little head hag. If anyone was going to be insolent and ill-mannered, it was me.

Ferris snatched my arm and walked us both toward the door.

"We're on it," he said with a quick nod to Dickhead and Boudreaux.

*Oh no, he did **not** just man-handle me.*

I broke his grip and spun on my heel. "What? What do you mean, *we're* on it? I—"

Ferris bulldozed me into the hall and Boudreaux shut the door behind us.

I banged on the solid oak panel. "Hey! I'm not finished yet."

"Oh, yes you are," Ferris muttered, herding me down the hallway. "We can keep our eyes peeled for Rico along the way. Dickhead was right. If these cases are related, all roads will lead to Toussaint. We'll intersect Rico along the way."

Damn Sam. I hate when I'm pissed off and other people are right.

We wound through the corridor toward the sea of tiny beige cubicles that belonged to the not-so-senior agents. Philip Mouton was already pulling up the DMV website.

Ferris grinned and clapped him on the shoulder. "One more favor. After you've shown Abellard's photo to Rip, how 'bout running Wiley's phone records and credit cards? And put a BOLO out on his car."

The fifteen-minute trip to the Hotel St. Marie would give me a few minutes to check on the terrible twins. I climbed into the passenger seat of the SUV and punched in Nonnie's number.

"Oh, Miss Allie," she moaned. "When you come home?"

"What's wrong?"

"Is Kulu."

"What did she do now?"

"She lay egg in your...lady pads."

"In my *what*?"

"In box of lady pads...the ones with wings, on bathroom sink."

"*Eww*. Gross." I stared at my phone, trying to process the visual. "Get that egg thingie out of there."

"Is her nest!"

"Yeah? Well, they're my maxi-pads, and I'm not sharing."

That freeloading feather duster. Let her poop out her eggs somewhere else.

"Stick the egg in a wad of toilet paper," I suggested. "Shove it into a paper towel. Plop it into crumpled newspaper. Something. Anything."

The fully-developed visual registered, making me shudder.

"On second thought, throw the box away."

"But the baby..."

"Unless you've been letting boy birdies in the house, there won't be a baby."

"Is miracle!" Nonnie gushed.

"Nope. No miracle. No baby," I sighed. "The egg is unfertilized. Never mind. Just leave the box where it is. When Kulu gets tired of sitting on the egg, we can throw the box away."

"Feh. Miss Smarty-pants-know-it-all. You so smart, how you pay back taxes? Huh?"

"I'm not worried. I'll figure it out."

"Good thing Nonnie worried. We open business. You raise the corpses—for peoples like Lucia."

"Yeah. 'Cause that turned out so well."

"You got monies, didn't you?" She giggled like a school girl. "I even have name: American Corpse Management Executives. ACME."

"ACME, like in...Wile E. Coyote ACME?"

"I be office manager."

My temples started to throb. "We'll talk later."

"I work your house. At kitchen table. No...how they say... over-the-heads."

"Sorry, gotta run. Zombies everywhere. Bye now." I clicked *end* and stared out the window.

Sweet baby cheeses. I'd just lied to Nonnie. Was it too much to ask for a freaking deadhead when you needed one?

The wrought iron balcony of room 411—Sherrod Wiley's room at the Hotel St. Marie—overlooked a torchlit tropical courtyard. Interesting choice, I thought. While most guests opted for street-side rooms with a view of The Quarter, Wiley choose a room on the opposite side. Why? Maybe working with the governor's office had brought him to the city a time or two...or ten. Maybe the twenty-four-hour party in the streets had grown old. Maybe he was simply tired and wanted a good night's sleep. Or maybe his mission required privacy.

Wiley's suitcase lay atop the luggage rack beside his bed, its contents still neatly folded and strapped inside. A single change of clothes and a dopp kit. He wasn't planning on a long stay, which begged the question: what exactly was he doing here? A better question still: what did Sherrod Wiley have that was worth kidnapping, or perhaps, killing for? Sex? No way. The guy was uglier than a mud fence. Money? Not likely. He was a glorified civil servant at best. Power? Too low on the totem pole.

Ding, ding, ding. Little Allie slammed the golden buzzer in my brain. *What he had was information.*

The point man would know the governor's schedule. Where he'd be, and when he'd be there. If Toussaint really was going for revenge, that info was worth its weight in gold.

Ferris listened to my theory and awarded it a grudging nod. "That sounds right, but a guy like Wiley could know a lot of things, that would be valuable to all kinds of people. Let's keep an open mind."

A quick look in Wiley's closet found it empty, so I ducked into the bathroom and nosed around. The sink was bone dry. Towels folded. Sanitary wrapper still circled around the toilet lid. Nothing.

Ferris's phone rang. He listened for a few seconds and then said, "Good job, Mouton."

I stepped out of the john so Ferris could fill me in, but he was already headed for the door.

"Looks like the BOLO paid off," he said. "Wiley's car, or at least what's left of it, turned up on Rampart Street."

Ferris drove us out of the Quarter and followed some ominous, rising plumes of black smoke to an abandoned parking lot in the 4700 block of Rampart Street. Firefighters had knocked down the flames, but the charred carcass of Wiley's late-model sedan billowed steam into the air.

Ferris flashed his badge and established FBI jurisdiction, asking one of the firemen to bust through the lock on the sedan's trunk with his shovel. Up popped the lid, along with the stench of burning flesh and hair. The tortured grin of a carbonized corpse greeted us.

"Jesus." Ferris winced and turned away.

"Wiley?" I asked.

"Hard to say. Probably. It's his car and he's missing. But whoever did this wanted us to find it, burning out a car in broad daylight."

The body was still smoldering, so we stepped upwind and contemplated our options.

"Don't look at me," I said, frowning at the trunk. "I'm not going in there."

"Neither one of us is," Ferris said, pulling out his phone to call it in. "That's the coroner's job."

As Ferris wandered a few more yards upwind, I considered asking him to hold off.

Odds were, the corpse was Wiley. We didn't have any witnesses. Trace evidence would be scant, if any, given the heat. And our priority-one time frame didn't give us wiggle room to grope around in the dark for clues. But I'd have hell to pay if I raised Wiley now and contaminated the crime scene. And if that charcoal briquette turned out *not* to be Wiley, I'd go down hard. Ferris was right. The coroner had to do his thing first. Besides, I wasn't all that keen on messing with this crispy-critter in situ anyway. He'd fall apart like an overcooked rump roast. Let the M.E. scrape him up and transport him. Once we had a positive ID, I could raise Wiley at the coroner's office before they autopsied him.

To be fair, I've had a few...incidents...with coroners over the years. Barely worth mentioning, really. They're a bunch of crybaby gossips, and frankly, they don't bring out the best in me. God knows Doc Blanchard, Cincinnati's coroner, hyperventilates at the mention of my name. I'm more about the end results than how I get there. But these elected official types are anal-retentive and downright squirrely when it comes to documentation, procedure, and cleanliness. They're *really* big on cleanliness.

Ferris had finished his call. "A penny for your thoughts," he said, breaking my reverie.

"Who's the coroner in these parts?"

"Dr. Slidell, or so I was just informed."

His name wasn't familiar—thank heavens. I'd learned my trade here in The Big Easy, but people in my line of work tend to keep it on the down low. The only official investigation I'd gotten caught up in was the "murder" of Toussaint's wife, and that was in Terrebonne Parish.

"Let's not bother Dr. Slidell with the ins and outs of raising. In fact, let's not even mention raising until he gets this corpse back to the morgue. He's a busy guy." Visions of the damage from my last raising at the Cincinnati morgue flashed through my head. "On second thought, don't even introduce me."

Ferris laughed. "What's the matter? Afraid the M.E.s office is behind on its Property and Casualty premiums?"

Freaking Ferris. Just because he could take a shot at me didn't mean he had to.

25

THAT DIMWITTED, SHIT-FOR-BRAINS HORNDOG

D r. Slidell arrived in a tricked-out Black Diamond Hummer and pulled up to the curb behind the burned-out sedan. He rolled his round body out from behind the steering wheel, adjusted his summer-white suit, and ran a hand through his shock of snow-white hair. His hooded eyes, neutral as they fixed on Ferris, narrowed considerably when they darted to me.

The brain bitch growled, causing the hair on my arms to stand on end. *Message received, Little Allie.* For all her quirks and inconsistencies, she'd never steered me wrong on a first impression.

Ferris, apparently noticing the change in Slidell's demeanor, ran interference by stepping in front of me and introducing himself. Slidell's weak attempt at a smile faded beneath his gray, overgrown goatee. He nodded at Ferris, then thumped a wooden walking stick by his side and pivoted toward me. "No need for introductions, Ms. Nighthawk. Your reputation, and your notoriety, precede you. Doc Blanchard and I are old fishing buddies. Sends his regards, by the way."

Holy crap on a cracker.

He snapped a pair of nitrile gloves over his balloon-like hands and peered into the trunk of the sedan. "Kind of you, young lady, to allow me to conduct my investigation before you turn our unfortunate friend here into a carnival freak show." He studied the charred body, then pursed his lips. "I doubt this gentleman started the fire and then locked himself in the trunk to die. I think we're safe to declare this a murder scene. ID and cause of death pending."

Ferris cleared his throat and leaned over the trunk beside Slidell. "We believe the corpse may be the governor's point man, Sherrod Wiley. He was reported missing a few days ago. I'll have our office email you his dental records."

"That'd be mighty helpful of you. If you're right, that'll put the identification issue to bed. Considering the thermal damage, we'll likely run a PMCT."

A what?

Ferris whispered over his shoulder, "A post-mortem CT scan. Helps with determining COD—cause of death."

"I know what COD is," I snapped.

Ferris sighed and turned to Slidell. "Non-contrast?"

"Absolutely. Given the tissue damage, injection of contrast agents would be impossible."

"Show-off," I hissed in Ferris's ear.

"Forensics 101, Nighthawk. Crack a book sometime."

The meat wagon pulled up alongside Slidell's Hummer. A few of his lackeys scampered out, and he waved them over with a swish of his hand. "Ready for transport, gentlemen. Our vic here is rather badly burned. Check for trace, and for God's sake, be mindful of dermal shedding."

Ferris leaned in close. "That's when the dead skin sloughs off. You know, 'cause they're burnt and...dead."

"Jesus," I said, punching his arm. "If anyone knows what dead bodies do, it's me."

Slidell climbed back into his Hummer and called, "Miss

Nighthawk? Just in case you had any ideas about raising Mr. Wiley, if indeed, he is Mr. Wiley, in *my* morgue, know two things. First, you will not touch this corpse, or go anywhere near it, without my express consent. Second, and I cannot stress this enough, as long as I live and draw air into my lungs, you will never *ever* raise a corpse in *any* morgue of mine. Have I made myself clear?"

He pulled away from the curb, not waiting for my answer.

"Crystal," I yelled.

Little Allie joined in, blowing out the few brain cells I had left. *Fuck you, Colonel Sanders! You arrogant pig-face.*

Ferris took a deep breath and watched Dr. Slidell drive up Rampart toward the morgue. "It could have been worse," he said.

"How so?"

"We could be hunkered in the trunk of that sedan, scraping up dermal shedding."

"Oh, bite me."

Ferris could be as glib as he wanted, I wasn't laughing. Slidell and his blanket refusal to allow me to raise Wiley in his morgue had thrown a monkey wrench into our case. We needed Wiley to confirm who killed him, and there was only one way to get that confirmation. I'd have to raise him. That meant someone was going to have to change Slidell's mind, and it sure wasn't going to be me. As we climbed back into the SUV, my eyes lingered on Ferris. Would he have a shot?

Ferris started the ignition and shot me the side eye. "Stop staring at me."

When I didn't respond, he sighed and put both hands on the wheel. "What?"

"Nothing. Well, maybe." I squirmed deeper into my seat.

"Do you think you could convince Slidell to let me raise Wiley?"

"Seriously? Not a chance. The guy doesn't know me from Adam."

"But you're an FBI agent. And he doesn't hate you the way he hates me."

"He does hate you, doesn't he?"

"More than the trots."

After a moment of silence, Ferris smirked. "What about Boudreaux? He's a local guy—and he's got the weight of the FBI behind him."

"What if Slidell hates him, too?"

"Only one way to find out." Ferris pulled out his phone and dialed Boudreaux.

"Put it on conference," I whispered. "*He* likes me. Kind of."

Boudreaux answered on the second ring. Ferris filled him in on the salient points, namely that Slidell had outlawed raising Wiley and had all but barred me from the morgue.

"Making friends as usual, Nighthawk?" Boudreaux asked.

"Apparently so, sir."

"I'll see what I can do. Percy and I go back a ways, but it hasn't all been rosy."

His name was Percy? Why didn't that surprise me?

"You know," Boudreaux said. "Without a court order, it's his call. I'll give him a shout and get back to you."

"Thank you, sir," Ferris said. "Before you hang up, can you transfer me to Mouton?"

"Sure thing. And Nighthawk," Boudreaux added. "Try not to make any more friends today. I don't think I could bear it."

"Wouldn't dream of it, sir."

After a brief pause, Mouton picked up the line. "Ferris, you must be psychic. Your man Rip just ID'd Henri Abellard's pic as the guy with the dreadlocks from the warehouse."

Ferris pumped his fist. "Be sure to let Agent Boudreaux

know—pronto. I'd like him to have that information before his conversation with Dr. Slidell. Any word from Fairchild or De Palma?" Ferris frowned and shook his head. "Okay, thanks. We're on our way back now."

"It's almost five," I said, glancing at my watch. "They should have checked in by now."

"They're fine. Stop obsessing."

Easy for Ferris to say. He didn't have the brain bitch pitching a hissy in his head. He threaded the SUV through rush hour traffic while I stared silently out my window, trying not to anticipate the worst. The air between us had grown thick and heavy. It wasn't until we pulled into the parking lot of the FBI office that Ferris finally broke the silence.

"Would you be as worried if it were me out there?"

If he thought that little bombshell was going to turn me into Chatty Cathy, he had another think coming. As soon as he put the car in park, I opened the door, jumped out and damn near sprinted for the door. Screw him. He could follow at his own pace.

I cruised through junior agent cubical land and stopped at Mouton's desk. "Nice job with the ID, Philip. Have you seen Babs—ah, Agent McMillen lately?"

"Last I saw, she was headed for the cafeteria, maybe an hour ago."

Boudreaux marched purposely up the hallway in my direction, sport coat over his arm, tie pulled loose; the look on his face, indecipherable. Heavy footsteps that had been pounding the Berber carpet behind me came to an abrupt stop. I knew without turning they belonged to Ferris.

"Update, folks," Boudreaux said from the corner of Mouton's cube. "Percy was in the process of conducting his examination of your corpse when I called. His admin relayed my message, asking for a sit down to discuss raising this fellow. Percy said he didn't have time for a meeting tonight, but he'll hold off on the autopsy. We have an appointment with him at nine tomorrow morning. I wouldn't be too hopeful, if I was you." Boudreaux sighed and leaned against the corner of the cube. "Sally—the admin—said he was only agreeing to meet 'cause it was me asking. She said he called you, and I quote, 'The mouth that roared.' Said he wouldn't let you raise that fella if you were the Lord God, Himself."

"Well, then," I said, refusing to swallow my sarcasm. "As long as there's hope."

Boudreaux smirked in spite of himself. "We'll give Percy a good night's sleep. He's a... Hell. What's the word? Irascible. An irascible old coot. I'll remind him of a favor or two I've got coming my way. I'll invite Director Horton to this soiree as well. Pick me up at my office, at eight-thirty." Boudreaux left us with a nod and continued his way out the door. Five o'clock had come.

I turned to Mouton. "Where'd you say Vinny was?"

"You never asked. I said Agent McMillen went to the cafeteria about an hour ago."

I shot him the Allie eye. "And where's Vinny?"

"In the conference room, last I saw him. But that was at least a couple of hours ago."

A chill snaked up my spine. Ferris and I bolted to the conference room before Mouton could even respond. Ferris threw open the door and we stared into the empty room. "Damn it!" he yelled. Vinny's computer was still logged in, but his phone was gone. He was kind enough to leave a note:

Sorry, I'm outta here. This ain't how the Vinster rolls. Be back later, V...

p.s. That whack-job babysitter you got me needs to get laid.

My head felt like it might explode. "She needs to get laid *out*, is what she needs!"

I sprinted from the conference room through the hallway to the cafeteria, with Ferris on my heels. We burst through the door and found Psycho Babs seated at a small round dining table with her nose stuck in one of her psychiatric journals.

She glanced over the top of her cheaters and studied us like some curious new organisms. "May I help you?"

"Where's Vinny?" Ferris boomed.

"I don't think I care for your tone." Sitting taller, she raised her brow and glared at Ferris. "Would you care to ask me again in a civil manner, or shall I simply ignore you?"

"Answer the damn question!" I said, straddling the chair across from her.

"I...he..." Babs blinked. "He's exactly where I left him—in the conference room."

"Bzzt! Wrong answer." I leaned in, getting nose to nose with her. "Care to try again?"

"Are you sure?" she murmured.

"What do you think?" I said, shoving Vinny's note into her perfectly manicured claws.

She scanned the words and blushed. I'd forgotten the part about her needing to get laid. Well, that's a lie. I didn't forget. I shoved it up her beak-like snout and rotated it.

Babs' cheeks blazed. "I hold multiple doctorates and I'm a trained profiler for the FBI, not a babysitter." She sighed and tossed up her hands. "We aren't well suited to spend time together. I needed a break, and he promised to stay put. The prepubescent monkey."

"He's not some snot-nosed runaway," Ferris snapped. "He's a grown man who could be in danger. And he disappeared on your watch."

Babs rolled her eyes. "He's a walking penis with the brain of a toddler."

My stomach churned at the thought of having to tell Boudreaux and Dickhead that we'd lost our vic. Correction, that *Babs* had lost our vic.

"Everybody relax. Just take a breath," Ferris said. "And think."

"Maybe he went back to his dorm room." I said.

"Possibly." Ferris rubbed his face with his hands. "Or maybe to The Boot, to hang out."

Babs shook her head. "No. We're grasping at straws. What would *Vinny* want, this pubescent college boy who just finished his exams? Pizza, beer, and girls?"

"Luna," I said, jumping off my chair. "He wants Luna."

Judging by the way he'd shoveled in his po' boys at dinner the night before, I figured he was looking for more of Mama's cooking too. I pulled out my phone and dialed the restaurant, tapping my foot, waiting for someone to pick up.

The voice that finally answered was soft and sweet. "Mama Femi's."

"Luna?"

"This is she."

"Luna, this is Allie. Is Vinny there with you?"

The line went quiet.

"It's okay if he is, we're just worried about him."

"Yeah," she giggled. "He's here. Eating Mama's cooking and waitin' on me to get off work."

"Would you put him on the line, please?" I sucked in the first good breath I'd had in at least ten minutes and swore to snatch him bald the next time I saw him.

Seconds later, Vinny whined in my ear. "C'mon, Nighthawk. Cut me some slack. I'm working here"

"Working your way to an ass-whooping."

"Give me a break! I'm in freakin' jail here. I—"

"It's for you own good, damn it." The dimwitted, shit-for-brains horndog. I closed my eyes and counted to ten, like that was going to help. "Stay where you are. I mean it, Vinny. We're on our way. God help your horny little ass if you aren't there when we walk in that door. Now, put Luna back on."

Ferris, tossing his keys from hand to hand, had been waiting for me to finish my rant. He finally gave up, walked to the door with Babs on his heels, and motioned for me to meet him at the car.

A hesitant Luna picked up the line. "How...how can I help you, Miss Allie?"

"Girl, you keep that bonehead in your sight until we get there. Do not let him leave. You feel me?"

"Yes 'um. I surely do."

"Tell Mama we'll have four for dinner—three if Vinny already ate. Be there in a bit. How 'bout saving me some garlic frog legs?"

"You bet. Have them hoppers ready and waitin' on you, Miss Allie. And don't you fret none. Vinny always got room for more."

I hung up, already tasting the garlic, but as I walked to the SUV and ducked into the back seat, an anxious Little Allie wouldn't let me be.

Where the hell is Rico, she wanted to know.

That made two of us.

26

SOMEONE CALL FOR A MURDEROUS, LIFE-SUCKING DEVIL?

I snatched my phone from my back pocket and speed-dialed Rico. The call went straight to voice mail.

"It's me," I said. "Where are you?"

I hung up, feeling even more anxious. Rico had gone off half-cocked, and was pissed for sure, but he would never ignore my call.

I tapped Ferris's shoulder. "You got Fairchild's number?"

He shook his head and handed his phone back to me. "No. But I've got Mouton's. He'd have it, or at least could get it for us."

I texted Mouton and two minutes later he texted me Fairchild's number. I dialed it and waited. One ring, two rings, three, four. The voice mail came on and my heart sank.

"This is Nighthawk. Call me as soon as you get this message. Thanks." I ended the call and leaned forward over the console. "Something's wrong and you know it."

"What's this?" Babs asked, craning her neck to peer back at me. "We have a new problem?"

I'd forgotten that she'd been with Vinny and had no idea what we were talking about. "Rico got antsy and went off with

Agent Fairchild to look for Jade. We haven't heard from either of them since noon."

Babs frowned. "That is a long while."

Ferris drummed his fingers against the steering wheel and sighed. "Let's corral Vinny and grab a quick dinner. If we haven't heard back from them by the time we're finished eating, we'll call it in to Horton and Boudreaux, and get a BOLO out on them. Sorry McMillen, but if we get called out in the middle of the night, you're back on Vinny patrol."

Babs closed her eyes and groaned. "Let's not borrow trouble, shall we? Maybe we'll get lucky and they'll turn up at the restaurant."

From the hangdog look on her face, it appeared that Vinny was more than the middle-aged desk agent could handle. To be fair, I could relate. There were days when Leo drove me crazier than a possum in a gunnysack. Those Abruzzi men—both cut from the same raggedy piece of coarse-grained jute.

Funny how they'd grown on me.

Luna rushed to greet us as we entered the bustling restaurant. Mama had a table set aside for us, the same table we'd had the night before, near the kitchen and more secluded than most. Vinny sat there waiting for us, straddling his chair as if he hadn't a care in the world. You'd think, with all the trouble he'd caused, he'd have had the decency to look contrite. But you'd be wrong.

"Finally. I'm starving here. Let's order already."

Luna giggled.

"You just ate," I said, taking the chair beside him.

"What can I say? Pretty ladies make me hungry." He winked at Luna, making me want to hurl.

A smiling Ferris flanked Vinny's other side, leaned in close and whispered, "If you *ever* take off again, the pretty ladies are going to have to scrape you up with a shovel."

The gobsmacked look on Vinny's face gave me my only laugh of the day.

Mama and Luna carried in platters teaming with crawfish, sausage, potatoes and corn. I filched a few pieces off the top, then trailed Mama back to the kitchen and put on an apron to help her. "You keep cooking like this, Mama, we're going to need a crane to get us out of our chairs."

She untied my apron, laid it across her arm and took my hands. "Someting troubling you, child. Tell Manman what it is."

There was no escaping her soulful brown eyes.

"Rico went off to search for Jade. He's not back yet."

"Ah. You worry for him. Maybe he is more than partner, eh?"

I glanced away to hide my feelings, as well as the tears in my eyes. "He'd be here by now if he were okay—or at least, he would have called. Where could he be?"

Mama held me and whispered a prayer for Rico's protection in my ear. Then she kissed my cheek and sent me back to my table with a motherly reproof. "We pray for his safe return, no? But for now, eat, my Little Bird. You will need your strength."

Leaving the kitchen, I felt Ferris's gaze on me. Little Allie chided, *He knows how you feel.* I smiled and involuntarily swiped at my eyes. He didn't need to see them pooling with tears—especially tears over Rico. I fell quiet and hoped that Vinny's mindless babble would fill the void.

Babs warily reached across the table and patted my hand, as if it might bite. "There, there, Ms. Nighthawk. I'm sure Officer De Palma is fine. He and Fairchild must have gotten caught up in the case. They'll be back soon."

I glanced up, silently cursing my transparency, and gasped. In the window behind Babs' head was Toussaint's reflection. I whirled out of my chair, expecting to find him standing behind me. But he wasn't.

"I'll be back," I mumbled, taking off across the restaurant.

After bursting through the screen door, I skidded to a halt on the porch. Something was...off. The night was still, too still, and eerily quiet, not a soul in sight despite the packed parking lot. But there, at the foot of the steps, was a message—a flaming message—meant for me.

I leapt from the porch and stomped out the flames consuming a fetish made of parchment and smelling of vinegar, with a tinge of something else. Peppermint, maybe? Although much of the paper had burned away, the charred remains contained a message written in red—blood, unless I missed my guess. The same two words covered the paper from edge to edge: Allie Nighthawk. The source of the flames? A slim black taper, its tip still glowing, resting beside the fetish. Smoke curling up from the candle smelled familiar—strong, sweet and musky. Patchouli oil. Just beyond the reach of the flames sat a small resin carving—a gray, winged monster with pointed ears, bulging eyes, a protruding red tongue, and the talons of a harpy.

It was a statue of a Voudon *diab*—a murderous, life-sucking devil.

Toussaint's message was simple. He'd invoked the *diab* to destroy me.

I turned my eyes to the porch where Ferris, Babs, and Vinny stood, mouths agape. Mama waddled out behind them, gasped at the smoldering fetish, and grabbed Ferris's arm to steady herself.

"Who do dis? Who bring this evil to my doorstep?"

My heart ached. "You know who, Mama."

"Say it! Say the name of my enemy."

I raised my head and willed the words to come out loud and strong. "Toussaint Anselme Le Clerc."

The pain in her eyes cut me to the quick. In that one swift, horrible moment, her *bway* had become dead to her. Some of the guests had funneled out to the porch to gawk at a sight they couldn't comprehend.

Mama straightened her apron and smoothed back her hair. "Go back inside, please. Enjoy your food. All is well." She shooed them to their tables with an offer of a free dessert for the intrusion.

Clueless but smiling, the guests returned to their seats, with Mama, Babs, and Vinny trailing in behind them.

Ferris and I searched the grounds, but Toussaint was long gone—if he'd really been there in the first place. More likely, someone had left the fetish for me on his behalf. Toussaint's astral projection had visited me before. Screwing with me was his favorite pastime.

We returned to find Mama pacing the creaky wooden porch boards, sprinkling a jar of red brick dust on the front steps and across the threshold. "Not in my house, Toussaint," she huffed, tossing handfuls of dust at the windows. "Not to the people in my heart."

Luna packed up our leftovers and handed them to Vinny for a late-night snack while Ferris paid our bill.

Mama anointed each of us as we walked out the door, offering her blessing and protection. "Little Bird," she whispered, cradling me to her chest. "Hold fast. Each day, I get closer to finding your antidote. Toussaint's magick is strong, but yours is stronger."

I wanted to believe she was right. I needed to believe she was right. So, what was stopping me?

Once we slid into the SUV, Ferris made good on his promise to report Rico missing.

"No, Director Horton, we haven't heard from either De Palma or Fairchild since roughly noon. I'll call Agent Boudreaux and ask him to put out a BOLO." Ferris paused then gave a quick nod. "Will do, sir. Goodnight."

Ferris called Boudreaux who instantly ordered the BOLO. After a quick reminder from Boudreaux about our nine o'clock meeting at the coroner's office, Ferris ended the call, and an oppressive silence blanketed the car. Even Vinny seemed solemn and withdrawn. Maybe the impact of all this was finally hitting home. Maybe he was worried for his safety, or Luna's. Then again, Vinny wasn't all that complex. He might have just been hungry again.

Ferris pulled into a parking spot at the hotel. "We have to pick up Boudreaux at eight thirty. Let's meet in the restaurant at seven-thirty.

Babs caught my eye and winked. "Come, Mr. Abruzzi. Let's get you inside before your libido leads you astray again."

She motioned him out of the car and took hold of his arm as they struck out across the parking lot.

"Hey, Vinny," Ferris called. "Remember. Your ass. Scrape, scrape."

Vinny kept walking and flipped him the bird.

"See you in the morning," I said, opening the door.

"Allie, wait." Ferris patted the passenger seat. "Come up here. I want to talk to you."

My eyes filled with tears despite me willing them not too. "It's late. I should go." I said, sliding out the car door.

"Allie. Please."

His voice sounded pleading. Almost desperate.

It's not his fault you're an idiot, Little Allie chided. *Talk to him.*

I ducked into the passenger seat, turned to face him, and froze. There was something in his ice-blue eyes I'd never seen before. When he spoke, his voice was soft and his words were measured.

"I'm worried about him, too...and Fairchild. But I'm worried about you more. I know you're conflicted about Rico and me. And this case, your history with Toussaint, the memories and emotions it dredges up, it's tearing you apart. But you act like you've got everything under control. Like you don't need anyone. I'm just saying, it's okay if you need to lean on me. I'm here for you. Even if I lose you."

That was the sweetest, most romantic thing anyone had ever said to me. Thank God, one of us was a girl, even if it wasn't me.

He leaned down for a kiss. I moved closer, but his lips landed on my forehead. "Time to go in and get some sleep," he said with a yawn. "We've got an early morning."

As we rode up to our separate rooms in the elevator, I wondered if he was as perfect as he appeared to be. Maybe he had an ulterior motive. Maybe his charm and sincerity were part of a calculated plan to win me over.

If so, he was doing a damn good job of it.

"Good night, Allie girl," he murmured from across the hall.

"Good night." *You blue-eyed bastard.*

27

THE SOUND OF FUBAR

F alling asleep was easy—after tossing and turning and
watching the digital clock on the nightstand strike three.
Waking up on time to make our 7:30 a.m. breakfast would have
been a challenge, but for Babs' morning ablutions—which,
according to said clock, began at 6:30 a.m.

Having zero ablutions (unless you count soap, deodorant
and toothpaste) I made it to the restaurant, dressed and ready
to rock at seven-thirty, on the nose.

Vinny, halfway through his second plate of pancakes,
peppered me with questions. "So, when you raise these corpses,
how does it work? Do your eyes roll back in your head? Are you
in some kind of trance?" He wiped syrup off his chin and took a
swig of milk. "Is there an extraterrestrial mineral that takes
your power away? Like kryptonite or something?"

"Really? Kryptonite?" I snickered and sipped my coffee.

"Vinny shrugged. "Hell, I don't know. I'm just psyched about
watching you raise this guy today. I've never seen a raising
before. Sure beats hanging out at the FBI office all day with Ba
—no offense, Agent McMillen."

The coffee spewed from my mouth. "Excuse me?"

"No way," Ferris said. "It's too dangerous."

Vinny pounded the table. "That's bullshit, man. I didn't do anything wrong, but I'm in freaking jail, all day, every day. You know what? I'd rather take my chances out there with the biters and that Toussaint guy."

"No. No, you wouldn't," I said, grabbing Vinny's arm.

Ferris closed his eyes and massaged his temples. "Okay, kid," he said after a pause. "Point taken. Agent McMillen, why don't you escort Vinny to the agency's shooting range? Let him fire off a few rounds."

Babs folded her journal and laid it down, squaring it with the edge of the table. "I'm not sure I—"

"C'mon, Agent McMillen." Vinny's eyes sparkled. "You and me, rackin' slides and lettin' 'em fly. Whaddaya say?"

Babs glanced at me, silently begging for help. But she could fend for herself. I had my own fish to fry once Ferris and I reached the coroner's office.

Not twenty minutes later, he and I picked up Boudreaux and headed for our visit with Dr. Slidell. Boudreaux climbed into the car and promptly reminded us that Director Horton would be joining us there.

Yippee.

Although I suspected I knew the answer, I asked anyway. "Any update on De Palma and Fairchild, sir?"

"Negative. But the whole city's looking for them. Keep a good thought."

Oh, I had plenty of thoughts. Not a one of them was good.

Ferris spotted Dickhead on the sidewalk in front of the coroner's office and parked the SUV at the curb. We'd barely made it out of the car before Dickhead's lips began to flap.

"Who does this jackass Slidell think he is? If the FBI wants to raise a stinking corpse, then by God, we're going to raise a stinking corpse."

Boudreaux's brow shot up. "Percy's been the coroner in these parts since Moses was a child. We have a decent working relationship, him and me. Tread lightly."

I *harrumphed* a little too loudly, earning me an elbow from Ferris. Dickhead—tread lightly? Sure. He could tip-toe, like an M1 tank.

Dickhead cocked his head and stuck out his chin. "I'll tread any way I see fit. Tell you what, agent. You got any influence over this shithead, I suggest you use it. He doesn't want to dance with me."

Between Dickhead's puffed cheeks and Boudreaux's narrowed eyes, there was way too much testosterone in the air for my taste. Somebody had to be the voice of reason. That person was so seldom me. I didn't want to miss my chance.

"Shall we get this over with, gentlemen?" I asked, opening the office door. "Or would you rather keep pissing on each other?"

I didn't win any points for diplomacy, but the message found its mark.

Sally, a tiny spindle of a woman with poofy gray hair, fake eyelashes, and nicotine-yellow fingers sporting Fuck Me-red nail polish strolled out to greet us from behind the receptionist's desk.

"Hiya, Jake." She winked at Boudreaux and then nodded to the rest of us. "Morning folks. Percy'll be with you momentarily. He's taking his, ah...daily...constitutional. Have a sit. Could be a while."

The available chairs boasted more stuffing than upholstery, and were a filthy shade of Big-Bird yellow. Refusing to sit, Dickhead tapped his shoe against the hardwood floor and checked his watch continuously.

Sally snatched a pack of Marlboro Reds from her desktop

and strutted toward the door. "Excuse me, boys. Think I'll step out for a puff. Mind grabbing the phone if it rings?"

The door swung shut behind her, and Dickhead began to pace. "Absurd. Freaking absurd," he muttered.

Moments later, the door to the men's room opened and Percy strolled out with a newspaper folded under his arm. His eyes lit up when they fell on Boudreaux.

"Jake, you ol' pole cat, how the hell are you?" Percy pumped Boudreaux's arm like a jack handle. "Where the Sam Hill is Sally? Come on in, folks. Take a load off."

He led us into his office, plopped into his worn leather chair, then leaned back and propped his feet on top of his desk. He steepled his fingers beneath his chin and waited until all eyes were on him.

"My preliminary investigation's just about complete. The dental records y'all sent over for Sherrod Wiley are a match. Tox screens won't be back for a few weeks, and the tissue samples were a crapshoot, given the extensive thermal damage. But based on the post-mortem CT, so far, I'd say the COD is a single gunshot wound to the heart. The body was burned after the fact."

"Well done, Doc," Dickhead said, springing to his feet. "Now that we have your confirmation on the ID of the corpse, we have a secondary issue to discuss."

He paused expectantly, like he was waiting for Slidell to respond. When he didn't, Dickhead hovered over the desk like a thunderhead ready to explode.

"Let's cut the *good ol'boy* crap, Doc. We need to raise Wiley to secure testimony not otherwise obtainable. That's the whole reason we're here this morning. You knew that when you scheduled this meeting."

Slidell laced his hands behind his head and chuckled. "'Testimony not otherwise available.' If that ain't a load of dung. Director, I have an MD, a PhD, and whole lot of baby Ds behind my name. Don't think you can waltz in here with your mumbo-jumbo legalese and bulldoze me."

A vein in the side of Dickhead's neck began to throb. "Bulldoze is such a strong word. I'm just saying that we're going to raise that corpse. Right here. Right now. With or without your approval."

"Sorry, G-Man. My morgue—my rules."

"It's a matter of national security. I've got the Patriot Act in my pocket. What do you have, hayseed?"

"Hayseed? Who you calling a hayseed? I'll litigate this 'til the cows come home. Won't be nothing left to raise by the time this goes to court, you arrogant blowhard!"

"Gentlemen!" Boudreaux jumped to his feet. "We're all on the same side here. No need for hostility." He turned to Slidell and sighed. "Percy, you got no dog in this fight. If they want to raise the corpse, why not let 'em raise the damn thing?"

"The hell you say!" Slidell huffed and puffed as he pulled his lard-ass from the chair. "No dog in this fight? The *dog* is my morgue. You know how much damage this Barbie-doll Hoodoo Queen did in Cincinnati? What she did to their morgue? Ask Doc Blanchard."

"Excuse me?" I said, vaulting to my feet. "Barbie-doll Hoo—"

Ferris shushed me and jerked me into my chair.

"Who's gonna pay that bill, Jake?" Slidell asked. "I'll tell you who. Not me. And not the good people of New Orleans." Then that good ol' boy, with a whole lot of baby Ds behind his name, finally put his cards on the table. "If Mr. Patriot Act here wants to raise that damn body, then by God, he can cover any damages this little Hoodoo Mama causes."

Hoodoo Mama? My, my. This Colonel Sanders wannabe certainly had a death wish.

The room fell silent, and all eyes darted to me. But I didn't know why. *What the hell had I done...today?*

The pulsing vein on the side of Dickhead's neck looked ready to blow. He stared at me with narrow, unblinking eyes. Sweat trickled down my hairline as I visualized my career fading into the sunset.

"Fine," Dickhead finally said. "You want indemnification from losses secondary to Nighthawk raising Wiley in your morgue, you've got it. I'll assume that's a reciprocal agreement."

"Oh, absolutely." Slidell called Sally on the intercom and asked her to join us. "Of course," he said with a smirk, "You won't mind signing off on our little agreement."

"No. Why would I?" Dickhead eyed me, a crazy-train smile sprawled across his face.

Little Allie shivered.

Sally typed up the indemnification agreement and handed it to Slidell and Dickhead for their signatures. As they scribbled their names on the dotted line, I wondered what kind of reciprocal damage Director Horton envisioned heading my way.

No need to borrow trouble, the brain bitch sniped. *It always finds you anyway.*

"We'll only get one pass at this," I said. "So, listen up. Doc, make sure all your corpses are in drawers or cold storage. Sally, get as many plastic drop cloths as you can find—and some potato chips."

"What kind of chips, hon?"

"Who cares? They're for Wiley."

"The *dead* guy?"

"It's either chips or your little red fingertips. You choose."

Sally huffed at me then sprinted off to gather the supplies. Ferris, Boudreaux, Dickhead and I followed Slidell down the hall. Once Slidell slid his keycard through the reader, the door to the morgue's administration office popped open. We funneled down the hallway, past a file room and the pathology lab. A barrage of bangs, clangs, and thumps clattered up ahead.

"What the hell is that?" Slidell whispered.

Ah, shit.

"That's the sound of FUBAR," I mumbled, peeking through the window in the morgue door. Our carbonized corpse, Sherrod Wiley, was tearing the place apart. Blackened chunks of flesh and tissue fell from his bones as he railed from one end of the operating theatre to the other, leaving a minefield of zushi in his wake. Bone saws, rib spreaders and scalpels sailed randomly across the room. Wiley stared back at us through the window, growling and licking his lips as though he could see us.

"Jesus, Mary and Joseph," Slidell whispered, craning his neck to gawk at the carnage. "How the hell...? I thought *you* had to raise him. How much more raised does he get?"

"Oh, he's plenty raised," I said, clueless as to how that had happened.

An instrument tray crashed into the window, causing us to duck in unison.

Slidell stuck his finger in my face. "Ask your damn questions, lady. That flambéed flesh-eater's making mincemeat out of my morgue."

Wiley flung a loaded gurney against the wall, catapulting its cadaver into the air. The cadaver crashed into a second gurney, and then a third, toppling them like a human bowling ball, and sprawling them across the floor. He grabbed one of the cadaver's arms and began gnawing the flesh from its bones.

Dickhead frowned. "That's not normal. Is it?"

"Not even close," I replied.

Wiley wasn't behaving like the usual freshie, craving junk food as a precursor to flesh. How long ago had he been turned?

And why had he appeared to be dead when we opened the trunk?

Wiley sprouted a gaping hole in the decomposed tissue of his torso. His intestines spilled to the floor and slithered across the tile like giant gray worms.

How the hell was this happening?

There were only so many variables in the equation.

I yanked Slidell away from the window and grabbed his face. "When you examined Wiley, did you find evidence of a bite wound, or an injection site?"

Slidell shrugged, darting his eyes back to the window. "His dermis and hypodermis were severely compromised."

"In English, Doc."

"Look at the crunchy bastard!" he sniped. "Who could tell?"

However it had happened, Wiley had been infected and from this moment on, the situation would only get worse.

I sucked in a breath, faced Ferris and said three words that, if I were lucky, I might live to regret.

"I'm going in."

28

THAT CRAZY HOODOO MAMBO

Sally bellowed from further up the hallway. "Percy? I've got the Pringles, baby."

"Bring 'em on down," he yelled. "That crazy Hoodoo Mambo's going in."

Sally rounded the hallway and stopped short at the sight of us huddled by the morgue room door. "Couldn't find any of those drop-cloth thingies, so I grabbed these instead," she said, holding out a box of trash bags.

"No worries." Boudreaux deadpanned. "The contamination ship has officially sailed."

"Okey-dokey, Jake. I'll just toss you the bags. Ain't coming any closer. Bye-bye now," she said, her voice already fading.

Ferris trotted up the hall, retrieved the supplies and carried them back to the morgue door.

Slidell handed me his keycard and patted my arm. "Best of luck, honey. You gonna need it."

"Ready?" Ferris asked.

"Always."

He grinned and handed me a trash bag. "You never know."

His baby blues bored into mine, confessing feelings that his lips didn't dare.

"You never know," I said, with a wink, tucking the bag in my pocket.

His eyes lingered on mine, as he unholstered his Glock. "I've got your six, Allie girl."

"Wouldn't have it any other way," I said, racking Hawk's slide. "Let's do this."

The keycard slid smoothly through the reader and the door buzzed open. We pushed inside, slow and easy, single file with me in the lead.

A loud *crunch* echoed as I stepped on a piece of debris. Wiley's head shot up and swiveled toward me like a charbroiled meerkat, the meat from the cadaver's arm still stuck in his teeth. Then Wiley did something he hadn't done before. He twitched.

Have I mentioned that I hate freaking twitchers?

I raised Hawk and put Wiley in my crosshairs. It would have been so easy to squeeze the trigger. But we needed information.

"Who kidnapped you, Mr. Wiley?" He snarled and sank his teeth back into the cadaver's bicep, gnawing on it like a drumstick. "Who did this and why?"

"Le-serk," he mumbled, tearing off another strip of meat.

"Le Clerc? Toussaint Le Clerc?"

Wiley dropped the half-eaten arm and swiveled toward me, nodding. His blank eyes locked with mine. Then he twitched a second time. The charred, bacon-like strips that used to be his lips curved into a hideous smile.

He smells you, Little Allie whispered.

"Where did Le Clerc hold you?" I asked, taking a half-step back.

Wiley didn't respond—probably because he'd stopped listening. The scent of fresh meat beats the stink of a rotting carcass any day. A long, low growl hummed in his throat. He bared his teeth then slid his fire-ravaged foot forward, reaching for me with blackened arms. Flecks of a blue checkered shirt that had melted into his skin caught my eye.

I swiped the sweat from my brow and cocked Hawk's hammer. "Why you? What did Le Clerc want?"

Wiley lunged. I side-stepped and spun, keeping him in Hawk's sights. Wiley's grisly smile returned. He seemed to enjoy the hunt.

Freaking twitcher.

"Answer me!" I shouted. "What did Le Clerc want?"

"Gov-ner's shed-ual. Fun-raser," he said, pouncing on me hard and fast.

I jumped backward and fell over the rest of the corpse he'd been noshing. My right hand slammed into the stainless-steel sink, sending Hawk airborne. I scrambled to my feet and rolled left, barely out of reach of Wiley's snapping jaws.

"Get clear," Ferris yelled, leveling his Glock at Wiley's head.

I waved him off. "Don't shoot! Don't shoot! We need more answers."

My eyes snapped back to Wiley as I slid my Ka-Bar from its sheath. "Focus, Mr. Wiley. Did you give Le Clerc information about the Governor's fundraiser?"

Most of Wiley's blackened skin and tissue had sloughed to the floor, leaving his body glistening, open and raw. The grisly mass of carbonized waste stared at me and slowly shook its head. "No," he croaked. "Wouldn't. Couldn't. Injected me... made me...tell."

Wiley roared and circled me from the right, stumbled and caught himself. I matched his pace and moved with him, maintaining the distance between us.

Hang in there, Mr. Wiley. Just a couple more questions, I thought. *Then I'll make this all go away.*

Wiley chittered his teeth and fixed me in his flat black stare.

I glanced at Ferris, waving my knife, and said, "If you have to shoot, stay clear of his head."

Wiley hurled himself at me. I dove to my left, but not soon enough. He clamped my leather boot between his teeth and crunched.

I swiped my knife at the gristle of his arm.

"I've got this!" I yelled to Ferris.

Wiley instinctively let go as the knife connected. I snapped my leg back and kicked, but he dragged himself forward and snagged my boot in his hand. I pulled up my other leg and drove the heel of my boot into his face, knocking him backwards.

He landed on his butt, up against the wall by the door.

"Where did Le Clerc hold you, Mr. Wiley? Was there anyone else there with you?" I asked, trying to catch my breath.

His face was caved in from the nose up, but his jaws still snapped, and his freaking teeth still clicked like a dead car battery. He'd lost more appendages than he had left, and his exposed organs were seeing the light of day for their first and only time.

"House," he murmured. "Big house. St. Ber-nard. No one... else." Wiley's breaths came in gasps. "Bas-tard. Le-serk. Kill. Kill him."

I had all the information I was going to get. It was time to put Wiley down—not just because it was the right thing to do, but because what had happened to him was an atrocity. Wiley never asked for this. When he refused to betray the Governor, Toussaint killed him and injected him with the Z-virus... because zombies can't lie. Toussaint got the information he wanted after all. Then, to get rid of the evidence, he'd set Wiley on fire. The problem was that Sherrod Wiley's brain hadn't been destroyed by the flames, and now all that remained of the governor's point man was this incinerated, skeletonized monster.

Wiley snarled and tried to climb to his feet, but there wasn't enough cartilage left to hold his bones together. His body folded into itself like a house of cards, splintering, and shattering his femurs and hips. But his jaws...those tireless jaws... continued to snap. Toussaint's conscripted, low-rent weapon of mass destruction that simply couldn't die, still wanted to eat me alive.

Screw that.

"He's mine, Ferris."

I crawled across the floor and recovered my 9mm from beneath a pile of debris. Bringing Hawk to bear, I aimed the muzzle between Wiley's eyes, and said, "I'm sorry Le Clerc did this to you. You're right. He is a bastard."

With a gentle tug of my trigger, Wiley's troubles faded into black. Ours, on the other hand, had grown exponentially. Jade Chen had been kidnapped, Rico and Fairchild were missing in action, we had no antidote for the Z-virus, and now Governor Thornton was in danger. Something needed to give.

I dropped cross-legged to the floor, head in my hands, trying to ignore Little Allie who wondered if I'd ever be strong enough to take down Toussaint. Boudreaux, Dickhead and Slidell shuffled in through morgue door and quietly surveyed the scene. They muttered among themselves, but had the good sense to let me be. Even the pissed-off Dr. Slidell.

Ferris stooped and briefly squeezed my shoulder. After strolling away, he spoke to the others in snippets and hushed tones. When the conversation ended, Boudreaux, Dickhead and Slidell left.

Ferris turned to me with eyes that were warm and filled with something I'd rarely seen in them before. Compassion.

"When you're ready, Boudreaux wants to debrief us back at the office."

He gave me his hand and I climbed to my feet, scanning the

room from top to bottom, side to side. Slidell's morgue had been reduced to a biohazardous heap of detritus.

"Here you go," I said, forcing a grin and pulling the trash bag from my pocket. "I don't do windows."

"Why don't you keep it," he said, eyeing the layer of zushi that slathered me like a second skin. "You can wear it in the car."

29

GLINTS OF GOLD AND STINKY YELLOW DUST

Afetr a quick stop at the hotel so I could shower and change, Ferris drove us back to the office for our meeting with Boudreaux.

"What exactly do we need to be debriefed about?" I whispered, as we marched past the junior agents' cubicles. "Wiley trashed the morgue. I put him down and everybody there saw it. End of story."

Ferris hushed me as we entered Boudreaux's office and joined Dickhead, Babs and Mouton at the conference table.

"Where's Vinny?" I asked.

"Not to worry," Babs said, "Young Master Abruzzi is reviewing some redacted case files used for training purposes. He seems to be drawn toward investigation."

"Huh. How'd he do at the shooting range?" Ferris asked.

Babs sighed and pushed her glasses up her nose. "He's quite the marksman."

"Better than you?" Ferris quipped.

"We weren't keeping score."

Boudreaux whisked into his office, closed the door, and

joined us. "Sorry to keep you waiting. We need to discuss the raising at the morgue this morning."

"Actually," I said, picking at the arm of my chair. "It wasn't a raising. At least, not by me."

Dickhead rolled his eyes. "Duly noted. Let's start with your Q and A session with Wiley."

"It wasn't rocket science," I said. "Toussaint kidnapped Wiley to access Governor Thornton's schedule. When Wiley refused to cooperate, Toussaint killed him and then raised him."

"To get the info he wanted," Dickhead interjected. "Because zombies can't lie. Brilliant."

"After Toussaint got what he wanted, he tried to destroy Wiley by setting him on fire."

Boudreaux frowned. "That's where I get lost. You've used fire to put zombies down. Why didn't it work this time?"

"Hell, I don't know." I rubbed my face with my hands. "What do we know for sure? The only way to put down a biter is to destroy its brain. Obviously, the fire didn't get the job done. Maybe Wiley's skull protected his brain. Maybe the fire didn't burn hot enough."

Dickhead shook his head. "That doesn't explain why Wiley appeared to be dead in the trunk and then popped up a day later like some...Roborotter."

"I know. I know." Little Allie had been nagging me with the same question. "Wiley's brain wasn't destroyed by the fire, but maybe it was damaged. Like his wires got crossed, or his synapses misfired. Look, I'm not a scientist, but something caused him to appear to be dead and then rise later."

"Wait," Babs said, typing furiously on her laptop. "As I recall, there is some historic, pseudo-scientific evidence to support the notion of a delayed rising among the undead." She scrolled a bit, scanning the pages and then beamed. "Yes, here it is. Consider the case of Clairvius Narcisse, a Haitian who claimed, in 1962, to have been administered a toxic concoction and subsequently lapsed into a coma-like state that mimicked death. Believed to be dead, Narcisse was buried and, as legend has it, later resurrected by a Bokor who enslaved him for a number of years."

Boudreaux wrinkled his brow. "But Narcisse never actually died. He just appeared to be dead. Fifty some odd years later, Wiley died, was raised, then appeared to die and rise again.

"True," Babs said. "But in one very important regard, their cases are quite similar. Both victims experienced a time lag between infection and raising. We must ask what would account for that similarity."

"You might be on to something." I got to my feet and began to pace. "According to our conversation with Dr. Christian, Toussaint's manipulated versions of the Z-virus contain puffer fish and toad toxins—the same toxins used to create Zombie Powder."

"Yes, of course," Babs muttered. "The same toxins purportedly used on Narcisse. Or what if Wiley's rising in the morgue was nothing more than a neurological backfire—simply his damaged brain recalling Toussaint's command?"

Ferris nodded. "The right combination of those toxins, neurological deficits secondary to fire damage, or a combination of both may well be responsible for the delayed rising."

Dickhead held up his hands. "Whatever the forensics may show, we have more pressing matters to deal with. Governor Thornton is in danger and he needs to be so notified."

"On it." Boudreaux pointed to Mouton. "Find out who's taken Wiley's place on the governor's staff. I want a copy of upcoming fundraisers and public appearances scheduled over the next two months." Mouton nodded and rose to leave, but Boudreaux motioned him back to his chair, saying, "Stay put, son. I'm not finished with you yet."

"Sir," I said, without a care as to where he wanted to take

the meeting. "What about Jade Chen? And Detective De Palma and Agent Fairchild. People on this case keep disappearing." I didn't have to say *I told you so*. My eyes said it for me.

Boudreaux didn't appear to notice.

"Thanks for the segue, Nighthawk. As I recall, Mr. Wiley said he was held at a big house somewhere in St. Bernard Parish. That ring a bell with any of you?"

"Absolutely," I said. "According to our source, Le Clerc bought a manse in St. Bernard Parish around a year ago."

Mouton pulled up the records on his laptop. "Just to confirm our findings, sir. We searched over a three-year time frame and found four manses changed hands, purchased under the names of Boucher, Durrand, Segal and The New Orleans Salvage and Restoration Group."

Boudreaux glanced around the room. "Names still don't mean anything to anyone?"

A table-full of blank stares gave him his answer.

"Can't help but think a secluded manse might be a decent place for Toussaint to keep his victims. That's where he kept Wiley. Mouton, pull up those addresses and Google Map each of those locations. On my desk in fifteen."

"Yes, sir." Mouton stood and hovered over the table like he was waiting to be dismissed.

Boudreaux looked up and sighed. "Now, son."

Mouton scattered and a momentary lull hit the room.

What the hell, the brain bitch muttered, throwing caution to the wind.

"About the raising this morning, Director Horton." I felt my face flush. "I just want to confirm, on the record, that we're all on the same page."

Horton smirked. "All of us except Percy Slidell, I suspect. Go on."

"I didn't raise Wiley. Most of that damage was done before I entered the room."

"Believe me, Nighthawk. That fact isn't lost on me."

"Good to know, sir." Silly me. What was I worried about? My innocence was his best defense against the mega-losses at the morgue.

We still had a few minutes until Mouton would return, so everyone scrambled. I called Nonnie, and instantly regretted it.

"What do you mean there are *two* eggs now?" Freaking Kulu. That was all I needed. A hormonal parrot plopping a pair of eggs in my box of maxi-pads.

Yack, yack, yack. Oh Miss Allie. Yammer, yammer, yammer. Duck's ass. *Oy.*

"Tell her not to poop any more eggs. Leave the nest alone until I get home. I don't know when. No. They won't hatch, they're unfertilized. You're seventy years old. How can you not know that?"

Thank God Mouton walked back in the room.

"Gotta run now. Bye, bye."

Mouton's face was uncharacteristically grim as he marched in with his laptop and a plastic-wrapped envelope tucked beneath his arm. Everyone settled into their pre-break places around the conference table, expecting him to pull up the address information Boudreaux had requested.

"This came in for you yesterday, Nighthawk," he said, holding the delivery in front of him, oddly, reverently, as if it were an ancient relic. "Whatever it is, it stinks. We ran it through the scanner...you know, for security."

His eyes darted around the room, looking everywhere but at me. "It failed the scan, so they opened it, hand-searched the contents, and then wrapped the envelope in plastic. I'm...I'm sorry."

He slid the envelope across the table.

I didn't—couldn't—touch it.

"What's in there, Philip?" I asked.

Bile rose in my throat as I stared through the plastic, at the white cardboard packet with its colorful logo, dreading its contents.

"What is it?" I whispered again.

My only response was the solemn look in Mouton's eyes.

You can do this, Little Allie crooned. *You need to do this.*

I watched in fascination as my hands appeared to move on their own, fueled by a strength I hadn't realized I possessed. They slowly picked up the packet, tore it open, and dumped its contents for everyone to see.

Dickhead reached across the table. "What the hell—"

"Don't touch that!" I snapped, sweeping it out of his reach. Dozens of long, thin stems with fringy yellow blossoms wound tightly around something at the center, obscuring it from view.

Little Allie gasped. *Asafoetida.*

She couldn't be right. But of course, she was.

I tore at the layers of stems with my fingers, working toward the middle. Glints of gold peeked out from the object beneath; a fine yellow powder dusted my hands and the table.

Ferris curled his nose. "*Jesus.* That stuff stinks."

I unsheathed my knife and began hacking through the stems.

"It's Devil's Dung," I said, never taking my eyes from the blooms. "A magickal herb. Used, in this case, to wage a curse. It's also Toussaint's calling card."

More golden glints popped through the endless layers of stems, followed by bits of black. A design began to take shape: the number 4581.

Through a haze of pooled tears, I brushed the remaining yellow blooms off of Rico's badge.

30

NEVER EVER ASK THAT QUESTION

"The bastard's screwing with us." Boudreaux said, swiping the herbs into the garbage can. He called maintenance to remove it, and then glanced around the table, connecting with the others before settling his eyes on me. "Don't let him into your head. Nothing's changed. We suspected Le Clerc was involved in the disappearances and now we know for sure. We stick with the game plan we have. Mouton, pull up those addresses and satellite pics."

Mouton fired up his laptop and keyed in the data while the rest of the team waited with bated breath. Me? I slipped down a deep, dark rabbit hole.

Three people missing (abducted by my nemesis Toussaint Le Clerc), another three dead, the governor in danger, and the Z-virus mutating with no antidote in sight. Not to mention a spate of black magick aimed at me, and now, at someone I loved.

The brain bitch cringed at me using the "L" word when it came to Rico.

Screw her.

I was too tired and too scared to argue. All those troubles

were a lot to bear. Maybe the brain bitch had been right. Maybe I wasn't equal to the task—especially when my partner wasn't there to lean on. The guy who saw through all my bullshit, who knew when to leave me be, or to kick my ass. The guy who pulled out the best in me in the worst of times. Times like now. So much at stake. How could I...how could anyone...

"Nighthawk."

I popped back out of my rabbit hole and discovered Boudreaux waving at me from across the table. "We boring you?"

"No, sir." I blinked and sat tall, swiping at my cheek to annihilate a tear that had dared to escape.

Stupid whiny-baby, wimpy-sue waterworks. Doubting myself had been unsettling, but crying, downright embarrassing. Finding every eye in the room riveted on me, was...what's the word? Oh, yeah. Mortifying.

Mouton shot me an awkward nod, then cleared his throat and began his presentation. "I'll email this to you for later reference, but as you may recall, there were four properties we zeroed in on, based on their St. Bernard locations and sale dates."

He popped their Google Earth pics onto the projection screen.

"The first manse, purchased under the name Boucher, doesn't fit the bill. The area's residential—offering a complete lack of privacy. Notice the bicycles and toys in the yard. Not to mention the owner, Theodore Boucher, is a parish council member.

"Our second location, in the Arabi area of St. Bernard, was purchased by Ned Durand, a retired historian who also serves as a professor emeritus at Tulane. Way too high profile and a little long in the tooth to be our man.

"The third house, in Violet, purchased by one Mr. Wesley Segal, smells more like what we're looking for. It's a handy-man's special in a secluded area, camouflaged by trees and vegetation. The sale went through last year, but the satellite pics aren't showing any signs of rehab work. It's in rough shape, still arguably viable. Let's put a pin in this one.

"The fourth place, in Chalmette, burned in 2015, and sold at auction to The New Orleans Salvage and Restoration Group. It sits back off the main road, surrounded by woodlands. It's secluded and wouldn't draw uninvited company. The satellite pics don't capture much because of the tree canopy, but the house looks to be under roof, more or less."

Mouton shifted his gaze back to the team. "Properties three and four appear to provide the best options for clandestine activity, sir."

"That's all well and good," Dickhead said. "But what about the governor's schedule? "That's our primary focus."

Two keystrokes later, Mouton popped a dossier onto the screen. "Meet Wiley's replacement: Evan D'Arbanville. Per Mr. D'Arbanville, the governor's biggest fundraiser takes place tonight at eight. Black-tie, invitation only."

"Where?" Boudreaux asked.

"The Guillory mansion in The Garden District."

Dickhead narrowed his eyes. "I assume you advised the governor's security team to cancel the event."

"Yes, sir. They thanked us for the heads up, and said they'd take it under consideration."

"Of course, they did," Dickhead muttered, straightening his tie and taking to his feet. "I'll call the governor personally to express our concerns. Since the threat is related to Le Clerc, it falls under the jurisdiction of the task force any way. Worst case scenario, if this event goes forward, Agent Boudreaux, as Senior Agent in this locale, I'd like you to coordinate the local HRT team."

Dickhead turned, singling out Ferris and me. "You two as

well. Once we've secured the fundraiser, you can get back to filming your episode of "Zombie House Flipping."

"You don't need us," I said. "You've got all the local FBI talent you need for backup."

"Oh, we'll have plenty of backup, but you'll be there too. No one knows Le Clerc like you." Dickhead checked his watch and frowned. "We don't have much time. Unless you hear from me to the contrary, meet at the Guillory mansion at six-thirty and run a sweep. Low profile. We don't want to alarm the guests. You heard the man. Black tie only." He gave me the once-over and sighed. "Nighthawk, you wear a...you know, a...dress. You do *own* a dress?"

"Sure. I keep one in my go-bag next to my tiara."

What an ass-monkey. Someday, somewhere Dickhead would pay for that. *But it won't be today*, I thought. *Because today, I need to buy a dress.*

Boudreaux directed Ferris and me to Magazine Street for our impromptu evening wear. We had approximately three hours to find some fancy duds and sandblast ourselves clean. Ferris ducked into Luca Falcone's to rent his tux and told me he'd meet me at The Red Carpet, a ladies' shop not far up the street.

Based on the number of dodgy stares I got from the sales clerks, I took it that most of their customers didn't shop in zombie-stomping boots and torn T-shirts that read *Please Don't Feed the Flesh-Eaters.*

I tried on at least ten dresses and couldn't find a thing that fit my...style. Whatever that was. After slipping on the last dress, I walked out into the styling area and found Ferris slouched in a chair, waiting for me.

"What is *that*?" he asked, staring at my gown, a tasteful little number—rows of flounced, burgundy taffeta, with a black sequined bow across the chest. His crinkled eyes filled with amusement. "You're a girl. How can you suck so bad at this?"

"What's wrong with it?" I asked, spinning in front of the mirror, swishing the skirt back and forth.

"Little Bo Peep called. She wants her dress back. Think... hot chick...like the red dress you wear to salsa class."

"Nonnie picked that dress out. It's the only dress I own."

"I should have known." He inspected the tag in the neckline and snorted. "This is a size six."

"And?"

"We're going to be here all night. Excuse me," Ferris said to a sales clerk, who was taking it all in from a safe distance. "Could you bring the lady something in black, that accentuates her... assets...and shows a little leg? Size two, please. Thank you."

"Size two! I have to breathe, you know."

"Trust me," he said, with a lazy smile.

Moments later, the clerk returned with a gown that fit all of Ferris's requirements. It was stunning, and would have looked amazing—on somebody else.

I felt my face flush. "I can't wear that. That's for somebody sophisticated. Somebody...elegant."

"Try it," he whispered. "I think I'm...you're...going to like it."

I ducked back into the fitting room and slipped it over my head, feeling a rush as the silk brushed against my skin. The person in the mirror staring back at me looked taller than me—more collected. Ferris was right. It fit like a glove and hugged me in all the right places. "What do you think?" I asked, stepping out of the dressing room.

Ferris sucked in a breath. "It's...amazing."

The halter top and thigh-high slit left little to the imagination. "Where would I put Hawk? Or even Baby?"

"In your purse."

"What purse?"

"We'll take it," Ferris said to the sales clerk. "And a silver clutch. And a pair of silver stiletto heels," he said, wincing at my zombie stompers, peeking out from beneath the dress.

"Size 10," I muttered.

Ferris stifled a snicker.

"Holy crap. Who's paying for all this?" I whispered. "I'm fighting Headbutt for dog biscuits as is."

"I've got it," Ferris said, brushing the top of my head with his lips.

"Oh, I can't. It's too much. How about we go halves?" I peeked at the tag and almost hyperventilated. "Maybe twenty-five percent?"

He shrugged and handed the clerk his charge card. "It's work-related. I'll expense it."

"But what if they don't cover it?" I asked.

He stared at the gorgeous black gown and grinned. "Then next month, for some reason, I'll run through a massive amount of ammo."

For better or worse, working with me seemed to be rubbing off on Ferris.

Babs got off easy that night, pulling Vinny duty again. And for once, she didn't grouse about it. That obsessive-compulsive stork knew when to keep her mouth shut. A night of standing in heels, chatting up fat cats and choosing the right fork? Give me biters any day. Besides, Babs and Vinny seemed to be getting along better, since Vinny discovered his new-found interest in investigative work.

He'd been devastated when, for security reasons, Babs put the kibosh on them going out to Mama Femi's for dinner, but she earned some mega-brownie points suggesting they order in from Mama's and have Luna deliver it.

After showering and borrowing some of Bab's ablutions and makeup, I slipped into my new dress and swirled my hair on top of my head. Pretty girls made that look so easy. My swirl looked like roadkill.

Babs strolled up behind me and stared into the bathroom mirror, tsk-tsking. "Here, let me," she said, sweeping my hair into her uninvited hands. "Think more Angelina Jolie and less...Daniel Boone."

After a few failed attempts, Babs twisted, turned, and pinned my hair into a respectable updo, then slipped a transmitter into my ear canal, covering it with a wispy curl.

Someone knocked on the door, and I jumped, nearly turning my ankle in those brand-new silver stilettos.

Babs bit back a laugh and moved for the door. "You look lovely. Happy hunting tonight." Glancing out the peephole, she announced, "Your escort has arrived."

Babs opened the door and Ferris's eyes shot to me. He wore his perfect, toothpaste commercial smile and a black tux that fit like a glove. Little Allie damn near swooned. Well, maybe that was me.

He silently held out his arm. I picked up my clutch with Baby, an extra clip, and my knife packed inside, and sashayed to the door without stumbling once. Babs nodded her approval, but the night was young. The smart money called for at least one face plant in those shiny shoes of death.

"I want her back by eleven," Babs said, tapping her watch. "And not a minute later, mister."

Ferris winked. "I'll do my best. You know how inconsiderate criminals can be."

"I'm old enough to come home when I want," I said. My foot slipped out from under me, and I grabbed the doorjamb for support. "Don't wait up."

Private security was already buzzing when we pulled up to the Guillory mansion. Ferris flipped his badge and after a brief once-over, a band of silent, sneering big boys ushered us through the gates. I caught sight of Dickhead further up the driveway, sporting his usual constipated face, identified by its flapping mouth and purple skin tone. I couldn't help but grin. For once, his tirade wasn't aimed at me. When I recognized the target, my grin grew into a smile.

Governor Andrew Thornton, a bear of a man, stood impassively, arms crossed, chin held high. Another man I'd never seen before, wearing a condescending smirk, hovered at the governor's elbow.

Judging by the volume of Horton's voice, the stranger's smirk had struck a nerve. "Let me assure you, Governor, the threat is considered credible and high. Call this event off, now, before it's too late."

"Horton...is it?" The governor sucked in his chest and sneered down his nose. "I didn't get to be governor by running away. I flew sorties in the Gulf War and retired from the military with the Bronze Star and Distinguished Service Awards. I can take care of myself, and just to make sure, I've got my own hand-picked security team watching my six."

Horton's eyes narrowed. "With all due respect, sir, you need—"

"What I need, Director, is money. Proud as I am of those military medals, they don't finance my campaign. It takes a lot of $10,000-a-plate donors to fill those coffers."

"Director Horton, if I may," said the stranger at the governor's elbow. "My name is Alpha Guillory, the host of this evening's event. We have over a hundred confirmed guests who, as Governor Thornton so eloquently pointed out, are bringing their checkbooks. It's far too late to cancel."

The vein on Horton's neck throbbed. "Just how many lives are you willing to gamble?"

Guillory swept his hand around his estate. "I'm an oil magnate, Horton. This dinner cost more than you make in a month. The governor's security is here, and so is mine. There isn't a terrorist motherfucker alive who stands a chance of getting to the governor tonight."

"What about *dead* ones?" I asked. "We're talking about biters here, not Ali Atwa. What do your men know about fighting the undead?"

Thornton eyed me like a bug. "Who the hell are you?"

"Allie Nighthawk, and this is my partner, FBI Agent Sean Ferris. Governor, you and I share a past with Toussaint Le Clerc, the man who's gunning for you."

"Le Clerc?" Thornton paused and then shrugged. "Afraid I don't recall the name."

"Think back to your days as a prosecutor, sir. Le Clerc's wife Sabine was infected with the Z-virus. When he refused to put her down, I did it for him. He wanted me charged with murder, and you refused to prosecute. He blames us both. Me, for killing Sabine, and you, for not punishing me."

"Ah, revenge, the hazard of being a prosecutor. I remember. But why now, after all this time?"

"I left New Orleans not long after your decision. Le Clerc has taken...great pains...to draw me back. Now he has us together—where he wants us."

Ferris nodded. "Le Clerc has killed before, sir. Director Horton is right. As important as this night is, for your safety and the safety of all concerned, you should cancel the event."

"Duly noted," Thornton said. "But the event is still on. I'm not one to cut and run. And I never kowtow to the whims of psychotic thugs. I'm confident that our existing security team can handle Le Clerc." He nodded to Horton. "I appreciate your concern. Ms. Nighthawk and Agent Ferris can stay as my guests and keep their eyes open for trouble. Discreetly. I don't want my guests alarmed. Good day, gentlemen, Ms. Nighthawk. If you'll excuse us, Mr. Guillory and I have a fundraiser to throw."

Governor Thornton marched back to the mansion with Alpha Guillory nipping at his heels, discussing the dynamics of the seating arrangements.

Dickhead stared after them, hands on his hips, looking like he was ready to chew the bark off a tree. "You heard the Governor," he snapped. "You'll attend the party as his guests, keeping a low profile. God help us if we spook his well-heeled patrons."

Dickhead leaned forward and pulled his lips back in a snarl. "You will also function as my internal eyes and ears. I will supervise from a remote location and coordinate with Agent Boudreaux to have the HRT folks in position and ready to respond should the need arise."

"Gotcha," I said. "Oh, and can we have a cool code word if we have to call for help? Like Zushi, maybe?"

"Knock yourself out," Dickhead mumbled, handing Ferris a lapel mic. Our fearless director stomped back to his car, leaving us alone in the middle of the driveway.

"We've got a lot of moving pieces here. What could possibly go wrong?" Ferris asked, running his hand through his hair.

"Never, *ever* ask that question," I said, drilling his bicep with my fist. "It's the surest way of finding out."

31

PRELUDE TO A CLUSTERFUCK IN D MINOR

With the governor's real guests due to arrive inside the hour, Ferris and I decided to poke around a little, running our own last-minute security check. As we strolled through the mansion, arm in arm, nodding at the strategically placed security monkeys, their eyes pegged us for the unwelcome and over-dressed interlopers we were.

The view from the arched palladium windows in the foyer found the guard at the gated entrance checking the arriving food trucks and vendors against his clipboard, and waving them through, with barely a glance inside them.

"That's a problem," Ferris muttered, as we swept deeper into the interior of the mansion.

The ballroom doors were propped wide open. The hardwood floor had been set up for the orchestra earlier. Musicians, dressed in their symphony black attire, scurried here and there, tuning their instruments, checking their plugs, and reviewing their sheet music.

How hard would it be to infiltrate the perimeter wearing a black suit and a hokey musician's union ID card?

A set of heavy wooden doors opened off one side of the

ballroom to a multi-level library, filled with thousands of books, and leather furniture covered with throws and nail-head trim, a crystal chandelier, and an antique Rookwood fireplace. Multiple sets of beveled glass doors on the other side of the ballroom opened to a veranda.

A passage, with security guards positioned at each end, connected the ballroom and the dining hall, where ten massive mahogany round tables were set with linens, fine china, silver and crystal.

We wandered to the back of the dining hall, toward a set of swinging wooden doors, and watched as servants bustled in and out, giving us a glimpse of the room that lay beyond.

"That's the biggest kitchen I've ever seen," I whispered.

Ferris pushed through the swinging doors and we slipped into the kitchen, unnoticed. The chef barked orders at the prep cooks, while the busy wait staff zipped past us, back and forth through the café doors, completing last minute preparations. In the far right corner, near the pantry, I spotted the partial logo of a delivery truck peeking through a swag-covered window in the kitchen door.

Little Allie's voice warbled in my brain. *The vendors have been using the delivery entrance near the old servant's quarters.*

Before I could get a better look, a human mountain barreled out from between the prep tables and blocked me.

"May I help you?"

None of these muscle-bound security monkeys had been pleasant, but this gorilla shot laser beams from his eyes. He closed the distance between us and puffed out his chest, trying to push me back. Ferris pulled his ID and shoved it at the man's nose. "FBI, big guy. Step off."

"Hiya, Clyde," I said, shoving past the over-grown ape. "This place looks fun. How 'bout you let us in?"

"How 'bout you take a flying leap?"

Alpha Guillory pushed the swinging door open from behind. "Bruno, that's no way to treat our guests."

"Sorry, Mr. G. They got no business back here, so I told 'em to scram."

"Thank you, Bruno. I'll handle it from here." Guillory pivoted toward Ferris and me, flashing an effervescent smile. "I apologize. Bruno has been with me for over twenty years. He's as loyal as they come, but a bit unpolished. Was there something you needed?"

Ferris feigned his own poster-boy smile. "Just checking the place. Discreetly, like you asked."

"The guests should be arriving soon. Perhaps you'd care to profile them as they enter the premises. Keep your eyes open for undesirables, carrying weapons and the like."

"The problem," I said, taking Guillory's arm as he escorted us back to the foyer, "is that these undesirables don't carry weapons—other than their teeth. They'll be easy to distinguish from your guests, though. They'll be the shambling, smelly ones with their flesh falling off."

Guillory blinked and opened his mouth as if he had something to say, but simply turned and walked away.

For some reason, I get that reaction a lot.

At the top of the hour, chamber music wafted out from the ballroom, and valets took their stations at the door. Moments later, guests drifted into the mansion under the watchful eyes of private security, as well as Ferris. Guillory, already a couple of drinks in by my count, circulated through the crowd, gladhanding and slathering on his southern charm with a trowel.

With Ferris rooted like a potted plant at the entry, I did a little circulating of my own, watching the body language of rich bitches and eavesdropping on their hoity-toity twaddle—all while standing on five-inch railroad spikes and wearing a tight black slinky. My toes cried for mercy, the balls of my feet blazed, and my ankles buckled like a newborn deer's. God help me *and* the seams on my dress if I had to run.

Little Allie thought a Jack Daniel's slushie would help. So did I. But when I joined the line at the bar, Ferris caught my eye and shook his head.

Spoil sport. Surely one of the princesses in that place had to have a Percocet.

Once the guests were accounted for and cocktail hour was in full swing, Ferris left his post at the entrance and sidled up alongside me. "Boudreaux's got his team in place."

I shifted my weight from one foot to the other. "Whatever's going to happen better happen soon, or I'll be crawling into action. Next time, you wear the slutty silver shoes."

The rest of the cocktail hour featured blue-haired saber-tooths circling the room, clawing their way toward Ferris, the hottest guy in the place and one of the few under forty. He knew how to work it, too, smiling his impossible smile and oozing that rakish charm.

Like he does with you? The brain bitch asked.

If that mouthy head hag wasn't careful, she'd end up wearing a silver stiletto like a fascinator.

When dinner was announced at 8:45 p.m., I nearly cried, knowing that food and a chair were in my future. I sat beside Ferris, slipped off my shoes under the table and rubbed my blisters. Any illusions I had about filling up disappeared when a bowl of lettuce soup arrived, along with three steamed green beans, and a quartered red potato.

No way," I hissed. "You can't tell me it took all those prep cooks to come up with this."

I pushed back my chair, feigned a smile and stood, slipping my silver clutch under my arm.

"Where are you going, dear?" Ferris asked, pulling at my arm. "Everyone else is *here*."

"That's right, dear," I said, bending to his ear. "I'm going to the kitchen to check out that delivery truck. And maybe snag a crust of bread while I'm at it."

Ferris and I slipped quietly away from the tables and wandered toward the foyer. Accessing the kitchen through the swinging doors in the back of the dining hall would draw too much attention, so we strolled out the front entrance and boldly walked the outer perimeter of the mansion, like the conscientious security minions we were. Once we reached the back of the manse, we darted behind the corner of the carriage house for cover.

The truck that had been backed up to the kitchen door was still there, but its doors were now swung wide open, obscuring our view.

"What the hell's in there?" I whispered.

"You twos shoulda listened to me earlier."

Ferris and I froze.

"Turn around, nice and easy like. Don't be makin' any moves."

I pivoted to find Bruno, the human mountain with an attitude, aiming a .45 at us. He'd taken off his jacket and rolled up his shirt sleeves since I'd seen him last. The tattoo worn by Toussaint's crew, a likeness of Baron Samedi, the Voudon Lord of Death, peeked out from beneath the rolled cuff of Bruno's sleeve.

I crossed my arms and glared at Ferris. "See? I told you this wasn't the way to the bathroom."

32

CODE ZUSHI

Ferris threw a roundhouse into Bruno's chest, sprawling him across the driveway. The .45 in Bruno's hand tumbled airborne, end over end, coming to rest on the grass beside the sidewalk. Bruno scrambled toward the gun but Ferris slammed his right Italian loafer into Bruno's jaw, knocking the thug into next Tuesday. Ferris twisted a stainless-steel bracelet around Bruno's massive wrist, cuffing him to the rusted remains of a long-forgotten basketball post that bordered the driveway.

We sprinted toward the kitchen entrance and peered silently through the gap between the hinges of the opened truck doors. The last three biters shambled from the truck, through the enclosed passageway, and into the mansion.

"How many deadheads you think came out of this sucker?" Ferris whispered.

"Two hundred."

"Really?"

"How the hell should I know? Too damn many."

Ferris rolled his eyes. "I can't believe what I'm about to say." He turned his head toward his lapel mic. "Code Zushi. Repeat Code Zushi."

I unzipped my new silver clutch, pulled out Baby and felt an instant pang of regret. "No disrespect, girlfriend," I said, kissing her muzzle. "But I wish this purse held a bigger gun. I think I'm gonna need it."

Ready or not, it was time to save the day. Ferris stood shoulder to shoulder with me and started the count. "On three. One, two..." Ferris paused and did a double take. *"Nighthawk, where the hell are your shoes?"*

"Under the table. Trust me, I'll run faster without them."

"Three!"

Pandemonium exploded from the direction of the dining room. Glass breaking, people screaming, furniture smashing, and zombies keening. We tore through the back door and into the kitchen, toward the source of the chaos, following a sickly-sweet smell I knew all too well.

Dozens of freshies, flesh-eaters, and corpsicles, frenzied by the smell of fresh meat, ravaged the dining room, stumbling and crawling over each other, snapping their jaws and chattering their teeth. Panicked guests, who had flipped over their tables to use as shields, were being overrun. The private security guards scattered across the room shot into the horde, creating a deadly crossfire. Flesh and body parts flew through the air like shrapnel. The screams of dying rich people came and went quickly, and then came again. The walls ran red like in some cheesy vampire flick, and the Persian rugs that covered the hardwood floors squished wet beneath my feet.

Boudreaux's HRT teams burst into the dining room from the ballroom and opened fire.

"Remember, head shots," I screamed. "Head shots."

In between rounds, the TAC agents pulled the survivors they could reach to safety. The governor, trapped on the far side of the room, brandished a broken table leg, defending a squadron of quivering blue-hairs behind him.

Baby had ten in the mag and one in the pipe. That wouldn't

last long. My Ka-Bar was more of a Hail Mary option. Hand-to-hand combat with a shit-ton of Zs, coming at me from all directions, would be beyond risky.

Ferris and I battled across the room, taking out more than a dozen deadheads as we made our way to the governor. Two down, four down. I snatched the extra mag and knife from my clutch and slid them down my cleavage for easy access, hoping I wouldn't hear an embarrassing clink against the floor.

A corpsicle latched onto my left ankle and damn near brought me down. I did a forward lunge to keep my balance, tearing my tight new dress to shreds. The stinking rotter refused to let go; it kept bobbing and weaving from one side to the other, snapping its gnarly teeth at my calf. A shot at the wrong time could end up with me bleeding out, so I used my bare right foot to disconnect the biter's head from its shoulders, punting it into the ballroom. Holy stank on a stick! Talk about trench foot!

I clambered to my nastified feet, hyperventilating and miffed. To hell with the damned dress and that stupid silver purse. It's hard to fight a horde when you're dressed like Angelina Jolie. There's a reason I do this shit in zombie stompers. I yanked out my Ka-Bar and shoved that piece of shit silver clutch into the mouth of the closest biter.

Sometimes, even zombie hunters have to vent. Now, I was ready to war.

Thornton drilled his table leg into a biter's brain, taking it out with one blow. But the wooden leg splintered, leaving him with nothing to defend himself. A rotter rushed him from the right, knocking him and several of the old biddies to the floor. Ferris nailed the biter between its eyes with his .45, while I took out a deadhead that shambled in from the left.

"I got two bullets, a shredded dress, and no shoes," I said. "You?"

Ferris slammed in a new mag. "A ruined tux and more kills than you."

Everything's a competition with this guy.

We were out in the open with no cover, but almost to Thornton's side. I got a twofer by drilling back-to-back corpsicles with one bullet. A biter blindsided Ferris, so I swung Baby into position and fired. Booyah!

"Cover me," I yelled, reaching down my cleavage for my last mag and praying I wouldn't come up empty. I fished it out with a sigh of relief and slammed it home, ready for the next round of rotters in the night's deadly game of Drill that Deadhead.

Ferris and I positioned ourselves in front of the governor, backing both him and his band of blue hairs up against the wall to eliminate any surprise attacks from behind. I fired into the horde time and again, uncharacteristically losing count along the way. My chest tightened; my vision skewed.

I shook my head, trying to end the blurriness, and block out Little Allie, who'd begun whining. Something about needing to look.

Look where? I thought. *I am looking.*

Look up, she screamed.

Toussaint's translucent face loomed below the massive eighteen-foot ceiling of the dining room, smiling on the waves of rotters that waged his war below. His eyes found mine, and his smile grew cold.

"Little Bird," he cooed inside my mind. "Why waste your time here, when I have what you seek?"

A snippet of Rico flooded my brain. He'd been beaten and tied to a chair, head lolled to one side, eyes closed, and jaw slack. But still alive. No doubt about that. If for no other reason than to draw me close.

"Nighthawk!" Ferris smacked my shoulder. "What the hell?"

He slapped me hard, and then resumed firing.

"What's wrong with you?" he screamed.

The visions melted before my eyes. No more Toussaint. No more Rico. Just an undeniable need to be somewhere else. But where? The bastard could have given me that much, at least.

I wiped a trickle of sweat from my eyes, raised Baby, then aimed and fired at the remaining Z's. Boudreaux's HRT guys and the remaining private security guards had taken out the bogeys that had infiltrated the ballroom and beyond. Soon, the firing slowed to a chorus of pops, and finally, to a few shots here and there. Thornton was safe. Alpha Guillory hadn't fared as well. He lay sprawled against a wall with his throat ripped out. Apparently, his blue blood tasted as good as any other. I ambled across the floor, pumping what was left of my mag into the brains of the slaughtered victims, saving the last bullet for Guillory. One of the nearby biters, whose legs had been shot out from beneath him, growled and swiped at me. With the last of my ammo gone, I had to drive my Ka-Bar through his skull and into his brain.

Amazingly, the table where we'd been sitting an hour earlier still stood upright, but like everything else in the room, it was stained red and slathered in several layers of zushi. I wandered over, reached beneath it for my shoes, and heard the unmistakable chatter of snapping teeth. A careful peek beneath the tablecloth revealed a snarling corpsicle, impaled by a broken chair leg, right beside one of my pretty silver stilettos. I picked up that shiny size ten shoe of death and spiked its five-inch heel straight through the brainstem of that decomped deadhead. Surely, that's what it was made for, 'cause it wasn't worth a damn for anything else. I jerked the shoe out of the biter's head and dodged the wad of zushi that seeped out with it.

Then I thought twice and rammed it back into the rotter's skull. What else was I going to do with it? It's not like I'd ever wear it again.

Ferris walked up from behind, grabbed my arm and hissed

in my ear. "What happened back there? You froze. You've never done that before."

I wrestled my arm away and thought about decking him. But he was right. And any explanation I gave would sound certifiable. Still, he deserved to understand.

"It's Toussaint," I said, sinking to the floor cross-legged, burying my head in my hands. "The bastard pops in and out of my head as he pleases. One minute I'm me; the next minute, he takes over, filling my brain with whatever the hell he wants. And it freaking *pisses me off.*"

I turned and punched a hole through the wall, darting my eyes to see if anyone had noticed, and then laughed like a loon. The room was toast. Most of the mansion was toast. My fist-sized hole paled in comparison, and the brain bitch reminded me that I could always chalk it up to collateral damage.

Boudreaux walked up, wiping blood from his glasses. "All told, one-hundred-thirty-three bodies. We don't have them categorized yet—rotter versus human, and bites versus cross-fire. That should be an interesting conversation with the media."

Ferris holstered his Glock. "It was an inside job all the way, sir."

Thornton, who'd been tending to the hysterical blue hairs, snapped up his head. "How dare you?" He stomped toward Ferris and stood him nose to nose. "I am the governor of the state of Louisiana. These people—both the dead and the living —were my supporters, my guests." He swallowed hard and stared at the body of Alpha Guillory. "And some of them my lifelong friends. How dare you suggest—"

"It was Bruno." The edge in Ferris's voice was hard to miss. "He tried to kill us when we stumbled onto his truckload of deadheads out back. He may have worked for Guillory for twenty years, Governor, but money talks. It makes people do stupid things. You know? It...skews their decision making."

I didn't need to be Psycho Babs to read between the lines. Ferris was angry. The body count could have been zero if the governor had listened to us and called off the fundraiser.

Boudreaux's eyes were unreadable as he clapped Ferris's shoulder and muttered something in his ear, steering him away from Thornton. I got the sense Boudreaux was using Ferris's rage as a teachable moment, so I turned away and found myself in the governor's sights.

"You blame me, too. Don't you?"

"Don't you?" I asked, dumbfounded. Who the hell else was there? But deep inside, Little Allie chanted Le Clerc's name over and over.

Thornton ambled away with his head in his hands, picking his way across the bodies, the wreckage and the gore. I wondered if he'd had time to realize that by now, the media would already be on the other side of the crime scene tape, waiting for a soundbite, waiting for an explanation that would satisfy...anyone. If the truth ever came out, the headlines would bury him. But I had my own hills to climb, starting with rescuing Rico, Fairchild, and Nancy Newshound.

Boudreaux motioned for me from the ballroom. The anger management lecture must have ended.

Sorry, Governor, I thought, as I navigated the minefield of human remains to rejoin them. *Not my circus, not my monkeys.*

"There's nothing more for you to do here," Boudreaux said, checking his watch. "It's after ten now. Horton's on his way. He and I can handle this clusterfuck. How 'bout you take down that psychopath and find those missing folks?"

He didn't have to ask twice. I nodded and broke for the door, with Ferris beside me.

"Count on it, sir," Ferris called over his shoulder. The edge in his voice had morphed into determination.

We hadn't made it five steps when Boudreaux brought us to a halt.

"Nighthawk, where in the hell are your shoes?"

"One of them is over there, under my dinner table, covered in zushi." I pointed toward the dining room. "The other is buried in the brain of a deadhead, also in there...somewhere. If it's okay sir, I'll just leave them where they are."

Boudreaux closed his eyes and pinched the bridge of his nose. "I should have known better than to ask. Carry on."

First things first, Ferris and I needed a quick clean-up. But before we dove all balls-to-the-wall into this rescue mission, we had an important stop to make. One that, if we were lucky, might save our lives.

33

'FOR LIKE THE GRASS THEY WILL
SOON WITHER'

F erris was quiet on the ride back to the Marriott. Maybe that was because of what we'd just seen. Or, maybe he was focused on what lay ahead. Either way, I figured he'd earned his space. Visions of Guillory slumped against the wall with his throat torn out flickered in my head like an ancient home movie, so I nipped it in the bud and turned my thoughts to Nonnie and the terrible twins instead. Over the years, I'd come to realize that the Dr. Phils of this world were generally full of shit. Sometimes, processing trauma was worse than simply blocking it out.

We rode the elevator to our rooms and agreed to meet back in the hallway in twenty. I slid the keycard in front of the reader and opened my door. Vinny levelled a gun at my face.

I dove back around the door frame. "Jesus! Put that thing down before you kill someone."

"Just making sure you're a friendly."

Babs scrambled out from the bathroom. "Vinny, who said you could touch my gun?"

"Someone jimmied the door. You were in the can, and I got

Luna sitting next to me. What do you want I should do? Heave the remote at 'em?"

I walked back in, slamming the door behind me. "You're lucky I don't ram that remote down your throat."

Luna clutched the couch pillow against her like a shield.

"Don't mind me," I said, grabbing some fresh clothes. "Be out of here in a few. Just need to clean up."

All eyes darted to the remains of my little black dress. Strangely, the only person to blink twice was Luna.

Babs snapped her fingers at Vinny and held out her hand.

"I know more about this piece than you do," he said, relinquishing her baby Glock. "And I'm a better shot. It's my life on the line. Stop treating me like a child."

Babs leaned in and murmured, "Then stop acting like one."

I headed into the bathroom and shut the door, a little bummed that I'd miss the rest of the show. When I came out after my shower, things had settled down. I strapped on my ankle holster, reloaded Baby and slipped her into place. Then I slid on my zombie stompers and grimaced as they rubbed against the blisters left behind by those godforsaken heels of death. Last but not least, I holstered Hawk and clipped extra mags to my belt. My ever-present Ka-Bar, tucked safely in its sheath, completed the ensemble.

"Wish us luck," I said, slipping both Mama's gris-gris bag and the obsidian necklace over my head. "Ferris and I are going to go check out the properties in St. Bernard. But first, we're going to swing by Mama's. I'll let her know you're here, Luna. It might be a good idea if you stay put tonight—in case things go sideways."

Luna's smile was soft and sweet. "Thanks, Miss Allie. You be safe now."

"I studied lockpicking this afternoon. Call me if you need me," Vinny quipped.

Not today, I thought. But never say never. The kid had grit, and he'd embraced the paranormal aspects of this investigation without a blink. Then again, he also had his daddy's sassitude. Nobody's perfect.

Babs' eyes held mine as I pulled the door closed behind me. We weren't the best of friends, but she'd been there for me when I needed her, and even when I hadn't realized I'd needed her. A lot was riding on this mission. Rico, Jade, Fairchild, Babs, Vinny, Luna, Mama, and Ferris. *And* taking down Toussaint? *Please God,* I prayed. *Don't let me fuck this up.*

Ferris, waiting in the hallway, pushed the elevator call button. "Ready?"

"No offense," I said, giving him the once-over. "I liked your tux better."

"Had to throw it out. Between the rips and the stains, it's seen its last black-tie affair."

"Tell me about it. What's left of my dress might make a good ShamWow."

As the elevator doors opened and we walked inside, I found myself wondering if we would ever make it back.

Ferris seemed lost in his own thoughts as he drove us to Mama's which gave me a chance to check in with Nonnie. I missed the old fossil and the terrible twins more than usual. *Enough with the squishy feelings shit,* I thought. But Little Allie had already pulled up my contacts and hit *send.* One thing I hadn't considered was that it was after midnight in Cincinnati.

Nonnie's muffled voice came on the line. "Miss Allie? Something wrong?"

"No. Sorry. Didn't mean to wake you up. How's everything?"

"No so good. Headbutt dug out under fence and chew up Mrs. Winstel's wisteria."

Crap. The latest salvo in the wisteria war. That feisty, fat, little zombie hunter would get me kicked out of the neighbor-hood yet.

"Mrs. Winstel very unhappy. Says she talk to home owners association. And Kulu...she lay another egg."

"So, we're up to three eggs now?"

"Yes."

"In my maxi-pad box?"

"Yes. She won't let me near nest. What you do about tax issue?"

I should have known better than to call. "We'll talk later. See if you can find something to stick in front of the fence-line. Tell Mrs. Winstel I'll buy her a new bush when I get home."

"Is vine. Not bush."

"Whatever. Go back to sleep." For some reason, I uttered an uncharacteristic, weenie-like platitude. "Nonnie, thanks. For everything. Give the twins an extra dog biscuit from me. I'll be back as soon as possible. I...miss you guys."

"Everything okay, Miss Allie?"

"No. But it will be soon. Goodnight."

"Is bad, bad feeling. Come home. Please? Someone else take case."

Poor Nonnie. The woman knew me better than to think I'd ever play it safe.

Ferris and I pulled into Mama's around 11:15 p.m. The restaurant was closed but the lights were still on. Mama would still be there cleaning and prepping for the next day. We climbed the steps and she opened the screen door, as if she'd been expecting us.

I couldn't suppress my smile. Of course, she had.

"Welcome, child. I know why you come." She placed her weathered hands on my cheeks and kissed my forehead, then quickly turned and wrapped Ferris's hands in hers. "And you, Mesye Ferris, faithful friend of my Little Bird, will always be welcome in my home."

She ushered us inside, guided us across the deserted restaurant to her kitchen, and then led us through the faded velvet curtain to her greenhouse. She paused at her workbench and regarded us with warm but worried brown eyes.

"Time has passed so quickly. I have done all I can. Toussaint's magick is great, but his darkness pales against your light. Perhaps together, you and I can undo what he has done. Listen carefully," she said, handing me three vials from her workbench. "This tonic will hinder Toussaint's virus, but it is *not* an antidote. It must be re-administered with each new moon, or the victim will begin to decline, and in time, turn." She closed my hand around the ampules, placed Ferris's hand on mine, then laid hers atop ours. "One vial per victim. Do you understand?"

Ferris and I both nodded.

"I will prepare more doses, and when time permits, I will teach you to concoct your own. I have someting more for you as well. Someting you use only in defense of your life, or the lives of those you seek to rescue." She held out a small leather pouch, synched tightly with a small gold cord, and asked, "Do you remember what it is that we use *only* in the defense of life?"

"Yes, ma'am."

My fingers trembled as she placed the pouch of Goofer Dust into the palm of my hand. The dry hoodoo blend, containing, among other things, graveyard dirt, snakeskin, and powdered bones, provided its holder with very powerful grisgris.

"Be strong, be centered, and do God's work," she said, escorting us back to porch. "Take all of my love and bring it back to me, child." She folded me to her bosom, gathering Ferris in as well, and blessed us with a Psalm: "'Do not fret because of evil men or be envious of those who do wrong; for like the grass they will soon wither, like green plants they will soon die away. Trust in the LORD and do good; dwell in the land and enjoy safe pasture.'"

Mama's strength and blessings surged through me. Judging by Ferris's wide-eyed expression, he felt that same power running through his veins.

Armed in every sense of the word, we lit out of Mama Femi's in the dead of night, ready for battle.

34

THIS ALMOST NEVER HAPPENS

Since two of the four mansions we had reconned could be credible targets, Ferris and I had a decision to make.

"Which manse should we hit first?" Ferris asked. "Heads, the one in Violet, or tails, the place in Chalmette?"

I yawned and stretched, settling into the passenger seat of the SUV. "Both are due East; Violet's further out. Let's start with the one in Violet and work our way back."

Google Earth pics showed the house sat off the road in a secluded area, surrounded by trees and vegetation. A real handy-man's special, sold over a year ago to somebody named Wesley Segal. Broken windows, missing shingles and dangling shutters gave it that haunted, abandoned look. The perfect candidate.

Ferris stifled a yawn of his own. "I'd rather be doing this in the daylight, but your buddy Le Clerc's set a wicked pace."

Ferris had a point. It was almost midnight. As someone who, more often than not, plied my trade in the dead of night, I knew the dangers of working in the dark more than most. Whether I was dodging headstones and flower vases in a cemetery, or traipsing through ramshackle old houses, there was always an element of the unknown. Chuck holes and open graves, or rotting floor boards and collapsing stairs always added a little *sumpin'-sumpin'* to the equation.

But at the end of the day, Ferris was right. We weren't running this investigation; Toussaint was running it, calling the shots, and leading us in a game of cat and mouse.

Talk about a red-hot poker up my ass.

The brain bitch fired off a message that was sure to find its mark. *Think this is a game, asshat? Let me show you how it's played.*

———

Ferris followed the Suburban's GPS from Meraux to an isolated corner of Violet, winding us through the city streets and into the woodlands. Paved roads transitioned into unpaved paths, swallowed by trees, kudzu and vegetation that grew unchecked.

"According to the coordinates, we're here." Ferris pulled the SUV to the side of the gravel road and parked, as if he was concerned about oncoming traffic. I pushed open the passenger door and tumbled into a tangle of saw grass, doubting he had much to worry about. Ferris popped the trunk and handed me a flashlight, then took his Buck knife from the sheath on his belt.

"Where the hell's this mansion?" I switched on the light and pulled my Ka-Bar to cut a swath through the weeds.

"Up ahead," Ferris said, pointing his flashlight through a grove of Cypress trees. "I see the roofline."

We hacked and whacked through a sea of deadfall and wound up on a gravel drive that led to the mansion. Even in the dark of night, sweat poured down my temples and dripped between my shoulder blades, giving me a chill. The air stunk of peat, decay and moldering vegetation. A cloud of mosquitoes whirred around us and whined in my ears.

I swatted my face and nailed one the size of a 747. "Nature sucks," I hissed.

With the mansion and a large *No Trespassing* sign now clearly in sight, we turned off our flashlights and navigated by moonlight. The house was pitch black and lifeless, still as a tomb. Ferris glanced up, then quickly squatted down, motioning me to join him.

He pointed to what appeared to be a camera fixed to a nearby tree and whispered, "I'm feeling all kinds of hinky about this place."

He was right. The place had *wrong* written all over it. But we had a problem of another kind.

"We don't have a warrant," he whispered. "So, before we knock on the door and ask to go inside, let's check this place out a little closer. Follow me."

I bear-crawled behind him, wishing we'd had enough evidence to get that missing warrant. But even now, as suspicious as the place looked, we had no proof we'd find Toussaint, let alone any of his victims or anything even remotely illegal.

Ferris bypassed the front entrance, and the first-floor windows with their drawn shades, and crawled around the side of the mansion, stopping by a collection of filled garbage cans —a strong suggestion that someone might be inside. An odd odor wafted up when he lifted a lid and shined his flashlight inside one of the cans. A combination of ammonia and rotten eggs, maybe? An acrid chemical fume kind of smell. Empty paint thinner cans, reddish stained coffee filters, dirty rags, and hundreds of empty cold medicine packets overflowed from trash bags and lay scattered across the gravel. On the far side of the drive stood a wooden picnic table, surrounded by a sea of cigarette butts. Whoever these people were, they smoked like fiends, coughed like Typhoid Mary, and smelled like egg farts.

"That's it," Ferris said, shining his light at the trash heap. "That's our ticket in."

I stared at him, wondering what he'd seen that I hadn't.

"All this garbage, the smells—they're cooking meth," he whispered. "You said yourself he was a wannabe chemist. What better way to finance his operation?"

It made perfect sense. "Just to be clear," I said. "I was going in anyway, but now because they're cooking meth, you say it's all hunky-dory?"

"It's called exigent circumstances. If someone is being held hostage, and the search is necessary to protect life or prevent serious injury, it's permissible. It's also permissible if we need to prevent the destruction of evidence or contraband. Either way, we're good to go."

I'd never been much of a rules person anyway, but if it was blessed by Ferris, then by God, it was good enough for me. We rounded the back of the manse and noticed a small light glowing in one of the rooms. Ferris crept beside the window and cautiously peered inside.

He circled back down and gave me a thumb's up. "It's quiet in there, no bogies in sight. We'll infiltrate through the back door. You go right, I go left, clearing each room as we go. Got it?"

Memories of slicing the pie at Perp Town flooded my brain. I'd done a face-plant into an open grave while chasing a dead-head, and banged up my wrist. Cap and Rico made me requalify at the range by shooting my way through Perp Town before they'd let me back to work. That was the first time I'd ever sliced the pie, inching forward and clearing a room, a sliver at a time. There was a distinct advantage that first time around: the bogies were cardboard cutouts as opposed to gun-toting douchebags. Today, I'd be dealing with douchebags.

Since I'm a left-handed shooter, I tucked the flashlight between the fingers on my right hand and held it just below the barrel. Ferris gently turned the knob on the back door. It popped open with a quiet squeak. I entered and went right, clearing the rooms quickly, listening for Ferris's voice. We met in the foyer, having found no bogey's in between, nor any sign of Rico, Fairchild, or Jade. But we had another floor to go.

"Somebody's here," Ferris whispered. "Careful with the gun. There's a fresh batch of meth cooking in the kitchen."

We climbed the steps and hugged the wall, clearing the upper hallway much as we had the first floor. I cut right; Ferris cut left. Nada. Not a single soul. What had we missed?

As we descended the steps, a quiet scraping noise caught my ear. Ferris pointed to the left side of the first floor. He went left, but this time, I took his back to be sure our bogey wouldn't double back from behind. A wall in what might have been the study at one time had been pushed forward, revealing a now empty hidden room. The back door made an audible click as it latched in place. Ferris sprinted forward and threw the door open, then raced outside, with me hot on his heels.

The moon had ducked beneath some clouds, leaving our flashlights as the only source of light. Our douchebag could be anywhere. Ferris inched forward with me covering the rear. A quick commotion to the left made me spin. Ferris and the bogey were on the ground in a death roll. Ferris's gun, knocked from his hand in the fracas, lay several feet away.

The moon peeked out from the clouds long enough to glint against the big-ass pig sticker in our bogey's hands.

"Knife!" I screamed, pinning the bastard in Hawk's sights. We were out in the fresh air, away from the cooking meth, but I couldn't get off a clean shot.

The douchebag scrambled to his feet and swiped his knife at Ferris, drawing blood from his arm. Ferris jumped back and drew his own knife. They circled each other slowly, eyes locked.

Ferris lunged; the bogey snap-kicked the knife from Ferris's hand then wrapped him in a headlock.

Ferris tucked his chin and leaned forward to throw the bastard over his shoulder.

"Ah-ah-ah." The bogey brought the edge of his knife to Ferris's throat. "I wouldn't if I were you."

"Put it down *now*, scumbag, and let him go." I cocked my hammer and pointed Hawk at the douchebag's head. "Where are Toussaint and the others?"

"Who?"

"Toussaint Le Clerc and the people he kidnapped."

"What the... I'm the only one here. I cook meth. That's what I do. I never kidnapped nobody. Freaking nutjob." He pressed the knife against Ferris's throat.

"I'm a zombie hunter, dude. I live for headshots. Go on. I dare you."

"I'll slit him ear to ear before you pull that trigger."

"And two seconds later, you'll be dead. You see the flaw in your plan, right?"

Something in the bastard's eyes told me he wasn't afraid to die. He adjusted his grip on the knife, leaned into Ferris's ear and murmured, "Say good night, Gracie."

The bastard flinched as I squeezed off a round, sending my bullet wide and into the garbage pile filled with paint thinner cans. The trash exploded, sending all three of us airborne, ass over elbows. Ferris, first to his feet, scrambled over to the douchebag, slapped him in cuffs, and dragged him down the gravel drive. I scuttled behind them, watching the flames growing closer to the house.

"She's fucking certifiable!" the bastard screamed, as he stumbled away from the flames. "Nobody shoots a gun at a meth lab."

Ferris glared at me. "Not to mention that was like the worst shot ever."

"He flinched, damn it! I wasn't *inside* the meth lab. I was *outside*. And I almost never miss." Holy Guacamole, I'd never live this down.

We watched the inferno from well down the gravel drive,

barely keeping our feet beneath us as the Violet mansion exploded in a magnificent blaze of glory. Shingles and flaming debris rained like fire bombs from the sky, making us bob and weave beneath them. An interesting change of pace and somewhat ironic, really. Usually, I was dodging zushi bombs.

Sirens wailed in the distance. I gave silent thanks that the blaze would be contained before it spread through the woodlands. While Ferris called it in, I practiced my speech—the speech I'd have to give to finagle my way out of this debacle. What can I say? Some things never change.

"Well, we've eliminated house number three," I said, planting my hands on my hips.

Ferris sighed. "That's one way to put it."

"Let's go. We're wasting time. You called it in and help is on the way. No need for us to stick around."

"What about Mr. Meth?"

"Give me the key to the cuffs."

The douchebag flinched when Ferris tossed me the key. "Dude, she's crazier than a shithouse rat. Keep her the hell away from me."

Ferris's eyes blazed. "No way, man. You tried to slit my throat. And look at my fucking arm," he said, staring at a gash in his bicep. "Did you do that, or did the explosion?"

I dragged the bastard to a Cypress tree and uncuffed him. "Turn around, wrap your arms around the tree and give it a big old kiss."

He swore under his breath as I cuffed his wrists around its trunk.

"There," I said with a nod to Ferris. "Call Boudreaux, tell him we left his Christmas present trussed up to a tree. Now, can we *please* get the hell out of Dodge?"

I set out through the brush without waiting for Ferris's answer. That flaming carcass of a mansion was the last place I wanted to be when Boudreaux and Dickhead showed up.

35

I'LL TRY TO BLEED SLOWER

Ferris trudged out of the brush a few minutes behind me and climbed back into the Suburban. "Boudreaux says thanks for the gift, but he didn't get you anything."

"My bosses never do," I said, inspecting the wound on Ferris's arm. It was still bleeding with bugs, sweat, and... nature...stuck to it. "Do these fleet cars come equipped with first aid kits?"

"Maybe. Check beneath the passenger seat."

I reached beneath me, felt the contour of a box and pulled it out. Ferris drove to the Chalmette location while I rummaged through the box, seeing what I had to work with.

"This is the end of the line," Ferris said, wincing as I pulled what was left of his sleeve out of the wound. "If Toussaint's not holding them here, we're back to square one with nothing to show for our efforts."

Little Allie begged to differ, pointing out that we...well, I... had successfully burned down an 18th century mansion—which was hardly *nothing*.

I flicked on my flashlight to get a better look at the wound and frowned. A gaping two inch-long gash straddled his bicep.

He wasn't having trouble moving his arm, so nerve or tendon damage seemed unlikely, but he needed stitches.

I opened a small bottle of hydrogen peroxide and poured it straight on the cut. Ferris grimaced but didn't pull away. After slapping a sterile pad on the wound, I tied it tight around his arm with a length of gauze and taped it in place. That would have to do for the time being.

I shoved the kit back under the seat and pulled out my phone to review the information Mouton had emailed us.

"Well here's a bit of luck," I said with a snicker. "This place already burned once in 2015, and judging by the Google Earth pics, I'd say they haven't started work on it yet. So, it's relatively Allie-proof."

Ferris snorted, but didn't respond. Maybe he was thinking what I was thinking. As much as I wanted to strike gold this time, the manse in Violet had seemed a more likely location. Chalmette was the most populated city in the parish. This place might sit off the road in a wooded area, but if Toussaint wanted real privacy, why would he choose a location under everyone's noses?

Bold. Then again, Toussaint's ego had always written checks he couldn't cash.

Ferris pulled into the River Road driveway and turned off the ignition. I climbed out of the car, took a long, deep breath, and stared at the moonlit mansion, part of me praying we were at the right place, and part of me dreading what would happen if we were.

The woodlands have a sound of their own in New Orleans, especially in the middle of the night. Frogs croaking, insects buzzing, and owls hooting; brush rustling and twigs snapping from dozens of unseen species whose eyes and ears have been trained on you since the moment you stepped from the car. I tried not to think about alligators, but then every shadow took on the shape of twelve-foot-long eating machine.

Ferris and I crept up the front steps of the mansion and peered inside through the sidelight windows. Our flashlights glared off the glass, doing little to illuminate what was on the other side of the door.

"No warrant, no probable cause." Ferris sighed. "Let's do a walkaround, see what we find."

"Let's not, and say we did." I tapped my flashlight against the window, breaking the glass.

"What the hell? You can't just brea—"

"Listen," I said, cupping my ear. "Hear that?"

"Hear what?"

"Rico and Jade calling for help."

Crickets chirped; flies buzzed. Tumbleweeds drifted across the porch while Ferris listened in vain and finally shook his head in disgust.

"You didn't hear a damn thing. Now, nothing we find here can be used as evidence. It's called fruit of the poisonous tree."

"We don't need evidence. If Toussaint's here, he won't be leaving alive."

I reached through the broken window to unlock the door but a voice inside me murmured, *Turn the knob.* The voice was cold, hard and new, definitely not the brain bitch's.

I turned the knob. The door popped open and swung back slowly, as if welcoming us inside.

That was way too easy, Little Allie whispered.

A menacing laugh echoed through the foyer.

Every muscle in my body froze, but Ferris sighed and pushed against me from behind. "Well? Are you going in, or what?"

I turned to tell him to back off, and the laugh boomed again, louder. Ferris didn't even blink. An ugly realization set in: Ferris hadn't heard the laughter because he hadn't been meant to hear it. That creepy little gift was for me alone.

"Toussaint's here," I hissed, pulling Hawk.

Relax. Breathe, damn it. I stuck my finger inside the coin pocket of my jeans, brushing it against the vials, stroking them, as if they were magic talismans that could save us.

Ferris drew his Glock and skimmed past me, planting his feet at the edge of the threshold, and knocked on the open door. "FBI. Is anyone here?"

He waited several moments then called out again. "This is Agent Sean Ferris, FBI. Is anyone here? Please identify yourself."

I scoured the foyer with my flashlight, and saw two people dead ahead. I raised Hawk, but then realized I'd seen our reflections in a mirror. I think I peed a little.

My light swept past something on the floor. When I looked again, it was a small pool of blood.

"Ferris," I hissed. He didn't hear me, so I called again, forcing out his name in a voice I didn't recognize as my own. "*Ferris.*"

His eyes darted to me, then traveled to the end of my flashlight beam and stopped. He stared long and hard, as if he couldn't make it out, then shot me a questioning glance.

"Blood," I mouthed.

He squinted at the spot again, blinked, then eyeballed me like I'd lost my mind. "*What?*"

"It's blood."

"Are you sure?" He heaved a sigh, but brought his gun to high ready. "FBI entering the premises."

Without waiting for a response, he crossed to the center of the foyer and shined his light on the blood. Only it wasn't blood anymore. It was a man's black wallet. My mind raced. *Had it always been a wallet?* Absolutely not. I was sure I'd seen blood.

Ferris rolled his eyes at me before squatting on his

haunches and flipping the wallet open with the tip of his Glock. Rico's driver's license stared at us from the center of our flashlight beams.

Ferris stood back up, yanked out his phone, and placed a call. "This is Agent Sean Ferris of the FBI requesting back up at 1416 River Road, Chalmette. Possible kidnapping."

My heart hammered; my spit went dry. I stepped across the threshold, and an odd but familiar stench seared the inside of my nose. Sick, sweet, decay with a side of mold, mildew, and rot. Weeds breached the splintered floorboards; algae snaked across the walls in endless green veins. Nature had taken over, adding a musty stink, but the underlying reek came from something darker. Something sinister.

Ferris stepped toward me, and the floor groaned beneath his weight. "This place is one big boobytrap. Watch where you walk."

I heard Ferris's voice, but another sound beckoned from deeper inside the mansion. Something distant, low like a whisper, but not. Something...urgent.

I froze and listened again, blocking out Ferris and the nighttime noises from the woods. The sound returned, much louder now and more defined: a series of shrill screams followed by a long, furious rant. The screams? Probably female. The rant? Definitely male. Definitely Rico's.

I bolted across the foyer and dashed down the hall, following the voices. Ferris reeled, yelling something about waiting for backup, but his words disappeared like smoke in the air. I didn't need to hear him anyway. The only thing that mattered was running deeper and deeper into the mansion, to get to where I was supposed to be—where I *needed* to be.

My feet pounded against the hardwood floor, one after the other, carrying me on a mission that wasn't my own.

Toussaint stepped out of the darkness and into my path,

laughing like a loon, and pointing at me, as if I were the butt of some sick, twisted joke.

I pulled up short, raised Hawk and fired, emptying my mag into his skull.

"Nighthawk!" Ferris's voice thundered in my ears. I spun to find him staring, slack-jawed, at the bullet-riddled wall in front of me. "What the hell are you shooting at?"

The floor creaked once, twice, then gave way beneath me. My arms flew up and I dropped like a stone, losing both Hawk and my flashlight.

I reached out, clawing at what was left of the floorboards, and stopped my descent. Sawdust and debris billowed through the room. Slivers of rotted wood snapped and fell, pinging against the bottom of the crawlspace below. But the floor held.

Ferris lay down near the closest joist and extended his hand. "You okay?"

"Never better." I grabbed his forearm and pulled myself along his body, scraping my hips and legs against the jagged floorboards as I struggled up and out of the hole, breaking off even more of the rotted floor.

Once extricated, I rolled away from the hole and onto my back, gulping air. But all the air in the world wouldn't change what had happened. My mind was no longer my own. Toussaint had burrowed into my head like a tick, making me see and hear exactly what he wanted me to see and hear. If I was going to save anyone, the first person I needed to safeguard was me.

I brought my fingers to my neck and held the obsidian necklace, silently asking Mama for protection.

Ferris scrambled off the floor and pulled me to my feet. "What's wrong with you? I tell you the floor's rotten, and you take off across it like a bat out of hell. Then you shoot the shit out of an empty wall."

"I'm okay," I said, dusting myself off. "I thought I heard Rico and Jade, that's all."

"Yeah. Like you heard them before, right? Enough with the games." He shined his light around the floor, locating my flashlight and Hawk. "Pick up your shit and get behind me."

"No. Really, Ferris. I thought I heard them."

He moved on without another word, making me feel like an even bigger nutjob than I already did. Explaining how Toussaint remote-controlled my brain seemed like an excuse, not to mention a waste of time. It didn't matter. We still had a job to do.

I stepped forward, following Ferris, and my ribs screamed out, bringing me to my knees. I ran my hand over my flank, feeling something sticky and wet. Ferris, already back at my side, pulled what was left of my shredded T-shirt aside and shined his light on my torso. Bruises were already blooming. Blood ran freely from several deep gouges in the front and on the sides. I didn't need an X-ray to tell me at least a couple of my ribs were cracked.

Ferris ripped off his shirt sleeve, balled it up, and pushed it into my side. "Keep pressure on that."

"Ah! Not so hard."

"You have to stop the bleeding."

"Whatever. I'll try to bleed slower. Just get that thing away from me."

While in the glow of his flashlight, I ran a hand over my hips and legs, checking for other damage. Assorted cuts and bruises, rips here and there along my jeans, including a missing belt loop in the front, near my right hip. The corner pocket had ripped at the seam. My heart sank as I stuck my hand inside and discovered only two of Mama's three vials remained; the third must have fallen into the crawl space.

Fuck me twice on Tuesday.

"You're hurt," Ferris murmured. "We should stop and wait for backup."

"Then stay, you big pussy. I'm good to go. If Rico and the others have been infected, every minute counts."

He snorted, but held his tongue and continued down the hall. I slipped in a new mag and prayed that between the brain bitch and I, one of us could keep Toussaint out of my head.

Ferris wrapped his fingers around the next door knob and twisted. When it didn't budge, he tried again, putting his shoulder to it. The door groaned but held. Voices chattered inside the room. I glanced at Ferris to see if he'd heard them too. The excitement in his eyes told me they were real.

He signaled a three-count with his fingers, then stepped back and kicked beside the knob, shattering the lock. The door slammed open. He went left; I went right.

Ferris downed a bogey with a single tap to the head, then whirled and took out another. A third skell crouched in the right front corner. I spun and fired, flinching at the pain in my side. Hawk's muzzle wavered; my bullet went wide. The bastard stood and set me in his sights, but never got the chance to pull the trigger. My second shot drilled him between the eyes.

Nothing to crow about. That was my second miss of the day and I was certain to hear about it. But three up, three down, and the good guys were still standing. That was a win in my book.

A muffled voice called from behind a door at the far end of the room. "Well, it's about damn time." The timbre and the tone sounded familiar, but given Toussaint's mind games, I took my cue from Ferris's reaction.

He bit back a smile, strolled forward and rapped on the door. "Anybody happen to see a cop, a rookie, and a reporter around here?"

"Son-of-a-bitch. Where in the hell have you—" Rico was having a meltdown and all I could do was smile.

I'd never been so happy to have my ass chewed out in all my life.

36

SHIT-OUT OF MIRACLES

The solid mahogany door required a skeleton key which, sadly, hadn't been left in the lock for our convenience. As if that weren't a big enough challenge, the hinges weren't visible on our side of the door, either.

Ferris frowned. "I could kick all day and not break this mother down. If I shoot the lock, the bullet could ricochet or hurt one of them inside."

"Occam's razor," I muttered. "Since the key isn't in the lock, surely one of the dead guards has it. Hold on."

I bent over and rummaged through their pockets, grimacing, as I pulled out Kleenex, cigarette packs, and loose change.

"*Yes,*" I whispered, wrapping my fingers around an old brass key.

With a wink at Ferris, I put the key in the lock and turned the knob. The massive door groaned in protest as I pushed it open and stepped across the threshold. Ferris moved beside me, joining his flashlight beam to mine.

I scanned the room from left to right, searching for Rico. He blinked furiously as the light captured his face. In that instant, I cataloged every cut and bruise, the circles beneath his eyes and the sallow tone of his skin. He was tied to a heavy wooden chair in the center of the room. Dried blood stained his clothes and peppered the floor around him. Ferris pulled his Buck knife, rushed to Rico's side and began sawing at the ropes to free him.

Fairchild lay in a heap, arms pulled behind his back and zip-tied to the foot of an old cast iron radiator. He didn't speak, but his swollen eyes tracked our movements. Jade, lashed to a chair beside Rico, was slumped over, ashen and covered in sweat. Her usually shiny hair hung in tangled strings around her face. Which one needed me more? Had either of them been infected?

Jade raised her head and rasped, "Help Fairchild."

I nodded and went to Fairchild's side, slicing though his zip-tie. Anticipating the pain, I sucked in a breath and bent over, propping him squarely against the wall. A wave of dizziness washed over me.

I straightened up slowly, released my breath, then scrambled back to Jade. Her eyes were hollow and dark.

"It's too late," she whispered. "Toussaint injected me with the virus. Take care of the others."

I pulled out one of the vials from Mama, opened it and held it to her lips.

"Drink this," I said, pouring it into her mouth before she could ask what it was. Every second counted.

Freed from his ropes, Rico rose slowly from his chair and grimaced as the blood rushed back into his limbs. He wobbled to Jade's side, swept her sweat-soaked hair from her face, and kissed her cheek. "What did you give her?"

"Mama made a tonic—"

"Mama, the magical Hoodoo queen?"

Under any other circumstances, I'd have knocked him into next Tuesday for taking a shot at Mama. But I bit my tongue instead. We had too big a battle in front of us to fight each other.

Jade's eyes glimmered with hope. "This is a cure, right?"

I busied myself, checking her arms and legs for injuries. Anything to avoid looking her in the eye. "Not exactly."

Rico fixed me in a long cold stare. "What do you mean, not exactly?"

"Let's focus on getting out of here, okay?"

He stepped closer and growled, "Let's *focus* on the truth."

The truth? We'd been down this road before with Leo. There had never been a cure, and he knew it.

I spun around, ignoring the pain—but not for long. My knees buckled; a gasp shot out my mouth. I grabbed the arm of Jade's chair to keep from falling, while Ferris shot to my side and put his arm beneath my shoulder.

Rico's eyes widened. "What's wrong?" He glanced from me to Ferris and back again, waiting for an answer.

So, I gave it to him straight.

"I fell through the fucking floor trying to save your ass. A simple thank you would suffice."

The sound of distant footsteps brought our squabble to a close. But they weren't the comforting, measured steps of the cavalry coming to save us. They were the frenzied, erratic steps of the undead.

"She's right, you know," Ferris said, guiding me toward the door. "Now is not the time. We're about to have company, and not the good kind."

I waited at the door while Rico helped Jade out of her chair, and Ferris lifted a woozy Fairchild to his feet.

"You with us?" Ferris asked, tapping Fairchild's cheek.

The rookie steadied himself and flashed a wobbly thumbs up.

Ferris winked. "Back up's on the way, pal. You hang in there, okay?"

Ferris and I had our weapons, but Rico's and Fairchild's were long gone. I forked over my Ka-Bar knife to Rico, while

Ferris busted Jade's chair into pieces and handed out the jagged legs like party favors.

When he was finished, he unsheathed his Buck knife and gave it to Fairchild. "I want this back, kid. It's my lucky knife."

Battered and bloodied, we formed a ragtag group of warriors; Ferris at my back, Jade and Fairchild next, with Rico batting clean-up. I felt good about our chances. What the hell? We'd made it this far. All we had to do was make it back out alive.

Okay. Maybe I didn't feel exactly *good*. But fair...ish. Heavy on the *ish*.

As we took our assigned places at the entrance to the hallway, I couldn't help but remember the last time I went up against a real horde—the undead kind that never tires, that keeps coming long after you're exhausted. The kind that destroys everything in its path. The kind that's driven by an insatiable hunger. Toussaint sent an army of rotters to overrun my house when we were safeguarding Leo. Rico and Ferris were with me then, too. So was Nonnie.

Too bad Nonnie isn't here with us now, I mused. She couldn't hit the broad side of a barn with a gun, but she swung a mean skillet.

The footsteps grew louder, thumping, scuffling and shuffling toward us, echoing down the passage that led to our escape. With no way past the horde but through it, we moved into the hallway to run the gauntlet.

The biters surged, coming in high and low, grabbing our shoulders and ankles. Ferris fought off a corpsicle that lunged in from the left. A rotter snagged my calf and took me to my knees. Jade stepped up and buried the business end of her chair leg into the rotter's head, spearing it like a redfish.

I got a twofer, jumping to my feet and firing into the forehead of the closest biter. The bullet burst through the back of its brain and into the eye socket of the bogey behind it.

We'd pass a room and think we'd cleared it, only to see a new round of rotters diving out into the hall, targeting the back half of the group.

Sirens blared in the distance. We battled down the hall, taking ground inches at a time. For every rotter we wasted, two more took its place. The narrow hallway echoed like a canyon, making it impossible to pinpoint where sounds came from. In front of us? Behind?

I had no way of knowing what was behind me. Was Rico holding his own? Fairchild? What about Jade?

I didn't dare look back to find out.

A surge from the rear drove Ferris into me, knocking me to the ground. I flipped onto my back as a biter dove on top of me, snapping its serrated teeth at my neck. I shoved Hawk into the rotting flesh beneath its chin, pulled the trigger, and blew its head off, driving its body back into the oncoming horde. They stumbled backward into each other and fell like a line of deadhead dominos, giving me the chance to check on the rest of the group.

My flashlight beam came to rest on Princess Jade, who wielded her chair leg like a Louisville Slugger, swinging away and bashing brains like she'd been doing it her whole life. She was hot on Ferris's heels, using him as a shield, the way she was supposed to. Rico, behind her, faced sideways with his back against the wall, head swiveling left to right, anticipating the next wave. He stepped forward, tripped over something, and fell to his knees.

Fairchild? Where was Fairchild?

Caught in the glow of my flashlight, Rico's wild eyes told me everything I needed to know. Fairchild lay motionless, mouth twisted in agony, eyes fixed and glazed, his raw, crimson throat ripped to shreds. Rico sprang to his feet with a roar and slammed his hand against the wall. He sucked in a breath, wiped his sleeve across his face, and then turned to me with resentful eyes.

Bile filled my mouth as he rammed the Ka-Bar into Fairchild's head.

My heart ached—for Fairchild, and for me, too. Would Rico ever stop hating me? Would he always blame me for what happened? Those were questions for another day. I worked my way to the back, to Fairchild, then bent over and picked Ferris's Buck knife off the floor and handed it to Rico. What the hell? Fairchild wouldn't be needing it.

The deadhead dominos, having righted themselves, churned forward in a rolling wave. Exhaustion had set in. My muscles ached. My ribs seared when I breathed. Soon, my mag would be empty, and we were shit-out of miracles. I tried not to dwell on the nasty end in sight. If it came to that, I had at least one bullet left. But did I have enough for Ferris, Rico and Jade?

Sirens screamed; flashing lights from police cruisers reflected against the foyer walls. *Thank God.* I thought. *Just a few more minutes.*

A bullhorn blared, "Chalmette Police Department. You inside, duck and cover. We're coming in hot."

As they entered, gunfire began to pop, sporadically at first, then quickly building to a hail of bullets that seemed to go on forever. Nobody wanted to duck and cover more than we did, but we still had the front-line biters surging toward us. Our best option was to flank each other, move forward in a crouched position, and pray for the best, taking the rotters down before they took us down.

Soon, the rain of bullets slowed to a deliberate series of calculated shots. The remaining deadheads fell one at a time.

Somehow, we'd survived. I'd never been more spent in my entire life.

I sat on the floor in the foyer and rested against a wall while Ferris called Boudreaux to tell him both the good news and the bad. When the ambulances arrived, I struggled to my feet and shined my flashlight into the crawl space, in search of the missing vial, but didn't find it. Jade and Rico passed by, strapped to their gurneys. On their way out the door, Jade smiled and kissed my hand, but Rico refused to look at me.

While the paramedics re-bandaged the knife wound on Ferris's arm, I asked Chalmette PD to look for the vial and then reclaimed my seat against the wall, leaned my head back, and nearly drifted off. The same odd, uninvited voice from earlier that night whirred in my ear. *Open your eyes.*

I didn't want to open them, but I needed to.

Directly across from me, on the foyer mirror, was a message written in blood. *Midnight. Tomorrow. Congo Square. Come alone.*

Could anyone else see the message? Or was it one of Toussaint's mind games? After watching first responders and the coroner's team walk past it without so much as a glance, I had my answer. The message was for my eyes only.

Toussaint needn't have worried. Come midnight tomorrow, I alone would be at Congo Square. And I wouldn't be leaving until I'd taken him down.

37

CASUALTIES OF WAR

Ferris needed stitches for the less emergent wound in his bicep, so I drove him to the St. Bernard Parish Hospital Emergency Room, the same place where Rico and Jade had been taken for assessment. After the nurse called Ferris back, I nodded off in the waiting room, awakening sometime later to the smell of coffee under my nose.

"Morning, Nighthawk." Boudreaux's eyes studied me, as if he were performing his own assessment.

"What time is it?"

"Five-ish"

"Go away." I rolled sideways and grimaced. Damned ribs.

Boudreaux stared at my bloodied T-shirt and the wounds that peeked through what was left of it. "Drink your coffee. We're going to get you checked out, just to be safe."

I hate doctors but I was too tired and in too much pain to argue. Not long after, Ferris, with his upper arm bandaged, strolled out from behind the double doors and sat next to me, leaning his head back against the wall and closing his eyes.

By the time I was called into the back, ninety minutes later, treated, medicated and discharged, Dickhead had arrived. He and Boudreaux stopped chatting when the hydraulic doors opened and I returned to my seat in the waiting room. Ferris lowered his gaze and squirmed like he'd been given an atomic wedgie.

Little Allie bristled and wanted to know what that was about. So did I.

Signed HIPPA consent forms in hand, Doctor Bailey met with us in a small conference room to discuss our litany of injuries with Horton and Boudreaux.

"Agent De Palma has a broken nose and multiple facial contusions and abrasions. He also has a bruised kidney with a small amount of associated internal bleeding. We're going to admit him, so we can monitor the bleeding and make sure it subsides on its own. As for Ms. Chen, I understand she's been infected with a synthetic version of the Z-virus." The doctor looked at me and frowned. "I also understand she was given some kind of...home remedy. You wouldn't happen to have a sample? We'd like to analyze the ingredients to prevent negative drug interactions."

I fished the last vial from my pocket and handed it to the doctor. "It's not a cure. It blocks the body's absorption of the virus. She'll need another dose in a month or so."

The doctor peered at me over the top op of his glasses. "A month *or so*?"

"Every thirty-ish days." Snarky bastard. Definitely not the kind of doctor who'd prescribe medicine in lunar doses.

Bailey scribbled something in his file and then continued his update. "Other than having contracted the virus, Ms. Chen is severely dehydrated and has pneumonia. She'll be admitted and administered fluids as well as IV antibiotics. Agent Ferris received six stiches in his bicep. He's got a nice assortment of soft tissue injuries, but he's good to go. Ms. Nighthawk has two broken ribs, several lacerations in her thoracic area, and the mouth of a longshoreman. We don't wrap ribs anymore; wrapping causes pneumonia. I've given her prescriptions for antibiotics and pain meds. She's not only good to go, I wholeheartedly invite her to leave—preferably, to never return."

Yeah? Screw you, Doctor Douche.

Boudreaux bit back a smile; Dickhead scowled.

"Geez. Awfully sorry for the potty mouth," I said. "How 'bout you lie down, Doc? I'll push on your broken ribs and we'll see if you've got any shits and fucks inside you waiting to escape."

"My ribs aren't broken."

"Not yet."

Boudreaux shot me the stink eye and escorted Bailey toward the treatment area. "Thanks for the recap, Doc. We'll take it from here."

Dr. Bailey disappeared through the hydraulic double doors. Dickhead glared at me and left the ER without another word, while the seemingly unruffled Boudreaux gave Ferris and me our marching orders. "It's been a long night. Go back to the hotel, take a shower, get some breakfast and some sleep. Debriefing in my office, four p.m." He walked out the door and called over his shoulder, "Been there, done that, Nighthawk. You'll be more comfortable sleeping in a recliner."

Rico and Jade were still waiting for their in-patient rooms, so we stopped to check in on them. Jade, sleeping, fluttered her eyes at sound of our voices. She smiled, flashed us a weak thumbs up, and drifted back off.

When I slipped around Rico's curtain, his eyes were open and staring at the ceiling. If he saw me, he didn't bother to blink.

Ferris walked to Rico's bedside and stared down at him. "Feel better, dude. We're heading back to the hotel."

Rico turned away and closed his eyes.

"Okay, later, man," Ferris said. He clapped Rico's shoulder, turned and left, to wait in the hall. Not me. I'd had enough of Rico and the stick shoved up his ass.

"You know, we almost died saving your butt, and Jade's too. The least you could do is nod."

He lay there like a dead mackerel.

Jerk. What had I ever seen in him? I snorted and turned on my heel.

"What did you mean?" he muttered.

"When?"

"You said the stuff you gave Jade wasn't exactly a cure."

"It's not. But it's the next best thing."

He pursed his lips and turned away. I was losing him again, but I didn't give up. "It stalls the virus. You know, keeps it from activating."

"Stalls it. So, she'll turn into biter in a couple of months, like Leo did."

"No, no," I said, sitting on the edge of his bed. "As long as she takes a monthly dose of the medicine, the virus won't take hold. She'll be fine."

Rico looked in my eyes for the first time since we'd left the mansion. "This medicine of Mama's, how's Jade going to get it back in Cincinnati?"

"Mama's making some extra doses, and she's going to teach me how to make it before I leave town. Jade will always have her medicine. I promise."

"Why would you do that—take on that responsibility? You don't even like Jade."

"Not one bit. But I like you. You're my partner. And she's important to you, so—"

"Wait a minute." Rico's eyes widened. "You'll actually have the power of life and death over Jade?"

"Yeah. I guess I will."

"Damn, that's gonna chap her ass."

"I know," I said, unable to check my grin. "Ain't it great?"

As Ferris drove us back to the Marriott, all I could think about was crawling into bed. My eyes were heavy and my ribs ached. *A pain pill would be nice.*

I relaxed against the seat, closed my eyes, and thought of Nonnie. The sun was up and she would be too. I reached for my phone. If I called her now, I wouldn't have to put off sleep once I reached the hotel.

Nonnie answered on the second ring. Kulu cawed in the background like a pissed-off pterodactyl, with Headbutt howling harmony. I jerked the phone away from my ear and yelled, "What's going on, Nonnie?"

Ferris side-eyed me in silence.

"They fighting over dog biscuits again."

"Sorry. I'll buy Kulu some food when I get back. A day or two, tops." I meant to get seed before I left, but didn't have the money.

"Miss Allie, this paper from county about back taxes. What you going to do?"

"I'll check with my tax guy as soon as I get home." Humongous lie. I have no tax guy, or guys of any other kind. Guys require money.

"Why you not tell me you have tax guy?"

"Because I really don't. I told you before, I'll figure it out, and I will, soon."

"They throw you in prison."

"No, they won't throw me in prison."

Ferris side-eyed me again. Freaking Nosy McNose.

"No worry," Nonnie purred. "I have lawyer guy. Help me register American Corpse Management Executives in Ohio. We incorporated, Miss Allie!"

Oy. Even Nonnie had a guy. "You know how I feel about opening a company. Anything else before I go?"

"Headbutt still peeing on Winstel's wisteria through fence."

I cursed under my breath and scratched my fingers across the phone.

"Interf...gotta...home...love...all." I hit *end call*, chafing at the sound of Ferris's laughter.

"Did I hear something about tax problems? And prison?"

What the hell. The cat was out of the bag. I shared my tax problem, brushing over the part that made me sound like a dolt, but Ferris picked up on it anyway.

"Three years? Jesus, Allie."

"No lecturing. Solutions only, or I'll break your face. You know I can."

"Obviously, you need money. What's this company Nonnie wants to open?"

I told him Nonnie's hairbrained idea about a fee-for-service zombie business model.

Ferris was no stranger to my rules. He knew how I felt about indiscriminately raising the dead for profit, but he wasn't above torturing me. "What would you call your company?"

I gave him a stony stare.

"How about *You Raise Me Up*? It's catchy and familiar. It's got—"

"Too late. Nonnie already named it: American Corpse Management Executives."

Ferris paused and snickered when it sank in. "No shit. ACME? Like in the Road Runner?"

"That's what *I* said." We were almost back to the Marriott when I noticed a 24-Hour Walgreens on our left. "Hey, pull in here. I need my prescriptions filled, and gauze and stuff."

Ferris parked the SUV along the curb and leaned his head back on the headrest.

I laid my phone on the console and swiveled out of my seat with a wince. "Need anything?"

"Nope." He paused, holding me in his unreadable blue eyes,

as if he had something more to say. "Here," he finally blurted, whisking out his FBI-issued credit card. "Pharmacies don't take dog biscuits."

"Thanks," I said, feeling my face flush. "I'll pay you back."

"No, you won't. I love you, Allie girl. Remember that."

I winked and brushed my finger across his, as I took the card from his hand. "Me too."

Walking into the pharmacy, I chided myself for not being able to say those three small words. But the pragmatic brain bitch wondered what Ferris could ever do to make me forget that he loved me.

Medical supplies in hand, I climbed back into the SUV with the speed of a snail and prayed for the sweet relief of death. Pain-pill thirty was a distant memory. I nudged a napping Ferris, jolting him awake.

Five minutes later, we arrived at the Marriott and I climbed out of the SUV even slower than I'd climbed in. After sharing an elevator, and a gentle kiss goodnight, I waved my room key over the card reader, rejoiced at the sight of the blinking green light, and opened the door.

Babs whisked across the room and gently wrapped her arms around me, mindful of my ribs. Apparently, Boudreaux had filled her in. I'd have been good with a fist bump; but her hug was nice in a warm, fuzzy, you're-breathing-my-air kind of way.

"Welcome back, Allie. You had us worried."

"Thanks," I said, easing myself into the desk chair. "There was a lot of that going around." I frowned at my boots, wondering how I would ever get them off. Spying my dilemma, Babs came over, knelt down, and slid them off for me.

"Where's Vinny?" I asked, alarmed and picturing him

passed out in an alley off Bourbon Street with a horde fighting over his body parts.

"Across the hall, reading *Fingerprinting 101: Ridges and Whorls*. He knew I was anxious to see you, so he promised to stay put and be on his best behavior." Bab's tone grew soft and empathic. "I...I was so, so sorry to hear about Agent Fairchild."

Her words landed like a punch to the gut. No doubt, she grieved for Fairchild, but I suspected her real intent was to draw me out—to get me to open up about my feelings.

What was the point? Fairchild was dead and wasn't coming back. I'd have done anything to save him but fate makes the rules. I just carry on, winning sometimes, losing others, always the good little corpse whisperer who never asked for any of it.

Right now, I needed my head on straight. Why did Babs even venture into the land of feelings? I wasn't in the mood for her psycho-babble bullshit.

"You're right," I said, matter-of-factly. "It is a shame. He was a bright kid with a great career in front of him. But now he's dead. And what I really want is a bath, a pain pill, and some sleep. Mind waking me up in time for the debriefing with Boudreaux?"

I grabbed a clean T-shirt and some underwear, walked into the bathroom, and shut the door. Wouldn't you know, the freaking pill bottle had a child proof cap. It took forever to get it open and toss back 10 milligrams of it-still-hurts-but-I-don't-care.

I turned on the water and climbed into the tub, peeling off my bandages. When the tub filled, I flicked off the faucet with my toes and leaned back into the hot, soothing water. After dozing for a bit, I woke up long enough to wash, redress my wounds, and put on my fresh T-shirt. Wandering out to the bedroom, I found Babs gone and noticed a recliner waiting beside my bed.

Settling in, I silently thanked Boudreaux, closed my eyes

and prayed for sleep. But images of Fairchild's flayed neck and visions of my midnight face-off with Toussaint loomed like thunderheads in the distance.

I was the only one who knew about that midnight meeting. And that's the way it would stay. Maybe I couldn't control fate. Maybe I couldn't save Fairchild. But nobody else was going to die on my watch—with the possible exception of me. And that was a risk I was willing to take.

38

HOW COULD YOU?

Three o'clock came far too soon and my ribs hurt before I even opened my eyes. Babs brought me another pain pill and watched while I staggered to my feet like the bride of Frankenstein. By the time I'd made it vertical, my hair was soaked and matted against my face. Babs and her blasted thermostat.

She threw me a pained glance and sighed, "How can I help you, Allie? Anything."

"Keep the temperature at sixty-eight, or I'll snap you like a twig." I took a lap around the room and crooked my finger at her like a grade school principal. "Don't let the ribs fool you. I still got game."

Aching chest aside, the more I moved, the better I felt. My body wasn't used to lounging in a recliner all day. After pulling myself together and making several more laps around the room, 3:30 p.m. arrived, and we all piled into the SUV for our 4:00 p.m. meeting with Boudreaux.

Ferris looked like he'd gotten some sleep. The shadows beneath his eyes had faded, but he still seemed weary and a bit distracted. Who could blame him after the night we'd had?

I hadn't seen Vinny since the rescue mission. He smiled as he slid across the back seat, mumbled a quiet hello and squeezed my shoulder, but his usual stream of Abruzzi-style banter was missing. I had the feeling he was uncomfortable—like he didn't know how to act in the wake of Fairchild's death. He wasn't the only one.

When we reached the FBI office, I climbed out of the car with a bit less pain than when I'd climbed in. That gave me hope. Midnight was right around the corner; I'd need to be in fighting shape and hide any weakness.

Once inside the office, Mouton's was the first face we saw. He'd been a close friend of Fairchild's. Babs crossed the room and hugged him tight. I kept my distance and gave him a solemn nod. With or without broken ribs, I'm not a hugger.

Vinny had no business at the debriefing, so one of the junior agents escorted him to an empty desk in cubicle land and provided him with a text on blood spatter analysis. Always excluded from our meetings, Vinny usually groused about being cut from the herd, but apparently, the lure of blood spatter appealed to him.

Boudreaux strolled into the conference room with Director Dickhead Horton on his six. Horton glared at me as he crossed the threshold and tapped the door with his fingertips, letting it drift slowly closed. I waited, eyes forward and mouth shut (at least for the moment), but Little Allie fumed. Dickhead and his mind games. Why he thought he could intimidate me was anyone's guess.

Pretending not to notice, Boudreaux flipped open his file and glanced across the table at Ferris and me. "Let's start with the house in Violet."

Silence filled the room while Boudreaux waited for one of us to fill the void. The moment was awkward and uncomfortable, and brought on by one of the oldest interrogation techniques in the book.

Jesus. Ferris and I weren't a couple of dip-shit skels. You answer the questions you're asked and don't volunteer anything. That boneheaded move cost Boudreaux a few brownie points. Seeing that he wasn't getting what he wanted, he changed his approach.

"Okay, from what I see in the file, you didn't have enough evidence to obtain warrants to go inside either of the properties in Violet or Chalmette. Let's start with the mansion in Violet. Agent Ferris, why did you enter the property without a warrant?"

Ferris cleared his throat. "We inspected the property from a public vantage point and found evidence of an active meth lab operation. Rather than delay entrance to obtain a warrant and call for backup, and risk losing tangible evidence due to intentional destruction, I made a judgment call to breech the residence."

"I see," said Boudreaux. "And how did that relate to the kidnapping case you were investigating?"

"Le Clerc is a wannabe biochemist by trade. He needs money to finance his operation. Cooking meth seemed a likely source of income. The pieces fit, sir."

"Where and how did you encounter the suspect?"

"Nighthawk and I cleared the house. As we descended the steps from the second floor, we heard a noise below and discovered the suspect was escaping, via a hidden room on the first floor. We gave pursuit. I engaged the suspect outside, near the garbage pile, and he pulled a knife."

Boudreaux made some notes and then turned his eyes to me. "Ms. Nighthawk, at what point did you engage the suspect?"

"As soon as I saw the knife, I pulled my gun and ordered the bogie to drop it. I..."

"You...what?"

"I asked the suspect where Le Clerc was and where the kidnap victims were being held. The suspect stated he had no idea what we were talking about. He was simply cooking meth and was in the wrong place at the wrong time. He refused to drop his knife and threatened to slit Agent Ferris's throat. He said, 'Say good night, Gracie,' and adjusted his grip on the knife. I took that as a direct threat to Agent Ferris, raised my gun and fired."

"What happened next, Ms. Nighthawk?"

"The suspect flinched, and the bullet missed his head by a couple of inches."

Boudreaux waited for me to continue, but that was my story and I was sticking to it. He leaned back, laced his hands behind his head, and asked, "Where did your bullet land?"

Shit, shit, shit.

"You know where it hit. It hit the garbage pile filled with combustible materials and blew the place to smithereens."

Babs grimaced.

"I, ah," Ferris cleared his throat and coughed. "I immediately called in the explosion. Believing that the kidnap victims were in grave danger, and being held at the Chalmette location, we handcuffed the suspect to a tree and continued on to the house on River Road."

Boudreaux placed his hands on his face and looked out from between splayed fingers. "Let's skip ahead, shall we? Once you arrived at the Chalmette location, you entered the premises without a warrant because...?"

I wasn't about to let Ferris go down for my error in judgment. "I thought I heard Jade and Rico calling for help from inside. Also, I saw blood on the floor."

Dickhead rose to his feet and loomed over the table. "And you didn't wait for back up because...?"

"Same reason. It's called excrement circumstances," I snarled. "You should know this stuff."

"Exigent, Ms. Nighthawk. Exigent circumstances." Boudreaux said.

"Whatever."

Dickhead cocked his brow. "And when you went inside without a warrant, *was* there blood on the floor?"

"No. As it turns out, what I thought was blood was actually Rico's wallet."

Ferris lowered his eyes and turned away.

"Allie," Boudreaux said quietly. "Why did you empty an entire mag into a blank wall?"

How did... Damn it, Ferris. How could you? Tears burned in my eyes, but I'd be damned if they'd fall. "I thought I saw Toussaint there."

Babs' face looked pained. "Was he there, Ms. Nighthawk?"

"No. No, he wasn't. But that's not really important, is it? What's important is that Rico, Fairchild and Jade *were* there. We made the right call going in, and we saved them."

"Well," Dickhead said. "You didn't exactly save Fairchild, did you?"

"You bastard! We did our best. We almost died trying to save them. All of them, including Fairchild."

"Director Horton," Boudreaux snapped. "I think we've gotten all we need. Have a seat."

"Not yet. Just a couple more questions, if you don't mind. Do you know where Le Clerc is, Nighthawk?"

"No."

"Are you sure about that?"

I didn't have any buttons left for him to push, or any more fucks left to give. "I have no clue where Le Clerc is."

"Would you tell us if you did?"

Ferris studied me with sad, empty eyes. Did he know I was lying?

"Allie," Babs murmured, reaching across the table. "You're stressed and tired. Maybe you're too close to this case."

"We're finished here, aren't we?" I asked, getting up and leaving the room before anyone could stop me.

I'd already made my decision. My sandbox, my rules. No one else was going to die because of Toussaint. This was my problem, nobody else's. And it was just as well. With one partner in the hospital, and the other one having thrown me under the bus, I was fresh out of partners anyway.

39

UPSIDE DOWN IS ONLY A POINT OF VIEW

I sat in the SUV, fuming, waiting for Babs and Ferris to realize that they could stick a fork in me. I was done. The meeting was over and I wouldn't be coming back.

Screw Ferris.

When push came to shove, I'd fessed up that it was my decision to enter the Chalmette residence without a warrant—to protect him. And what did he do? He threw me to the wolves, sharing, outside of my presence, that I'd shot at the wall, like I'd been caught in the throes of some psychotic vision. And Babs, with her soft, patronizing voice, intimating that I was crazy, exhausted, or in over my head. Or maybe all three.

Well, to hell with both of them. I'd seen Toussaint; if not because he'd physically been there, then because he'd been inside my head.

It all came down to their inability to believe in things they couldn't see. Things from the spirit world where Voodoo and Hoodoo are real—the world in which I operate.

My own partners didn't believe in *me*.

Way to leave me hanging, guys.

Within moments, Ferris and Babs climbed back into the car,

with Vinny in tow. Silence screamed; tension reigned. Vinny started to speak but paused, eying us uneasily. "I'm hungry. Let's head to Mama's for dinner."

"Good idea," I muttered, staring out the window.

Even a corpse whisperer needs her mama when the world turns upside down. Besides, with the night's battle still ahead, another dose of Mama's magick couldn't hurt.

"Mama's it is." Ferris glanced in the rear-view mirror. "What sounds good tonight?"

"A double shot of Luna." Vinny's stupid grin reminded me so much of Leo, it hurt.

Ferris stared into the mirror again. "Anybody else?"

I zipped my lip, but the brain bitch had a dying duck fit. *How 'bout a bowlful of Benedict Arnold with a big, ol' side of shut-your-pie-hole-you-backstabbing-Judas?*

It's a good thing one of us has a filter, even if we never know whose day it is to use it.

As Ferris pulled into Mama's, Babs swiveled in the front passenger seat, turned and locked eyes with me. "Maybe you and I could have a drink later tonight. You know, really let our hair down. Woman to woman."

The only answer I gave was the slam of my car door after I slid across the seat and climbed out. Freaking Psycho Babs. Almost had me sucked in, thinking she might have actually been a humanoid life form. All she wanted to do was pull out her DSM-5 book and diagnose me. Good luck with that, sister. And who would *ever* want to get to know Babs unplugged, hair down, woman to woman? I could barely stand the uptight, bun-headed bitch-bot I'd come to know and battle with over the thermostat.

Mama waited for me at the front door, propping open the screen-door with her arm. Eyes narrowed, lips taut, chin down. I'd seen that look before. For some reason, my ass was about to be grass.

"Welcome, my friends." Mama smiled at Ferris and Babs, and then nodded at Vinny. "Miss Luna is busy working, young man. You can make eyes at her all you want, but you leave her be until after she off the clock."

Vinny winked at Mama and kissed her on the cheek as he slid past her through the doorway.

She snickered and waggled her finger in his face. "Don't tink you can win me over with those bedroom eyes. You treat my Luna like a lady, or you deal with me."

Mama dug her nails into my arm and held me captive, while Luna appeared with menus and escorted the others to our table. "Aliyah Marie, why you come here with your soul all black and ugly? Such rage inside you. No one come into my home this way."

She pulled a decorative bundle of sage hanging from a calico ribbon beside the door. "Stand still, missy," she hissed, as she lit the bundle with a match and wafted it through the air, smudging me. "You can't be doing battle like this tonight, all tied up in knots."

"Doing battle?" I stared down my nose at Mama. "What do you know about tonight?"

Mama shook her head and sighed. "You have no secrets from me, child. I know where you go come midnight."

Shit. Shit. Shit.

"Don't mention this in front of them," I said, nodding to Ferris and Babs. "They won't be there. This is my battle, not theirs."

"Then center yourself, Little Bird. Tell me what vexes you."

"Everything, Mama," I whispered. "Everything is upside down."

Mama placed the bundle of sage inside a clay pot on the porch to cool and wrapped me in a bear hug. "Tings are not always as they seem. Upside down is only a point of view, no? Go eat with your friends." She bit her lip and smiled. "You not see it, but they *are* your friends—and that Ferris? He love you like no other. Oh, how that man worries for you. Lord knows, he ain't the only one."

"Really? Well, *my friends* have a funny way of showing it."

"Get your nose out of the clouds, missy. Everybody need help once in a while—even the great and powerful Aliyah Marie Nighthawk."

Little Allie winced.

"Nobody calls me that, Mama."

"Don't sass me, child. I turn you over my knee as soon as look at you."

She patted my backside and sent me to my table, having dressed me down in a loving way that was somehow worse than Dickhead had ever done. Could it be that Ferris and Babs had ratted me out because they were concerned about me?

Never one to hold back, Little Allie added her thoughts: Did my running back to Mama mean that I was concerned about me too?

Stupid head hag. If she was going to be so judgmental, the least she could do was run her thoughts by me *before* I plowed headfirst into a steaming pile of poo.

No matter his reason, Ferris had thrown me under the bus and then backed over me. He had to own that. And despite everything they had seen, if neither he nor Babs could accept that Toussaint had actually planted those visions in my brain, they were in too far over their heads to be of help tonight.

So, for the time being, Babs could keep analyzing me like a bug under her microscope, and Ferris, who had yet to apologize, was still in the doghouse. Nothing had changed. When midnight came, I would be on my own.

Ferris's eyes were on me as I wound through the restaurant toward our table. Was he hoping I would give him a pass and let him off the hotseat? Fat chance, pal. He snapped his eyes toward his menu as I flounced into my seat. Babs scowled and shook her head at me.

Like I cared.

She was parked on the same shit list as Ferris, and needed to dial back her eyeballs before I reached behind her cheaters and squished them like grapes. Vinny, no doubt tired of the melodrama he'd stumbled into, turned his attention to Luna, who quickly filled our table with all our favorites.

Food was the furthest thing from my mind. Even the smell of Mama's red beans and rice couldn't lure my taste buds to life. I ate what I could, and moved the rest around my plate to avoid another lecture.

Babs asked Ferris about his background and how he got into the agency. He answered politely, darting his eyes my way from time to time, although I pretended not to notice. Either Babs wasn't picking up on his signals, or she felt the need to fill the awkward silence with equally awkward small talk.

Little hearts floated out of Vinny's head every time he looked at Luna. I didn't want to bring his evening to a premature end, but I was exhausted and needed more rest before I took on Toussaint. I got to my feet and told the group not to end their evening on my account, that I would Uber back to the hotel. Ferris wasn't having it. He jumped out of his chair, nodding Babs a quick goodnight.

"Stay here and relax," I said. "I'm heading to bed any way."

Ferris whipped the car keys out of his pocket. "No problem. I'm tired myself." He turned to Babs and asked, "Think you can grab an Uber later, and make sure Don Juan here gets back safely?"

"No problem. You two must be exhausted after last night. Get some rest."

Ferris fell in step beside me as I threaded through the tables.

"You can't avoid me forever," he murmured. "We need to talk."

I pushed through the screen door and nearly bowled over Mama, who was sweeping off the porch with an ancient corn-husk broom.

Her eyes twinkled as I grabbed her arms to steady her. "Off so soon?" she asked. "With no kiss goodnight?"

"You know how cranky I get when I'm tired," I said, shooting her the Allie eye.

"I know *everything*, child. And I sees everything, too." She folded me to her chest and whispered a quick prayer in my ear. I kissed her cheek and continued down the steps, grateful for her blessing. But I stopped in my tracks when she turned to Ferris and said, "I have someting for you, young man."

Mama turned her broom upside down, pulled out a husk, and ground it to powder between her palms. Chanting a spell I'd never heard before, she divided the powder between her hands, blowing one handful onto Ferris and pouring the rest into his hands. "You keep this," she said, gazing into his eyes. "When the time come, you know what to do with it."

A wide-eyed Ferris turned to me, as if awaiting further instructions. I shrugged and motioned for him to slip it into his pocket. When he finished pocketing the dust, he thanked Mama and hugged her awkwardly, as if she were made of eggs. She blew us a kiss goodnight and waddled back inside.

"What was that for?" he whispered, as we trotted down the steps.

"Hell if I know."

Ferris was determined that I wouldn't ignore him on the ride back to the hotel. "It's not what you think," he said, winding through the streets of Meraux.

"What's not what I think?"

"The reason I told Boudreaux you shot at the blank wall. I didn't tell him to discredit you."

"Call it what you want. You threw me under the bus. The guy must think I'm a lunatic."

"He's worried about you, Allie. Me too."

I stared at him, feeling my heart break. "You don't believe I saw Toussaint."

He fidgeted in his seat and flipped on the wipers to clean off a fresh round of rain that had begun to fall. "I know you believe you saw Toussaint."

"But you think it's because I was stressed, or under pressure, or something. Not because he was actually manipulating my brain."

Now it was Ferris's turn to shut down, which actually hurt worse. I never should have let him try to explain. The hole he'd dug, and the chasm between us, had only grown deeper.

He pulled into a parking spot at the Marriott and shut off the engine. "I'm trying to wrap my mind around this stuff. I really am. I love you, Allie girl."

"You just don't believe me."

He closed his eyes and sighed. "Just promise me one thing. Promise me you won't go off to fight Toussaint on your own."

"It doesn't matter what I say. You won't believe me anyway." I jumped out of the car and slammed the door.

Ferris had enough sense (or was it compassion) to let me run inside and hit the elevator button before he climbed out of his car. When the door opened, I stepped inside, pressed the second-floor button and watched him walk slowly across the lot, until he disappeared behind the closing shiny brass door.

Once in my room, I stepped into the shower and let the hot

water soothe my aching muscles. Babs would be back soon. I didn't want to risk waking her when I left, so I lay down fully dressed, Mama's gris-gris bag and her obsidian necklace clasped around my neck, boots and weapons on the floor within easy reach. The thought of calling Nonnie popped into my head, but the brain bitch took a hard pass. On a good day, conversations with Nonnie required both concentration and imagination. I was shit-out of both.

It was 8 p.m. If I hit the rack, I could get three hours sleep before I slipped out into the night to face down Toussaint. As I set the alarm on my phone and closed my eyes, Little Allie wondered if Toussaint would haunt my dreams, but all that came was the blessed relief of a dreamless sleep.

40

A MAMA'S LOVE

I woke before my alarm sounded, the room pitch black and still except for Bab's rhythmic breathing and an occasional sputtering snore into her pillow. I stared at the lighted dial on my watch and counted the minutes passing by, trying to visualize my battle with Toussaint. But the images in my brain disintegrated into a gelatinous pile of zushi, faster than a microwaved corpsicle.

Ah, what the hell. Visualization has never been my thing anyway.

When eleven o'clock finally arrived, I sat up and eased out of bed. The springs protested with a sharp squeak, but Babs rolled over and continued snoring.

I stepped into my boots, slipped into my shoulder rig and sheathed my knife. Then I strapped on my ankle holster and grabbed some extra mags. Afraid that turning on the bathroom light would wake Babs, I stood in the dark and tucked my hair beneath my Ungrateful Dead cap, then ran my fingers across Mama's necklace hoping to feel her presence.

The fact that I didn't made me uneasy.

The pouch of magickal Goofer Dust that Mama had given

me sat on the night table, waiting to join the rest of my arsenal. Shoving it into my pocket, I crept across the room, opened the door and slipped out into the night to meet my destiny.

Lightning breeched the late-night sky; thunder roiled. I jogged to Congo Square beneath a steady mist, letting the rhythm of my footfalls clear my mind. *Center*, I thought, channeling Mama. *Center*.

With each step closer to the square, the air grew more hushed. Less than a week earlier, when I'd faced Toussaint at this same place, the sound of drums and the chatter of the spirits had echoed off the white stone pavers and filled my ears. The spirits were 'rejoicing.' That's what Toussaint had called it. But on this ugly, expectant night, the revenants were nowhere to be found.

Why? Little Allie whispered.

Never mind, my thoughts answered. *We're better off not knowing.*

The mist became a steady rain as I strode slowly across the pavers—skin tingling, senses acute, every noise and every sensation magnified a hundredfold. The air beside me whirred. I spun, coming face to face with Toussaint. His emerald eyes gleamed in the darkness.

"Little Bird," he whispered, brushing his hand against my cheek. "After all these years, I still yearn for you. How is it that we've come to this?"

"I put down your wife. Remember? And then you turned my dad into a fucking rotter."

Toussaint's eyes flashed. Good. I'd hit a nerve. But he wasn't finished baiting me.

"It's true," he conceded. "You and I, we've done...unspeak-able...things to each other. But before all that, there was love. I was your first, *shar*. And now, before I kill you, I will be your last."

Mama's voice wafted through the thick night air. *Center. Center.*

Toussaint stared into my eyes and stretched out his hand. Energy arced from the tips of his fingers and filled the space between us. Within seconds, my body, through no effort of its own, inched closer to Toussaint's.

An ugly smile crossed his face as he waggled his fingers toward my chest. Mama's necklace lifted up over my gris-gris bag, snapped at its clasp, and floated through the air into Toussaint's palm.

"A fitting souvenir for me, eh, *Ti Kras Zwazo*?"

I channeled my anger and summoned every ounce of power inside me. My mind pushed against his, plowing him backward onto his ass.

He leapt to his feet with a snarl, opened his arms wide and then swept them back together.

Something stirred.

Something in the darkness, beyond my line of sight, shuffled and scraped toward me across the stone pavers. Closer and closer it came, shambling out from the storm, coming shoulder-to-shoulder with Toussaint—a band of biters, snapping their gnarly teeth at me in anticipation.

I planted my feet shoulder width apart, drew Hawk, and leveled him at the nearest deadhead.

With a single nod from Toussaint, the rotters surged forward in an unrelenting wave.

I exhaled, centering myself, aligning each shot, and took the biters down, one by one, closest to furthest away—until my ammo ran out.

"Letting your minions fight your battles for you?" I shouted, slamming in a fresh mag and racking the slide. "Wow. That's weak. You're not the necromancer I remember."

Toussaint jerked as if I'd slapped him, but recovered quickly and flashed an inexplicable grin. "Yes. That isn't worthy of either one of us, is it? Forgive me." He raised his hands into the night sky and then flung them wide, silently scattering his biters back into the darkness from where they'd come. "It is only fitting that you should die by my hand alone, Little Bird."

Hawk's grip instantly blazed red-hot in my palm. Toussaint flicked his wrist and sent the 9mm sailing across the pavers.

I pulled my knife, but Toussaint locked onto it with his eyes and sent it airborne.

Unseen fingers constricted my throat and lifted me, suspending me inches above the ground. The more I struggled, the more the fingers contracted.

Lightning streaked across the midnight sky; thunder cracked on its heels. Memories of Mama and Nonnie, Headbutt and Kulu, Ferris and Rico, and my old partner, Harry Delk, swirled through my mind.

My vision began to blur. *How had things gone so horribly wrong?*

Mama had said that the light in me was stronger than the darkness in Toussaint, but he'd tossed my weapons aside like tinker toys. *Where was Mama when I needed her?*

Mama's astral voice raged above the storm. "*Enough, Bway!*"

Toussaint spun, mouth agape, eyes raised to the heavens. He dropped me into a crumpled heap onto the rain-soaked pavers, gasping for breath.

"Mama, is that you?" Toussaint called, wiping the rain from his face and staring into the storm. "Mama?"

Head on a swivel, he railed like the madman he was, calling out to the only mother he had ever known. Had he wanted to destroy her too? Or to simply beg for her forgiveness?

Hell, if I cared. Mama had given me an opening and that was all that mattered.

Biting back the pain, I dug into my pocket, yanked out the pouch of goofer dust, and hurled it up into Toussaint's face.

He howled and tore at his cheeks as the powder settled onto his skin, raising blisters that instantly burst, leaving behind glimpses of bone.

While he was swiping at the powder, I reached into my boot and pulled Baby from her holster. With my right hand steadying my left, I rolled onto my stomach and moaned as my fractured ribs compressed. On raised elbows, I levelled the gun and squeezed the trigger.

Toussaint slammed to the ground, flat on his back, unmoving. Blood seeped from his body into the ponding water on the stark white pavers, turning them red.

I gathered my knees beneath me and crawled toward his body. *Had I shot him in the head?* I couldn't be sure. My bones screamed; my muscles burned and the world grew gray. Every inch I gained seemed like a mile.

Just a quick rest, I told myself, closing my eyes.

Babs voice whirred inside my ear. "I'm here, Allie. You're going to be okay."

She uttered a few more words I didn't catch, and I smiled in spite of the pain. *You know she isn't real, right?* I thought. *She has no way of knowing you're here.*

The world went black.

I opened my eyes and silently darted them from side to side. From the looks of things, I was in a hospital, hooked up to an IV. Ferris was there, as well as Babs, and Vinny. Rico and Jade too, sitting in some crappy folding chairs, holding hands, looking closer than ever.

What the hell? Was I dying?

"Welcome back." Ferris leaned over the bedrail and

brushed his lips on my cheek. My left hand was bandaged and my entire body was on fire, but I had a good buzz going, and it didn't seem like I was dying. At least, nobody was crying anyway.

"Care to fill me in?" I croaked.

Rico poured me a glass of water and put the straw to my lips. That water tasted better than any Jack Daniel's slushie I'd ever had, and yet, that slushie was at the top of the list of things I wanted once I got out of there.

Ferris ticked off my injuries like a laundry list. "Let's see. You've got an assortment of broken ribs, a contused trachea, second-degree burns on your hand and a rocking concussion. But you'll live. Anything else you're fuzzy on?"

I eyeballed Babs. "How did you know I was at Congo Square?"

"Actually," Ferris said, squatting beside my bed, "I should probably be the one to explain that. Boudreaux was worried about you for, ah, for taking shots at the blank wall in the Chalmette house. He ordered me to put a tracker app on your phone, to, you know, keep an eye on you."

I felt heat rise in my cheeks. "I'll deal with Boudreaux later. Just when did you install this app?"

Ferris cleared his throat. "When you went into the pharmacy to buy bandages. You left your phone laying on the console in the car."

My head began to throb. I pressed the PCA pump and waited for sweet relief. But no sooner had my eyes drifted closed than they snapped back open.

"Where's Toussaint?"

Rico flanked me on the other side of my bed. "He's dead, Nighthawk. You nailed him."

"Head shot, right?"

"Dead as a door knob." Ferris said, glancing away.

I pinched the bridge of my nose. "Where is he now?"

A stony silence fell over the room. Ferris, Rico, Babs and Vinny all looked at each other in one big circle jerk.

My teeth clenched so tight I thought they'd break. "I want to see his body. *Now*."

Babs stepped forward and gently lay her hand on mine. "You can't."

"Why the hell not?"

She closed her eyes and sighed. "Because it's...gone."

"What do you mean, *gone?*"

Ferris tossed up his hands. "For Christ sake, Nighthawk. Toussaint's dead. I even felt for his pulse, to be sure. Then, I called it in, scooped you up, and drove like a bat out of hell to get you here. When the backup team arrived at Congo Square, Toussaint's body was gone."

I was released from the hospital the following day, in enough time to say goodbye to Ferris, Rico, Jade and Babs before they flew back to Cincinnati. Ferris wanted to stay in New Orleans with me, but Mama insisted that she'd send me back to him once she'd nursed me back to health.

He'd stopped by Mama's to visit me privately before he left town. He pulled the handful of dust that Mama had given him from his pocket, poured half of it into my hand, and then kissed me long and hard.

"Mama told me I would know when to use this. It's a lover's blessing to bring you back to me, Allie girl. I'll be waiting."

He left town having never heard those three little words that I struggle with so much.

For the time being, Mama allowed Vinny to stay with her too. School was out. He had nowhere to stay, and you couldn't stick a crowbar between him and Luna, anyway. I'd been thinking about asking him to come back home with me, maybe help Nonnie run American Corpse Management Executives, Inc. Why not? Somebody had to keep an eye on that crazy, blue-haired huckster. And down deep inside (a place I try not to visit), I figured Leo would get a kick out of us working together—if we didn't end up killing each other first.

Healing quickly is a requirement for corpse whisperers. In two days, I was up and about, following Mama, and driving Vinny crazy. After Mama showed me how to make Jade's medicine, I was so bored, that when my phone rang and Nonnie was on the other end, I didn't roll my eyes or sigh.

"When you coming home?" she asked.

"A day, maybe two, tops. How are the terrible twins?"

"Is triplets now," she said. "One of the eggs, it hatched."

I frowned at the phone. "Unfertilized eggs don't hatch, Nonnie."

"Fertilized, unfertilized, who tracks such things?"

"You let my bird get knocked up? We don't have enough dog biscuits to feed us as it is."

"Bah! Who know when the knocking happen? I take baby home—be his momma. I call him Hyrum."

"Perfect. That's one problem down. Now for that property tax issue..."

———

Two days later, when the time came to say goodbye to Mama, the words refused to come. I stood on the porch of the house I'd loved since I was a child, knowing that once I left, the chances were I would never see her again. But as all good mamas do, she guided me gently down the steps and shooed me back to the life I'd left behind. The life I was destined to live. The life of a corpse whisperer.

Vinny agreed to come to Cincinnati and work for me after he finished summering with Momma and Luna. He'd have a home with me for as long as he wanted. We could figure out his last year of college and ongoing training later. He had a long and exciting life ahead of him, working beside me in the corpse management business.

Ferris would be there waiting for me, and Rico too, each of them wanting something different from me, and each determined to get it.

I wished I knew what I wanted from them.

And I wished I could have seen Toussaint's body—to *know* he was dead—to *feel* the complete and utter absence of life inside him.

Until I could do that, I would never be sure he was truly gone.

ACKNOWLEDGMENTS

I would like to express my gratitude to the many people who helped bring this book to life:

Christiana Miller, your drive and focus have given The Corpse Whisperer series wings. Thanks for believing in me and Allie Nighthawk.

Robert M. Burdick, who reviewed, suggested, and corrected this manuscript—thanks for giving Corpse Whisperer Sworn copious amounts of your time, your literary expertise, and your devotion.

Ms. Logan Ashley, lifelong resident of New Orleans, who served as my local flavor and Creole consultant. I couldn't have written this without you!

Officer Scott Burdick who has stepped into his father's shoes as my police/weapons expert. Thanks for your expertise and for answering my ridiculously civilian questions.

And a special shout out to Don Moon and the network of authors and beta readers who critiqued Corpse Whisperer Sworn, as well as to friends and fans who encouraged me. You are too numerous to mention individually, but you know who you are. I will treasure your support and friendship always.

ABOUT THE AUTHOR

H.R. Boldwood, author of the Corpse Whisperer series, and finalist in the 2019 Imadjinn Awards, is a writer of horror and speculative fiction. In another incarnation, Boldwood is a Pushcart Prize nominee and winner of the 2009 Bilbo Award for creative writing by Thomas More College.

Boldwood's characters are often disreputable and not to be trusted. They are kicked to the curb at every conceivable opportunity when some poor unsuspecting publisher welcomes them with open arms. No responsibility is taken by this author for the dastardly and sometimes criminal acts committed by this ragtag group of miscreants.

You can send H.R. Boldwood a message at hrboldwood@gmail.com. To learn more about H.R. Boldwood, visit her website at: www.hrboldwood.com.

 facebook.com/hrboldwood

 x.com/BoldwoodH

 bookbub.com/authors/h-r-boldwood

ALSO BY H.R. BOLDWOOD

NOVELS

The Prodigal

The Corpse Whisperer

Corpse Whisperer Sworn

Corpse Whisperer Torn

ANTHOLOGIES

Killing it Softly (Volume One)

Killing it Softly (Volume Two)

Hyperion and Theia's Saturnalia

Toys in the Attic

Floppy Shoes Apocalypse II

Carnival of Horror

Bete Noire

Pilcrow and Dagger

www.ingramcontent.com/pod-product-compliance
Lightning Source LLC
Chambersburg PA
CBHW050529110726
47899CB00005B/1649